Beast of War

A thirty-foot-long iguana—its ancestors had been iguanas—poked its head through a mass of reeds and came on at a rush. Green Prime was staring straight at the creature when it began its charge.

Green Prime knelt and aimed his weapons pod. Johnnie, struggling to free himself from his pack, saw the four rocket nozzles staring back at him. He flung himself to the side, abandoning his rifle.

"Watch it, you damned—" shouted Sergeant Britten.

Green Prime's first rocket ignited. The man who'd been beside Johnnie hadn't moved. The backblast caught him, and his flamethrower reload exploded.

The scream and white-hot glare of fuel threw the rocketeer off. The remainder of his ripple-fired pod raked foliage to the side of the intended target.

The first missile glanced from the lizard. The beast clamped its jaws over the rocketeer's torso, then spewed out the remains in a froth of blood as it twisted for another victim . . .

SURFACE ACTION

DAVID DRAKE

ACE BOOKS, NEW YORK

For Mark L. Van Name
Who has made my life easier
as well as more interesting.

This book is an Ace original edition,
and has never been previously published.

SURFACE ACTION

An Ace Book / published by arrangement with
the author

PRINTING HISTORY
Ace edition / October 1990

ISBN: 0-441-36375-X

Prologue.

And we are here as on a darkling plain
Swept with confused alarms of struggle and flight
Where ignorant armies clash by night.

—Matthew Arnold

FIVE HUNDRED YEARS before the first colony ship landed on Venus, an asteroid which had been expanded into a fat nickel-iron balloon impacted with the upper Venerian atmosphere. There it spread its filling of tailored bacteria to graze among the roiling hydrocarbons.

That was the start of the terraforming process.

Thousands of asteroid casings followed the first. All the early ones were loaded with bacteria which broke down the poisons, forming free water through biochemical processes and creating mulch as they died and their bodies drifted toward the surface.

The upper layers of the atmosphere cleared and no longer trapped the sun's heat. The blankets of bacteria moved lower, following the hellish temperatures and poisonous hydrocarbons in which alone they could exist.

Rain fell—and vaporized again, long before the huge lashing drops had reached the surface. Furnace-hot layers of air cooled and cleared, and the rain continued to fall.

Even before the Venerian highlands rose above the remaining strata of hydrocarbon haze, asteroids spewed seeds, spores, and Earth-standard one-celled life into the atmosphere. The new cargoes spread and fell with the rain; and mostly died, but not quite all.

Men sent more asteroids filled with more life, and the life flourished.

The sheen of water-vapor clouds reflected the dangerous majority of sunlight from the re-formed planet, but the short, higher-energy end of the spectrum penetrated the clouds most easily. The actinic rays aided mutation, and the virgin surface of the planet permitted adaptive radiation on a scale never imaginable on Earth.

Asteroids strewed eggs; at first invertebrates, then those of backboned life forms, though none so advanced that the young required parental care.

The colony ships arrived.

In a degree, the planners who seeded Venus with life had been too successful. Land and sea both teemed with a savage parody of 'Nature red in fang and claw.'

The seas proved easier to colonize—'at first,' the planners said, though the temporary expedient quickly hardened to permanence. Domed cities sprang up on continental shelves a few thousand feet down—beneath the sunlight and the light-driven violence of the surface layers, but well above the scarcely less fierce competition in the deep trenches where all organic matter at last settled.

Seven days, four hours, and thirty-four minutes after the last colony ship landed on Venus, Earth's final war triggered a fusion reaction in her oceans. By astronomical standards, the resulting star was both small and short-lived; but it would smolder for thousands of years, and its first milliseconds had been enough to cleanse the planet of life.

Mankind survived in the domes of Venus.

Only in the domes of Venus.

The individual cities were independent and fiercely competitive, though the causes of their conflicts had no more logic to those not involved than did the causes of

men's wars through the previous ages. Earth's blazing death
throes imposed order of a kind on the wars of Venus, but not
even that warning trauma could bring peace.

Nuclear power and weapons were banned, as guns had
been banned in Japan during the Shogunate. The ban was
enforced with absolute ruthlessness. Domed cities were
vulnerable to conventional weapons of the simplest sort. A
dome which was believed to harbor nuclear experiments
was cracked so that water pressure crushed its inhabitants
into ooze before they could drown.

Apart from that, war on Venus was fought on the surface,
and by warriors.

Independent contractors, like the condottieri of Renais-
sance Italy, built bases and fleets with private funding and
staffed them with volunteers. They fought one another for
hire, and in the interim they fought the jungles for their very
lives.

Domes went to war according to set rules. When battle
and mercenaries' blood had decided the point at issue,
the losing city ransomed itself to penury. The winning dome
recouped the cost of the fleet it hired, and the winning
military entrepreneurs collected a comfortable victory bonus.

The losing mercenaries had the amount of their original
hire and whatever they had managed to save from the wrack
of defeat. That might be enough for them to go on to lesser
contracts, desperately trying to rebuild their fortunes; or
they might be forced to merge with another company on
unfavorable terms.

Sometimes they merged with the fleet which had just
defeated them. Business was business.

The fleets seemed a romantic alternative to life in the
climate-controlled safety of the domed cities. Civilians aped
the dress and manners of the mercenaries or scorned them,

but no one in the domes could ignore fleet personnel in their uniforms and their dark-tanned skins.

There was no shortage of volunteers to take up the reality of the romantic challenge. . . .

1.

A taster of wine, with an eye for a maid,
Never too bold, and never afraid. . . .

—Bliss Carman

THE CROWD IN Carnaval finery burst apart with a collective shriek.

The man forcing his way toward Johnnie through the revelers had a stubble beard and a wild look in his eyes. His left arm clamped a woman against his chest like the figurehead of a packet ship. Her domino mask hung from one ear. There were scratches on her collarbone, and the gauzy blouse had been shredded away from her breasts.

The man's right hand waved a butcher knife with an eight-inch blade.

"All right, you whore!" the man screamed. His dilated pupils weren't focused on anything in his present surroundings. "You want to spread it around, I'll *help* you spread it around!"

The knife slipped like a chord of light-struck ripple toward the woman's belly.

Johnnie's right hand dropped as he swung his hips to the left. The hem of his scarlet tunic had tiny weights in it, so that the ruffed flare stood out as his body moved—

Clearing the pistol holstered high on Johnnie's right hip.

The woman's body shielded all of the madman except his arms and the wedge of face including his staring, bloodshot eyes. The Carnaval crowd was a montage of silks and shrieks surrounding the event.

Johnnie's hand curved up with the pistol; faster than a snake striking, faster than the knife. For an instant that trembled like the sun on dew, the line of the pistol barrel joined Johnnie's eye and the madman's.

The muzzle lifted with a flash and a haze of clean-burning propellant. The sharp *crack!* of muzzle blast slapped through the screams. The madman's right eye socket was empty as his body spasmed backward in a tetanic arch. His arms lashed apart, flinging the woman to one side and the butcher knife to the other.

Johnnie took a deep breath and loaded a fresh magazine from the pouch on his left hip, where it balanced the weight of the pistol. The holographic ambiance faded, leaving behind a large room whose walls were gray with a covering of vitalon, a super-cooled liquid which absorbed bullet impacts within its dense interior.

A red light glowed on the wall above the door. Somebody was in the anteroom, watching the sequence through closed-circuit cameras.

The muscles of Johnnie's lean face set in a pattern scarcely recognizable as the visage of the good-looking youth of a moment before. He holstered his weapon and touched the door control.

"Well," he said as the armored door rotated and with-drew, "are you satisfied, Sena—"

The man in the anteroom wore a Blackhorse dress uniform, with the gold pips and braid of a commander. His only similarity to Senator A. Rolfe Gordon was that both men were in their mid-forties—

And they'd been brothers-in-law before the Senator's wife ran off with a mercenary not long after she gave birth to Johnnie.

"Uncle Dan!" cried Johnnie. He started toward Commander Daniel Cooke with his arms wide . . . before he remembered that what was proper for a boy of nine should have been outgrown by nineteen. He drew back in embarrassment.

Uncle Dan gave him a devil-may-care grin and embraced Johnnie. "What's the matter?" he demanded. "Did I develop skin-rot since I last saw you?"

He stepped back and viewed the younger man critically. "Though I won't," he said, "offer to swing you up in the air any more."

"Gee, it's good to . . . ," Johnnie said. "I wasn't expecting to see you."

"I have a meeting with the Senator this morning," Dan explained. "And I thought I'd come a little early to see my favorite nephew."

"Ah . . . shall we go somewhere comfortable?"

"If you don't mind," replied his uncle, "I'd like to watch you run through a sequence or two."

Dan's smile didn't change, but his voice was a hair too casual when he added, "The Senator comes to watch you frequently, then?"

"No," said Johnnie flatly. "Not often at all. But too often."

His face cleared. "But I'd love to show *you* the set-up, Uncle Dan. The screens in the anteroom—"

"I'd prefer to be in the simulator with you," Dan said. He lifted his saucer hat and ran his fingers through his black, curly hair. "Though I won't be shooting."

"There's some danger even with the—" Johnnie began until his uncle's brilliant grin stopped him.

Right, explain the danger of ricochets to Commander Daniel Cooke, whose ship took nine major-caliber hits three months ago while blasting her opponent in Squadron Monteleone to wreckage.

"Sorry, Uncle Dan."

"Never apologize for offering information that might save somebody's life," Dan said. "Got a jungle sequence in this system?"

"This system's got about *everything*!" Johnnie answered with pride as the gray walls dissolved into a mass of stems, leaves, and dim green terror. As the holographic simulation appeared, the climate control raised sharply the temperature and humidity of the air it pumped into the environment.

They were on the edge of a clearing, a dimpled expanse of yellow-brown mud. The surface was too thin to provide purchase for any plants save those which crawled about slowly on feather-fringed roots. Creatures with armored hides had trampled a path around the periphery of the clearing, through the brambles that were now curling to reclaim the terrain.

A bubble rose from the mud and burst flatulently.

"The trouble with the simulator," Johnnie said in a whisper, "is that you *know* there's something there in the mud."

The air was still and as moist as a sponge.

"Which makes it exactly like the land anywhere on Venus' surface," said his uncle, also speaking quietly. "Go on, then."

Johnnie took a step forward. If he'd been expecting to run a jungle sequence, he'd have equipped himself with a powered cutting-bar and a more powerful handgun. . . .

His left arm brushed aside a curtain of gray tendrils, roots hanging from an air plant to absorb water from the atmosphere—and to entangle small flying creatures whose juices would be absorbed to feed the plant. The simulator couldn't duplicate the touch of vegetation, but a jet of air stroked Johnnie's sleeve to hint at the contact.

A swamp-chopper exploded toward them from the oozing muck.

Johnnie drew and fired. His thumb rocked the grip's

feed-switch forward even as the first two rounds of explosive bullets cracked out, shattering the creature's stalked eyes.

Johnnie threw himself sideways. He fired the remainder of the magazine as solids which could penetrate the swamp-chopper's armored carapace while the blinded monster thrashed in the vegetation where Johnnie had been.

Genetically, the swamp-chopper was a crab, but ionizing radiation and the purulent surface of Venus had modified the creature's ancestors into man-sized predators. They retained lesser arthropods' unwillingness to die. Despite eighteen rounds into its thorax, the creature was still trying to claw through the bole of the holographic tree with which it had collided in its blind rush.

Johnnie slapped a fresh magazine into his pistol and aimed.

Dan put a hand on his arm. "Forget it," he said. "Don't worry about the ones that can't hurt you. Let's—"

"Cooke?" boomed an amplified voice. "Cooke! What are you doing here?"

Both men turned. The red light which glowed in the heart of a thicket of holographic bamboo indicated that someone was in the simulator's anteroom.

"Duty calls, lad," said Dan, rising to his feet. Johnnie shut the system down, just as something green, circular, and huge sailed toward them from the middle canopy.

Dan opened the door. Senator Gordon stood in the anteroom with his legs braced apart and his hands in the pockets of his frock coat. He neither stepped forward nor offered to shake hands.

Dan offered an ironic salute. "Good to see you again, Senator," he said.

"If I'd known you had nothing on your mind but playing foolish games with my son, Commander Cooke," Gordon said, "I wouldn't have bothered making time in my schedule to see you. Particularly at *this* juncture."

Dan ostentatiously shot his cuff to look at the bio-electrical watch imprinted onto the skin of his left wrist. He didn't bother to say that he was still twenty-three minutes early for his appointment because Gordon was already well aware of the fact.

"The games I've come to discuss aren't silly ones, Senator," Dan said coolly.

"For that matter," he added with a raised eyebrow, "these simulations aren't silly, either. Which is why I offered to buy Johnnie a membership to a commercial range."

"Yes, of course," the Senator said. When he was angry, as now, a flush crept up his jowls and across the hair-fringed expanse of his bare scalp. "You'd have had John spending all his time in the warehouse district. No thank you, Cooke. I can afford to accommodate my son's whims in a less destructive way."

"Right," said Johnnie in a brittle voice that sounded years younger than that in which he had been speaking to his uncle. "You got me the simulator, all right. *After* you knew Dan had already taken out a membership for me at Action Sports!"

"Something I've learned over the years," Dan said mildly, "is that the reasons don't matter so long as the job gets done."

He smiled at his nephew, but his face cleared to neutrality as he focused on Senator Gordon again. "But that's not what we're here to discuss . . . and I think your office would be a better location."

Johnnie nodded. "I'm really glad to see you again, Uncle Dan," he said. "Maybe if you have time—"

"No," said his uncle, "I'd like you to accompany us, Johnnie. You see—" and his face segued again from smile to armed truce as his eyes locked with those of his ex-brother-in-law "—this concerns you as well as the Senator. And everyone else on Venus."

Gordon's face was just as hard as that of Commander Cooke. "Yes," he said after a moment. "All right."

As Johnnie followed the two older men into the elevator to the Senator's penthouse office, his heart was beating with a rush of excitement greater than that he'd felt minutes before in the simulator.

He didn't know what was going on.

But he knew that it wasn't a simulation.

2.

There is a Hand that bends our deeds
To mightier issues than we planned:
Each son that triumphs, each that bleeds,
My country, serves Its dark command.

—Richard Hovey

SENATOR GORDON'S OFFICE befitted the most powerful man
in Wenceslas Dome—and mayhap in all of Venus. The
penthouse windows commanded a sweeping vision, down
across the city and up to the black ceramic dome.

In the center of the dome hung a ball of white light,
framed in black swags: an image of Earth as she had
become, and a warning to the generations of Venus why
nuclear power had to be banned if Mankind were to survive
in this her remaining refuge.

"Sit down, sit down," said the Senator as he stepped
behind his broad, ostentatiously empty desk and seated
himself.

Johnnie obeyed, his face expressionless. He'd only been
in his father's office a dozen times during his life, and he'd
never before been invited to sit.

The cushion sagged deeply beneath him. He looked
across the desk at the Senator and found that he was looking
up.

Uncle Dan, moving as gracefully as a leopard, sat on the
arm of his chair. The mercenary officer smiled frequently,
but there was more humor than usual in his expression as he

winked at Johnnie and then returned his attention to Senator Gordon.

The Senator spread his hands flat on the desktop in a pattern as precise as the growth of coral fronds. He didn't look at them. "I want to make it clear before we begin, Commander," he said, "that negotiations between Wenceslas Dome and the Blackhorse are conducted between the Military Committee and your commanding officer, Admiral Bergstrom. *Not* between me and you."

Dan raised an eyebrow. "And you can't speak for the Military Committee, Senator?" he said in false concern. "There's been a coup, then?"

The Senator became very still. "No, Commander," he said. "But there hasn't been a change of leadership in the Blackhorse, either. Has there?"

"No, quite right," Dan said. He spoke easily but with no attempt to feign nonchalance. "Admiral Bergstrom talks about retirement, but I think it'll be years—unless he dies in harness."

The soft cushions made Johnnie feel as though he were cocooned and invisible. Neither of the older men seemed aware of his presence.

"Whereupon," the Senator continued, "he'll be succeeded by Captain Haynes . . . whom you hate rather more than you hate me, don't you, Commander?"

Dan shrugged and turned up his left hand in a gesture of dismissal. "Oh, I don't hate Captain Haynes, Senator," he said. "He's as good an administrative officer as a mercenary company could have . . . but a little too much of a traditionalist, I think, to become Admiral of the Blackhorse at a time when Wenceslas Dome is overturning so many traditions."

It was like watching a scorpion battle a centipede. Uncle Dan feinted and backed, but his manner always hinted of a lethal sting, waiting for the right moment. The Senator drove on implacably, trusting in the armor of his certainty; absolutely determined.

"Now, if you said Captain Haynes hated *me* more than any other man on Venus . . . ," Dan added. "In that, I think you might be correct."

The Senator sniffed. "A distinction without a difference," he said. "And in any case, Blackhorse internal politics are of no concern to me. All that matters to Wenceslas—to the Federated Domes—is that the Blackhorse stand ready to earn the retainer we pay you. If there's a problem with your side of the bargain, perhaps it's time for us to engage some other fleet."

Dan pouted his lips in agreement and said, "Yeah, that's the problem, all right, Senator. That's just what I came to talk to you about."

Nobody in the office breathed for ten long seconds.

The Senator checked a security read-out on the corner of his desk; found it still a satisfactory green. "Say what you came to say, Daniel," he said, speaking as flatly as if his words clicked out through the mandibles of a centipede.

"Heidigger Dome has hired Flotilla Blanche," Dan said. "Carolina's got the Warcocks. We could handle either one of them without problems. If Blackhorse *alone* faces both of them together, then that's all she wrote. For us. And for you."

Johnnie expected Dan to undercut the weight of his words with a shrug or a grin. Instead, the mercenary officer's voice was as emotionless as that of the dome politician a moment before.

"Yes," said the Senator, "of course. So you'll have to associate another fleet for the duration."

Senator Gordon's penthouse was designed to impress, but it was a working office as well. Johnnie flipped up the right armrest of his chair to expose the keypad there. His

fingertips began to summon data while his eyes flicked back
and forth between the older men.

"We *need* to associate another fleet," said Dan, the
emphasis making clear there was more than agreement in
the words. "But no other fleet will deal with us. Nobody I
trust."

Holograms of the three fleets sprang to life in the air on
either flank of the desk: Blackhorse to the Senator's right in
blue symbols, Flotilla Blanche and the Warcocks to the left
in red and orange respectively.

Senator Gordon looked startled. He glanced about the
room for a moment before he noticed his son's hand on the
keypad. Dan's eyes narrowed, but there was no other
change in his expression.

The Senator's focus returned to the core of the discussion.

"That's not good enough," he said, slapping the words
out like a poker player showing his hand a card at a time.
"The retainer Wenceslas Dome has paid you over the past
five years has made the Blackhorse the most powerful fleet
on Venus . . . and the most profitable. If you're trying to
cut corners *now,* you're going to regret it."

He pointed his index finger. It looked white and pudgy
compared to the mercenary's sinews and mahogany tan, but
there was no doubting the reality of the threat the gesture
implied. "You will, Daniel. And Admiral Bergstrom. And
every member of the Blackhorse."

"I didn't say the other fleets rejected the deals we were
offering, Arthur," Dan answered calmly. "I said they
wouldn't deal with us at all."

For an instant, his lips curved into a grin as humorless as
the edge of a fighting knife. "We of the Blackhorse have
done very well from our association with Wenceslas, as you
say. Unfortunately, others have noticed that and decided
to . . . do something about the matter."

Dan pointed at the columns of blue ships. "Leaving us with that," he said. "And you with that as well, Arthur . . . because I don't think your idea of a Federation of Venus is any more popular among your peers than the Blackhorse is with ours."

There were eighteen dreadnoughts in the display's first blue column, but two of the symbols were carated: ships so seriously damaged in battle three months before that they were still out of service.

Across from the Blackhorse array were twelve red battleships and ten orange. One of the latter symbols was marked with a flashing carat, indicating it was doubtful. Because of the long association, Wenceslas Dome's data bank had much better information on the Blackhorse than on any of the other fleets.

In light forces, the disparity of strength was even more marked. Each of the three companies had a pair of the carriers which bore gliders and light surface vessels into the battle zone. The orange and red columns showed an advantage of two to one in cruisers and three to two in destroyers.

Only in submarines did the Blackhorse rise to near equality with its combined opponents. *Near equality* is a synonym for *inferiority*.

"Why hasn't Admiral Bergstrom told me this?" the Senator asked quietly. Before there could be an answer, he rephrased the question: "Why are *you* telling me this, Daniel?"

"Admiral Bergstrom doesn't like to bear bad news," Dan said. "He thinks there must be a way out, though he doesn't see one. Captain Haynes thinks there *is* a way out. Haynes was one of the founding members of the Angels, and he's convinced that he can bring Admiral Braun into an agreement with us."

Johnnie's fingers tapped the keypad.

"And *you* think?" the Senator prompted in a voice as dry as the sound of a rattlesnake sliding over leaves.

"I think there's a way to win, yes," said the mercenary. "But neither Bergstrom nor Haynes are going to find it."

The Angel forces now hung in slate-gray holograms alongside those of the Blackhorse. The smaller company was lopsidedly weak in cruisers and destroyers, and they had no carriers at all. When the Angels operated alone, they had to depend instead on skimmers launched from their dreadnoughts to keep hostile hydrofoils and surface-effect torpedoboats at bay.

But the Angels *did* have five battleships; and the nine 18-inch guns mounted on the newest of them, the *Holy Trinity,* made her a match for any ship on the planet in a one-to-one slugfest.

The Senator, his eyes on the blue and gray columns of the display, said, "You don't believe your forces, strengthened by the Angels, can successfully engage the fleets hired by Heidigger and Carolina, Commander?"

The question mark curled in his voice like the popper of a bullwhip.

"I wouldn't believe Admiral Braun if he told me the sea was wet, Senator," Dan said. "Captain Haynes is a perfectly truthful man, making him—"

"Making him very different from you, Commander!" Senator Gordon's face was gorged with blood. Watching him, Johnnie suddenly realized that 'shooting the messenger who brings bad tidings' had not always been an empty phrase.

"Making him unsuitable as a negotiator with Admiral Braun," the mercenary continued. "And making him an unsuitable choice for Admiral, in my opinion; but that's neither here nor there. The present problem is that whatever Haynes thinks, the Angels *won't* be supporting us when it comes to the crunch."

Uncle Dan's voice was calm only in the sense that an automatic weapon shows no emotion as it cycles through the contents of its feed tray.

"I see," said the Senator. "You believe that because Wenceslas Dome is pursuing a *practical* plan of confederation, the leaders of the other domes are concerned at their potential loss of power—"

"As you already knew, Arthur."

The Senator nodded. "As I already knew. And the fleets, equally concerned that a Venus united in peace will have no further need for them, are refusing to ally themselves with the Blackhorse. Making it impossible for the Blackhorse to engage the forces hired by Heidigger and Carolina."

"Not quite, Arthur," Dan said. "We'll engage Flotilla Blanche and the Warcocks, all right. And whichever additional companies join them—as I expect may happen."

Johnnie flinched to see the grin which suddenly distorted the mercenary's face.

"The thing is," Dan continued, "we'll lose. You'll lose. And Venus will lose, Arthur. Unless . . ."

"Go on," said Senator Gordon.

"Unless you let me take Johnnie here to the surface tomorrow as my aide," Dan said, and his grin became even more of a death's-head rictus.

3.

When the stars threw down their spears
And watered heaven with their tears
Did he smile his work to see?
Did He, who made the Lamb, make thee?

—William Blake

THE SENATOR BEGAN to laugh—honestly, full-throatedly.

When Johnnie *understood* what his uncle had just said, his whole being focused on what the Senator would do. He heard the peals of his father's laughter, but he still couldn't believe it. *Any* other reaction was more likely!

The Senator got up from his chair, wiped his eyes with the back of a pudgy hand, and walked to the windows. "Oh, Daniel, Daniel," he said to the man behind him, "you had me worried there for a moment. You must really hate me, don't you?"

Even Uncle Dan seemed nonplussed. "Arthur, this isn't a joke," he said.

"No?" said the Senator, glancing over his shoulder. "Well, I suppose that's too innocent a word for it, yes."

His face changed into a mask of white fury. "Come here, Commander—and you too, John. Come and look. Come!"

Dan obeyed without expression. Johnnie followed him, silent but as nervous as if a portion of the floor had just given way. Too much was happening, too suddenly, and he didn't understand the rules. . . .

The array of warships distorted as Johnnie's body

blocked portions of the projection heads, then re-formed behind him.

The Senator pointed out the window. "Do you see those people, Commander?" he said. "Do you?"

There was nothing abnormal about the figures below. Parents chatted on benches in the Common as their children played; couples found nooks in the foliage, better shielded to passers-by than they were from above; on the varied strips of the powered walkways, shoppers and businessfolk sped or loitered as their whim determined.

"They depend on my decisions, Commander," the Senator explained. "Their children will depend on the decisions I make today."

"I see th—"

"They depend on *me*. And all *you* care about is destroying my family, piece by piece—first my wife, now my son. Because you never had either one!"

"Arthur, don't be a bigger fool than God made you," Dan said in a tone of quiet menace.

"I'm not such a fool that I—"

"Arthur, *shut up*," the mercenary ordered. His voice rose only a little, but it took on a preternatural clarity that could have been understood through muzzle blasts and the crash of rending metal.

Dan crossed his hands formally against the small of his back. He didn't step forward, but the pressure of his personality lifted the Senator's chin like a chop to the jaw. "Senator, I always argued with them when they said you didn't have any balls, but—"

The Senator blinked. "*Who* said—"

"Everybody! Everydamnbody!"

Dan raised his right hand and snapped his fingers dismissively. The Senator flinched; Johnnie edged back, wishing that he were anywhere else in the world.

"You joined the Blackhorse when I did," Dan continued. "but you didn't have the balls to stick with it. You—"

"If you think courage is just shooting—"

"You didn't have the balls to make your marriage work!" the mercenary snarled. "You didn't have the balls to be a father to your son! And I kept saying, 'Yeah, but he's putting his whole *life* into a dream, so the other things don't matter to him.' "

The Senator's face was blank and as pale as unpainted marble.

"Only now," Dan concluded, "it turns out that you don't have the balls to save your dream, *either*. So they're right, you *don't*—"

"Get out of here," the Senator said. "Get out of Wenceslas Dome within an hour. Get out of—"

"Right, Senator," Dan said in a ham-fistedly ironic tone. "Right, you can dismiss me. But remember: when I go, so does the last real chance of uniting Venus before somebody decides it's better to use atomics than lose—"

He gestured with his thumb toward the glowing ball that hung above the Common, the reminder of Man's first home and its glowing death.

"—and Venus joins the Earth."

Johnnie sucked in his first breath for . . . he wasn't sure how long. "Senator," he said, "I'm an adult. If Uncle Dan wants—"

"John," said the mercenary in a voice as hard as the click of a cannon's breech rotating home, "sit down."

"But—" Johnnie said in amazement.

"Is this a foreign language?" his uncle demanded. "Listen, *boy*, I could find a dozen officers who have your skills. I needed *you* because I need somebody I can trust implicitly—but if you think you can argue about orders, then you're no good to me and your father, and you're no good to *any* fleet!"

Johnnie backed to his chair, then stumbled into it over the right armrest. It wouldn't have done him any good to look where he was going, because his eyes were glazed with shock.

"I think perhaps we'd all better sit down," said Senator Gordon. His expression had returned to normal: cold, distant; and, beneath the soft flesh, as hard as that of his former brother-in-law.

He sat calmly, then touched a switch. A pump whirred as it sucked fluid from the cushion beneath the Senator, dropping his eye level to that of the men across the desk from him. "Precisely what is it that you think my son can achieve for you, Daniel?" he asked.

"I can't tell you that, Arthur," Dan said.

His voice caught and he cleared his throat before he went on, "That's partly because I'm going to have to play the situation as it develops . . . and partly because it's not something that you need to know about. You have the political side to deal with. That's enough for any one man."

The Senator watched Dan without speaking.

"Arthur," the mercenary said, "I can tell you this: I'll be risking everything I have to save your plan of confederation."

"Your life, you mean," the Senator amplified.

"I've been risking my *life* for twenty-five years now, Senator," Dan said with the edge returning to his voice momentarily. "That's just my job. What I'm talking about is the chance—the certainty if I fail—of being cashiered from the Blackhorse and banned by all the other fleets."

"I see," said the Senator.

He looked at Johnnie, watching his son without speaking for seconds that seemed minutes. At last he said, "John, I won't claim to have been a good father . . . but you are my son, and you're important to me. Is this something *you* want to do—not to spite me, not to please your uncle?"

Johnnie licked his lips. "Yes, Father," he said.

"I want to be very clear about this, John," the Senator continued. "You aren't simply being asked to join a fleet. You're being requested to take part in an enterprise which—whatever the details—is far more dangerous than ordinary mercenary service."

He glanced at Uncle Dan. "That is correct, is it not, Commander?"

Dan nodded, still-faced. "That is correct. And the danger is increased by the fact that Johnnie won't have time to go through the ordinary training procedures."

"Father, I want to go," Johnnie said.

The Senator rose. "Then may God be with you, John," he said. "And may God be with us all."

4.

THE SQUALL DUMPED gray water in sheets and ropes across the clear roof of Wenceslas Dome's surface platform. Where the rain met the sea, there was a chaos of foam.

Below that margin, shifting with the swells that buoyed the platform, was the water of the ocean itself. It was green with nutrients and microscopic life.

Very occasionally, a streamlined vision of fins and fangs brushed along the edge of the platform and vanished again into the farther reaches of the ocean. One of the visitors took almost a minute to cruise past as Johnnie watched in amazement.

The hydrofoil that would take them to Blackhorse Base was occasionally visible also—through the homogeneous waters of the ocean, not the streaming wall of rain. The hundred-ton vessel rocked on her main hull with her outriggers raised. Her helmsman kept her headed into the wind with the auxiliary thruster. It was running just above idle, creating a haze of bubbles in the sea beneath the hydrofoil's stern.

The squall's fury could not have prevented the hydrofoil from operating at full speed had the situation required it; but the few minutes the passengers for Blackhorse Base would gain by loading now were outweighed by the needless discomfort of going out in the brief storm.

Besides, some of the passengers still hadn't finished their goodbyes.

Dan wore baggy khaki utilities instead of his dress creams, but he looked as crisp as if he'd been sleeping innocently for the past twelve hours. He grinned at Johnnie and said, "How's your head?"

Johnnie managed to smile back. "My head's fine," he said, more or less truthfully. "My stomach, though. . . . Is this what shipboard's going to feel like?"

After Commander Cooke enrolled his nephew at the Blackhorse recruiting office, he had gone off 'on personal business'—leaving Johnnie in the charge of his servant, Sergeant Britten, with orders to have a good time. Britten's notion of what *that* meant involved at least a dozen of the dives in Wenceslas Dome's warehouse district.

His uncle shrugged. "This dock's got an unpleasant period," he said. "The dampers are set to smooth tidal lift and fall, but they've got too much stiction to be comfortable in a storm."

The landing platform was as large as the Common thousands of feet beneath it on the sea floor. It was a closed, buoyant structure—of necessity, since the elevator tube joining the platform to the Wenceslas Dome had to adjust to variations in sea level.

The platform could hold a thousand people. Fewer than twenty were present now, scattered in clots and morose handfuls across the clear metal like litter on the floor of an empty amphitheater.

All the uniformed passengers were men. The fleets and their surface bases were male enclaves, though the mercenary companies employed some women as technicians and administrative personnel in the domes.

Sergeant Britten was a stocky man whose shaved head

made him look older than his years. He played privy
solitaire with his back discreetly turned to his master. His
seat was the powered pallet holding the slight kit which
Dan, Johnnie, and the sergeant himself were taking to base.

Over the past five years of association, Wenceslas Dome
had become a second home for the men of the Blackhorse.
Most of them kept a fully-stocked apartment in the dome for
the time they spent on leave and administrative duty. There
was no need to carry luggage between here and the base.

When men died, their effects were sold to the survivors
and replacements. No need for transport in that event,
either.

"A destroyer's a lot worse, of course," Dan went on. He
was letting his eyes slide across the landing platform;
concentrating on nothing, missing nothing. "But as my
aide, you'll be stationed on one of the dreadnoughts, and
your stomach won't mind that."

He grinned again. "Even when you're hung over."

"I'm fine," Johnnie said.

A couple sat on a bench a hundred yards from the stage
at which the hydrofoil was berthed. The man wore khaki; he
was middle-aged, balding and powerful. If Dan's hard
features suggested an axe blade, then this man was a sledge
hammer.

The woman was only a few years younger, but at least
from a distance she looked beautiful rather than pretty. They
sat side by side. Each had an arm around the other's
shoulders, and their free hands were intertwined on their
laps.

"Captain Haynes," Dan said, though his eyes seemed to
be on the gray, bobbing hull of the hydrofoil. The rain was
slacking off. Patches of white sky appeared briefly through
the roof before further spasms of rain obscured them. "And
his wife Beryl."

"Companion," Johnnie said. "None of the domes recognize legal marriage to a mercenary."

Dan raised an eyebrow at the venom in his nephew's voice. "Companion," he agreed.

Johnnie licked his lips. "Like my mother. Now."

"Yeah, like Peggy," the older man said. "It's been—too long, six months, I think. Since I saw her. But she's doing pretty well."

Dan checked/pretended to check the clock on his wrist. "She's with Commander LaFarge of Flotilla Blanche," he added. "A good man for executing orders, though maybe not the best choice to deal with the unexpected."

Johnnie looked at his uncle. "He's the one she ran off with?"

"That was a long time ago, Johnnie . . . ," Dan said. He shrugged. "No, that one didn't work out. He was killed later, but Peggy'd already left him. She's been with LaFarge for a couple years now."

The sky was definitely clearing, but the western quadrant—the direction of Blackhorse Base—was still gray.

"If a destroyer's bad," Johnnie said, "then that little thing's going to turn me inside out, huh?" He nodded toward the hydrofoil.

"Don't you believe it," Dan replied. "When one of those is up on its outriggers, she's the best gun platform you could ask for. Stable as a rock. I remember once . . ."

His voice trailed off when he realized that his nephew was staring fixedly at the Haynes couple again.

"He looks like he loves her," Johnnie said in a low, grating voice.

"Haynes?" Dan said. "I'm sure he does. Beryl's . . . well, I won't insult her by calling her his lucky charm. She's an estimable woman. But she's also the thing Haynes *trusts* when it's all coming apart and it doesn't look like there's a prayer of surviving."

He chuckled. "Something we all need, Johnnie. That or another line of work."

"But she's just a prostitute!" Johnnie snarled. "A *whore*!"

Sergeant Britten looked toward them. The sergeant's face was expressionless, but his big scarred hand was already sliding the cards away in a breast pocket where they'd be safe if he had to move suddenly.

Dan put his arm around Johnnie and turned him away. When the younger man resisted the motion, the mercenary's fingers pinched a nerve in his elbow. Johnnie gasped and let himself be manhandled to face the hydrofoil again.

"That was a long time ago," Dan repeated quietly. "If you get wrapped up in some minor problem of your father's from twenty years ago, then the real stuff's going to steamroller you right into the ground. And the world won't even know you existed."

"I'm sorry, Uncle Dan," Johnnie whispered.

"Don't be sorry," the mercenary said. "Be controlled."

He gave his nephew an affectionate squeeze. "That's the best advice you'll ever get, lad. Follow it and you'll rise just like me and the Senator."

A klaxon blatted above the docking valve. "El-seven-five-two-one, ready to ship passengers for Blackhorse Base," warned a voice distorted by the echoing vastness of the platform.

Men sauntered toward the valve. Some women waited; some turned and walked toward the elevator even before the mercenaries had boarded the craft which would take some of them away for the last time.

As Johnnie walked beside his uncle, his mind repeated, ". . . *me and the Senator* . . ." It was like pairing fire and ice.

5.

West and away the wheels of darkness roll,
Day's beamy banner up the east is borne,
Spectres and fears, the nightmare and her foal,
Drown in the golden deluge of the morn.

—A. E. Housman

THE DOOR BEHIND the dozen passengers closed, sealing the surface platform from the spray or worse that would enter when the outer lock opened. The air was hot, not warm; the humidity was saturated.

Captain Haynes turned in the passageway and stared first at Johnnie, then at his uncle. "Who's the civilian, Cooke?" Haynes demanded.

"John Gordon, Captain Haynes," Dan answered in a polite rather than merely correct tone. "He's a recruit."

The passageway rose and fell with a teeter-totter motion that didn't disconcert Johnnie as much as the slower rocking of the platform itself. The wet floor was treacherous, despite its patterned surface and the suction-grip soles on Johnnie's new sea boots.

"I believe Personnel still falls within the duties of the XO, doesn't it, Cooke?" Haynes said with heavy sarcasm. "Have I signed off on him? Because if I haven't, he shouldn't be in uniform."

The outer door opened with a slurping sound and a gush of algae-laden water. A rating from the hydrofoil looked in and shouted, "Will you get your butts—" before he realized that the hold-up in the passageway was caused by the

Blackhorse executive officer. He ducked back out of sight.

"Captain," said Dan quietly, "this isn't something I want to discuss without Admiral Bergstrom, and it isn't something I want to discuss *here*."

He nodded over his shoulder to where the remainder of the passengers, enlisted men and junior officers, waited blank-faced. A few of them pretended not to listen.

Johnnie was rigid. He'd spent his life thus far training to be an officer in a mercenary fleet. His studies and simulations ranged from small arms to fleet fire control, from calisthenics to the logistical problems of feeding thousands of men with the usual assortment of dietary quirks, taboos, and allergies.

But he'd always been the son of Senator A. Rolfe Gordon. He'd never been treated like an object: like a side of meat of doubtful quality.

The passageway rose and fell; and rose. More seawater sloshed in. The sky was a hazy white like glowing iron, and the atmosphere weighed on Johnnie's shoulders like bags of wet sand.

"His name's Gordon?" Haynes said.

"That's right."

Haynes grimaced, then turned. "We'll discuss it with the Admiral," he muttered over his shoulder as he stomped aboard the waiting vessel.

L7521 was a torpedoboat. There were three long grooves on either side of her main hull, like the fullers of a knifeblade. For the hydrofoil's present duty as a high-speed ferry, those weapon stations were empty, but torpedoes could be fitted in a matter of minutes by trained crews in a carrier's arming bay.

A tub forward held a pair of .60-caliber rotary-breech machine guns, while at the stern was a cage of six high-velocity ramjet penetrators which could punch a hole in anything lighter than the main-belt armor of a battleship.

Several additional automatic weapons were clamped to L7521's railings, perhaps unofficially by crewmen who wanted to be able to shoot back with *something*, even if the rational part of their minds knew it was something useless.

It was an impressive display, though Johnnie knew the vessel's gun armament was minor compared to that of the hydrofoil gunboats whose duty was to keep hostile torpedoboats from pressing home their attacks on the main fleet. And compared to a dreadnought of sixty, eighty, or a hundred thousand deadweight tons. . . .

The hydrofoil's real defenses weren't her guns, of course, or even her speed—though her ability to maintain seventy knots as long as there was fuel for the thrusters was certainly a help. The thing that had kept L7521 alive through previous battles and which might save her again was the fact she was so hard to see.

Powered aircraft played no part in the wars which puffed in brief fury across the seas of Venus like so many afternoon squalls. No combination of altitude and absorbent materials could conceal from modern sensors an aircraft's engine and the necessary turbulence of powered flight. And after the quarry was seen—

Battleships and cruisers carried railguns as secondary armament. The slugs they accelerated through the atmosphere hit at a significant fraction of light speed; significant, at least, to anything with less than a foot of armor plate to protect it.

No powered aircraft could survive more than three seconds after coming within line of sight of a hostile fleet. Gliders, travelling with the air currents instead of through them and communicating with their carrier through miles of gossamer fiber-optics cable, were a risky but useful means of reconnaissance; but under no circumstances could a glider become a satisfactory weapons platform.

Light surface craft could be designed to carry out most of the tasks of an attack aircraft and survive.

Survive long enough to carry out the attack, at any rate. War is a business of risks and probabilities.

The advantage a boat had over an aircraft was the medium in which it operated. Unlike the air, seawater is neither stable nor fully homogeneous. Swells, froth, and wave-blown droplets all have radically different appearances to active and passive sensors.

If the vessel was small—in radar cross-section—over-the-horizon systems could not distinguish it from the waves on which it skittered. Look-down Doppler aircraft radars were a technically possible answer, but an aircraft with a powerful emitter operating was even more of a suicide pact for its crew than an aircraft that *wasn't* calling attention to itself for a hundred miles in every direction.

Torpedoboats like L7521 were skeletonized blobs built of plastics which were transparent through much of the electro-optical band. Their only metal parts were in their gun mechanisms and powerplants, both of which were shielded by layers of radar-absorbent materials. If a hostile emitter did manage to lock on at short range, the little vessels mounted an electronic suite that could be expected to spoof the enemy for up to ten seconds—

Long enough to drop all six torpedoes before counterfire ripped the launch platform to shards of plastic and bloody froth.

The best countermeasures were teams of similarly-designed hydrofoil gunboats to extend the fleet's sensor range. Vicious battles were fought on the rolling wastes of No-Man's-Sea between opposing fleets. The gunboats' heavy armament meant that these blazing encounters almost always spelled death to the torpedoboat—but a regularly-spaced line of patches across L7521's main hull proved that she'd survived once; and therefore might survive again.

"Sir," said the young officer in the central cockpit, nodding to Captain Haynes. "Sir . . . ," and a nod for Commander Cooke.

The hydrofoil's cockpit had seats for four and room for several more standees. It looked like the best place to stay reasonably dry and still see what was going on, though the countermeasures/torpedo control station within the main hull forward was probably more comfortable.

Seamen among the passengers were already snapping lifelines to the vessel's railing. The small-boat men seemed cheerful, but the battleship sailors were grumbling seriously.

"Morning, Samuels," said Uncle Dan. "Get me a couple helmets and you can stand down the forward watch for this run. I'll take the gun tub with Recruit Gordon here."

The young officer's face blanked to wipe his incipient frown. "Ah, sir . . . ," he said. "One of the scout gliders thought he saw some activity along our route back. I think I'd like to keep a qualified crew at the weapon stations."

"Ensign Samuels," said Dan sharply, "I was qualified on hydrofoil twin mounts before you were out of diapers. Commo helmets, if you please."

Captain Haynes had appropriated one of the cockpit seats. He looked up from the control console with an unreadable expression. Johnnie expected him to speak, but apparently the XO wasn't willing to argue against the privileges of rank—even when it was Commander Cooke's rank.

The hydrofoil's commander gave Dan a flustered salute. "Aye-aye, sir," he said.

He turned and called forward, "Alexander and Jones, you're relieved. Give, ah, give your commo helmets to the director of Planning and his assistant."

Two ratings had climbed out of the forward position

before Johnnie and his uncle reached it along the narrow catwalk.

One of them grinned as he handed Johnnie a helmet made of the same gray-green plastic as the torpedoboat itself. "Enjoy yer ride, kid," the seaman said. "It's just like the battlewagons—showers in every stateroom."

Johnnie donned the helmet and started to sit in the low-mounted assistant gunner's seat. The AG's job was to pass fresh magazines and take over if his number one—necessarily more exposed—bought it. Dan smiled and waved his nephew to the main seat instead.

"Go on," Dan said. "You've got simulator hours on the twins, don't you?"

"Yeah, but I'm not qualified—"

The older man waved a hand in dismissal. "*I'm* qualified to judge," he said. "Maybe you'll—"

He touched the keypad on the side of the helmet he wore. "Set your helmet on 3," he continued, his voice now coming through the earphones in Johnnie's helmet. "That'll give us some privacy."

As Johnnie obeyed—hesitating, but managing to find the correct button without taking the helmet off to look at it—Dan continued, "As I say, maybe we'll find you something more interesting than a simulator target."

L7521 got under way, rumbling away from the dock on the single thruster at the stern of its main hull. The outriggers, one at the bow and two at the stern—the latter with thrusters of their own—began to crank down into the sea. When waves clipped the foils' broad vees, rainbows of mist sprayed about the vessel.

Johnnie thumbed the gunsight live. The holographic sight picture was exactly like that of his simulator back in Wenceslas Dome: a rolling seascape onto which the data banks would soon inject a target.

Reality might do the same.

The vessel worked up to about ten knots on the auxiliary thruster alone. The bow started to lift in a sun-drenched globe of spray. The stern-foil powerplants cut in and L7521 surged ahead.

"You think we're going to have to fight on the way to the base, then?" Johnnie asked, wondering if his uncle could hear him over the wind and drive noise.

The helmets did their job. Dan's chuckle was as clear as it had been in the Senator's office. "I think there's usually something on the surface of Venus that'll do for target practice," he said. "Why? Are you worried?"

Johnnie checked the traverse and elevation controls in both handgrips. The action felt normal, natural. The simulator had prepared him very well, though the amount of vibration through the seat and the baseplate was a surprise.

"I'm . . . ," Johnnie said. The wind pushed his head and shoulders fiercely, but the boat continued to accelerate. They must already be at fifty knots, though the absence of fixed objects disoriented him.

"Uncle Dan," Johnnie said, "I'm afraid I won't be good enough. I'm afraid I'm going to embarrass you. . . . But I'm not afraid of fighting."

"That's good, lad," Dan said in a matter-of-fact voice. "Because you're going to be fighting. If not on this run, then real soon. *That* I can promise."

The vibration of L7521's drives and hull reached a harmonic. For a moment, it seemed as though the vessel herself were screaming with mad laughter as she rushed toward the western horizon.

6.

*Rolled to starboard, rolled to larboard, when the surge was
seething free,*
*Where the wallowing monster spouted his foam-mountains on the
sea.*

—Alfred, Lord Tennyson

JOHNNIE REFLEXIVELY SET the gunsight controls to search
mode—then realized he wasn't alone in a simulator where
he'd be graded by electronics. He looked at his uncle in
embarrassment, poising his hand to switch back to direct
targeting.

Dan raised an eyebrow.

"Ah, was that right?" Johnnie asked. "The sights?"

In search mode, the holographic sight picture relayed the
image from the masthead sensors above the cockpit, the
highest point on the little vessel. At the moment, their
image was a three-dimensional radar panorama: 320° of
empty sea, with a sprinkling of low islands on the northern
and northwestern horizon.

"Sure," said his uncle. "Isn't it what your simulator told
you to do?"

"Yeah, but. . . ."

L7521 was running at speed, slicing over the swells like
an amusement-ride car on rails. Froth and flotsam snapped
by to either side of the hydrofoil at startling speed, con-
trasting queasily with the large-scale hologram which
scarcely changed at all.

"John, I designed your training programs myself," Dan

said. "They couldn't cover everything, but what they taught you is Blackhorse standard."

He grinned, devil-may-care Uncle Dan again. "Life can't cover everything, either, lad. Though it took me a while to figure that out myself."

Johnnie traversed the guns ten degrees, using the left-grip control, to swing them to the marked bearing of one of the distant islands. He then touched the right grip, bringing the sight picture back to direct.

For a moment, the hologram was an electronic image of the sea itself. Then the hydrofoil crested a swell and the sights centered on a blur of a gray slightly darker than that of the water. Johnnie dialed up the magnification to its full forty powers and thumbed in stabilization. The gun barrels rose automatically as L7521's bow slid into another kilometer-wide trough.

Just before the gunsight's direct viewpoint was covered by waves, the men in the gun tub saw something with jaws of yellow fangs lift above the vegetation and stare toward them. Nictitating membranes wiped sideways, dulling the eyes.

An image of seawater rose to fill the gunsight. Johnnie switched back to search mode.

He looked at his uncle, hunched below the tub's armor in the assistant's seat. The halo of spray from the steerable front foil soaked Dan as thoroughly as it did the younger man, but there was no sign of discomfort on his smiling face.

"You've been planning for . . . for years to do this, haven't you?" Johnnie said. "Bring me into the Blackhorse as soon as you could—twist the Senator's arm."

Dan shrugged. "The training programs? I wouldn't have forced you, lad. You wanted to learn, so you might as well learn the right way. Even the Senator agreed with that.

Otherwise you might have run off and joined some jackleg outfit that'd get you killed—if you were lucky."

The implications of what he'd just heard spread across Johnnie's mind like the base of a slime mold, then burst into feculent words: "You don't think I'm good enough for a real company, Uncle Dan? You don't think I could get into the Blackhorse without you pulling strings?"

The older man shook his head. "Wrong wording," he said calmly, as though he were unaware of the shock and horror behind his nephew's flat statement.

"*You* don't think that any real company's going to enlist the son of A. Rolfe Gordon against the Senator's will, do you?" Dan explained. "War's a business, Johnnie. Admirals put their lives on the line, sure; but they're gambling on a lot more than the chance of getting killed. Nobody competent—nobody competent enough to command a successful company—would offend the most powerful politician on Venus."

"He may not be for long," Johnnie said in mingled regret and anger. "Heidigger and Carolina won't let him stay if they win."

"Even then no fleet is going to offend the Senator for nothing," Dan continued. "Nobody in the history of Venus has been able to do what your father's already managed—a free association of three domes, forced by the populace and against the will of the oligarchs who'd been running the show until then."

"But if he fails—" Johnnie said.

"If he fails *this time*," his uncle said, riding over the interjection, "there's still the chance he'll be back in power later. Politicians have long memories—and so do admirals."

Dan focused on the sight picture, then frowned and rose from his seat to look over the armor. "Cover that," he ordered, pointing off the right bow. "Samuels is going to pass too close."

The sights went direct when Johnnie swung the guns with his right-hand control. The panoramic blur of land against sea became a huge mass to the left—probably the sub-continental Omphalos Sathanou, though that meant the hydrofoil's speed had been above the seventy knots Johnnie was guessing. To the right was an unnamed islet from which trailed a fur of water-brushing tree branches.

"All weapon stations, track right," Johnnie's earphones ordered in a voice that wasn't his uncle's.

The strait separating Omphalos from its minor satellite was a quarter mile broad, but only within a hundred feet of the islet was there a band of water which had enough current to clear it of mud and tannin. To the islet's right—south—clumps of reeds warned that the water there was danger-ously shallow also.

Dan charged and aimed the automatic rifle which had been placed between his seat and the armored tub. "Bloody cowboy," he muttered.

"What is it?" Johnnie asked, trying to scan both the holographic image and the expanse of green/brown/corpse-finger white beyond it. "What am I looking for?"

"Any damn thing that moves."

"Watch it," the ensign in the cockpit ordered.

Dan glanced sideways toward his nephew. "Remember," he said, "this is who you get crewing hydrofoils. Don't ever pretend people are going to be other than you *know* they're going to be."

L7521 slammed past the islet, her drive noise echoing as a *thrum/thrum/thrum* from the vegetation. The vessel's outriggers threw up triple roostertails. The wakes hunched waist-high across the shallows, churning mud from the bottom.

A ripple of fans waved nervously, the raking gills of giant barnacles or tube-worms.

A tentacle—a tendril?—shot out of the forest toward the L7521. It was gray and featureless, suggesting neither the plant kingdom nor the animal. Everything behind the rounded tip was a twisting cylinder a yard in circumference. The creature's lunge carried it a hundred feet over the water churned by the disappearing hydrofoil.

A sailor on the stern rail fired his machine gun. The pintle-mounted weapon wobbled, throwing its helix of golden tracers above the creature. Johnnie, glancing over his shoulder at the target his own weapons wouldn't bear on, thought a few of the bullets might possibly have hit.

Possibly.

"What was it?" Johnnie asked.

"Cover your sector," his uncle ordered, gesturing the twin mount forward as his right hand returned the rifle to the slot beside his seat. "Don't worry about the stuff that's over."

"Yessir," Johnnie muttered, his face cold. The hydrofoil banked slightly, hiding the creature which was already withdrawing into the vegetation from which it had sprung.

Uncle Dan grinned. "Good job, John," he said. "A lot of veterans would've shot off ammo they might need later."

"I won't get out of position again . . . sir," Johnnie said.

"Wish I was sure that *I* wouldn't," Dan said.

The older man looked back past the stern, where even the islet was rapidly disappearing. "What was it?" he added. "Something big and nasty and fast. But not fast enough. May all our problems be like that."

"Uncle Dan," Johnnie said, keeping his eyes rigidly on his sight hologram. "Is the Senator a coward?"

"Arthur?" the mercenary officer said. "Hell, no! Where did you get that idea?"

"He joined the Blackhorse when you did—"

"Right. He met your mother when she was seeing me off for training."

"—but he resigned after his first battle. He was afraid."

"He wasn't any more scared than I was," Dan said. "The *Elizabeth* got hammered out of line. Damned lucky we weren't sunk. . . ."

He put his arm on Johnnie's shoulder and kept it there until the younger man met his eyes. "Listen to me, Johnnie," Dan went on. "Arthur's first battle convinced him that Venus had to be united, so that some day there wouldn't *be* any battles. That doesn't make him a coward."

Johnnie nodded. "But he was wrong, wasn't he? I mean, you can't change human nature, can you?"

Dan grinned without humor. "I hope Arthur wasn't wrong," he said. "Because that battle convinced me of the same thing."

7.

The Devil is driving both this tide, and the killing-grounds are close,
And we'll go up to the Wrath of God. . . .

—Rudyard Kipling

FIFTEEN MILES FROM the Braids and an hour after they'd brushed past the tip of Omphalos Sathanou, Johnnie cranked up the gunsight magnification and added computer enhancement to eliminate the haze. He panned the guns slowly for an early view of the band of swampy islands and shallow channels through which L7521 would pass. Beside him, Dan dictated into a pocket workstation.

A command overlay pulsed slowly in the upper right quadrant of the gunsight hologram, then disappeared.

Johnnie blinked. He reached for the keyboard—and remembered he was in a gun tub, not at a control console. He slapped down his visor, manually keyed his helmet's access channel, and said to the artificial intelligence, "Review past minute's visuals."

The helmet went *eep* and projected into Johnnie's visor what he had seen a minute before. The visor image formed a ghost over the nearly identical view currently in the gunsight, but this time Johnnie was ready for the warning pulse.

Dan put the pocket unit away and watched intently as his nephew worked.

"Sir," Johnnie said, "we've been painted by radar."

As he spoke, the pulsed overlay reappeared in the gunsight, echoing the data sent to the main unit in the cockpit.

Dan touched his helmet keypad and said, "Twin mount to bridge. We're under radar observation. Over."

"Bridge to twin mount," replied Ensign Samuels in a wary voice. "We're approaching the Braids. You're—"

Samuels remembered who was on the other end of the link. "You may be seeing reflections scattered from islets. Over."

"Negative!" Johnnie hissed, bending close to his uncle to avoid using the intercom. "That's—"

"Bridge, that's a negative," Dan said sharply. "That's track—"

"—track-while-scan!" Johnnie concluded, identifying the pattern of high-power and low-power pulses which swept the torpedoboat.

"—while-scan," Dan continued. "Who the hell do you have on your EW board? Over."

Details sharpened in the view of the islands toward which L7521 sped. Computer enhancement at long range smoothed objects into a calculated sameness. As the need for enhancement lessened, the foliage appeared in its spiky, curling multiplicity.

There were mangroves and a breeze riffling reed tops into amber motion; but there was no sign of man.

"Shit!" said Ensign Samuels.

Then, in a controlled voice, the torpedoboat's commander continued, "Bridge to twin mount. Sir, the electronic warfare console was disconnected. The console is operating again now. You—"

Operating now that it's too late, Johnnie thought. Whoever was sitting at the console had found the constant buzzing both irritating and needless on a passenger run.

"—were right, of course. Over."

"Samuels," Dan said, "ask Captain Haynes to lock into Intercom 3, please. *Soonest!*"

The click of another station joining Johnnie and his uncle cut off the first syllable of Captain Haynes' voice saying, "—mander, is this some joke of yours?"

Dan rose to his feet and looked toward the cockpit. Haynes was standing also; their eyes met. Johnnie glanced from one man to the other—and turned back to the holographic display.

"No joke, Captain," Dan said. "If you haven't decided to lay on an escort for us—"

". . . f course not!" Haynes' protest was stepped on by the ongoing transmission.

"Then we have to assume that somebody's stationed here to make sure that you and I don't get to Blackhorse Base," Dan said. "Tell Bradley to turn ten degrees to port so we're headed toward Channel 17 instead of 19. That should get us more sensor data."

Johnnie ran a chart of the Braids on his visor. If he flexed his helmet to the tit on the gun mount, he could convert the sight into an omni-function display—

But right at the moment, it looked as though having the gunsight working was more important.

"I can't believe either the Warcocks or Flotilla Blanche would act so dishonorably!" Haynes said.

L7521's front foil nosed into the turn. The port stern outrigger telescoped enough to keep the deck more or less perpendicular to the 'down' of centrifugal force; the torpedoboat heeled like a motorcycle.

The Braids were a thousand square miles of weathered pillow lava over which the sea had risen at the end of the terraforming process. The result was thousands of islands, ranging in size from specks to narrow blotches that straggled along for several miles at low water.

None of the land rose more than ten feet above the level

of high tide; none of the channels wandering through the
mass was more than twenty feet deep when the solar tide
was at its lowest; and the sum of land and water together
was very nearly mean sea level. The through-channels were
numbered, but no one had bothered to name any of the
swampy islands.

"Do you think the people running Carolina Dome are that
honorable, Captain?" Dan said sharply. "You know as well
as I do that some of the smaller mercenary companies are no
better than pirates, picking up salvage on the fringes when
the big fleets engage. A few politicians could hire one of
them under the table. . . ."

Johnnie touched his helmet keypad and whispered orders
to the artificial intelligence. His gunsight, at full magnification, was centered on the point at which the target should
first appear. The sight picture was still an empty channel
choked from either side by black mangroves, but the
electronic warfare suite was beginning to draw a picture of
the ambusher.

Radar signals from the other craft located the emitter but
could not identify the hull on which the radar was mounted.
When the waiting vessel started its engines in reaction to the
torpedoboat's course change, L7521's passive sensors fed
back the faint sound signatures for comparison to known
templates.

When the vessel moved—out of Channel 17 and away
from the hydrofoil rather than on a direct interception
course—the torpedoboat's data bank achieved a 98 percent
probable identification. The lurking vessel was a surface
skimmer whose flexible skirts balanced it above the water
on a cushion of air.

The air cushion worked as well on land as on water. In
shifting away from L7521, the skimmer slid over a neck of
land which the chart showed as being above water level at

the present tidal state. The ambusher settled again in a slough connected to Channel 19.

"Sir," Dan said, "I have small-craft experience that you don't. Ensign Samuels will of course command his vessel . . . but with your permission, I'll take overall control of the operation."

Johnnie risked a glance around to see the captain's face, raised above the cockpit coaming. The rivalry between Cooke and Haynes was as bitter as many religious conflicts; but the men were, literally, in the same boat.

Haynes licked his lips. "We can't turn and run, then?" he said.

"From their acceleration," Dan said, proving that he'd kept an eye on his visor display while talking to his superior, "they're running light—no torpedoes. They'll have at least thirty knots on us, flat out. Our best hope is that they don't know we've noticed them."

"All right, Cooke," said Captain Haynes. He swallowed. "You're in operational command. I'll make room here in the cockpit."

"No time, Captain," Dan said as he tried to unscrew the cap which protected the hard-wire connector on the gun mount. It stuck. "I'll run it from here, if—"

Johnnie rapped the cap twice, sharply, with the butt of his service knife.

His uncle twisted again. The cap spun loose from the grip of microlife which had managed to root into the threads of supposedly impervious plastic.

"I'll run it from here," Dan concluded as he pulled glass-fiber line from the tit and connected it to his helmet.

L7521 rushed toward the Braids at seventy knots. Channel 17 wasn't an ideal route, since it narrowed halfway through the mass to little more than the width of the torpedoboat. That was something to worry about *if* they got so far.

Dan converted the gunsight display to a holographic chart of a square mile of the Braids. A blue line and a red bead plotted the torpedoboat's planned course and the ambusher's location respectively.

Johnnie swallowed and flipped up the twin mount's mechanical backsight. Blurred vegetation hopped and quivered through the sighting ring. The mechanical sights were for emergencies only—

And the Lord knew, this was an emergency.

"Three to bridge," Dan said. "Is the Automatic Defense System"—

As the commander spoke, the miniature four-barrelled Gatling roused on the centerpost of the cockpit coaming.

—"right, we need it live," Dan said approvingly. "Now, take us up Channel 18 instead. Over."

"Sir," Samuels blurted, "that's blocked—" Then, "Aye-aye, sir. Sorry."

The ADS fired high-velocity 50-grain fléchettes. The unit had its own scanner and, when live, operated independently to engage any target that came within a hundred yards of the torpedoboat on an intercepting course. The weapon was switched off at most times—it would riddle an approaching admiral's car in harbor as cheerfully as it would bat a hostile missile—but it gave the torpedoboat a modicum of protection against guided weapons in combat.

"Sir?" Samuels added. "We'll have to throttle back to make the chicane at the mouth of 18. Over."

"That's fine, Ensign," Dan replied absently as the AI ran possible scenarios, one after another, on the sight display. "So long as we don't try to run, it'll just look as though we're having problems with our charts. Over."

He looked at Johnnie, keyed intercom, and muttered, "Which, thank God, we're not. These charts—"

Dan nodded toward the holographic web of waterways. The glowing blue line—L7521—maneuvered against the red line of the surface skimmer, until a line of red dots joined the two.

The blue line ended.

"—are all that's going to save us. If anything does."

He grinned at his nephew. "That and you spotting the radar signal when whoever was at the EW console slept."

"Is Haynes sitting at that console?" Johnnie asked.

Dan shook his head. On the display's next scenario, the blue line cut across a reed bed that Johnnie didn't think was a channel.

It *wasn't* a channel. The line carried forward on inertia, then stopped—hopelessly aground. Red dots indicating gunfire from the ambusher touched the point which marked the torpedoboat.

A new scenario began.

"I don't like Haynes," Dan said. "But he's a fanatic about getting whatever job's in front of him done. By the book—but done."

The low-lying islands formed a mottled backdrop to the display now. Through the cut-out in the hologram for the iron sights, Johnnie scanned the foliage for any sign of the surface skimmer.

Nothing. Of course nothing. You could hide a battleship, much less an air-cushion vehicle, among the dense vegetation of the Braids.

The ambush might very well have gone unnoticed—until it was sprung. Personnel on a boat ferrying people back from leave couldn't be expected to be very alert.

And as Dan had noted, the surface skimmer could run the hydrofoil down if necessary.

L7521 heeled hard to starboard, slowing and juddering as her wake overran the decelerating foils. Sailors swung and cursed. They were trying to hold on with one hand while their real concern was for the weapons they might have to use at any instant.

The mouth of Channel 18 was lost to sight among scores of mangrove-dripping notches in neighboring islands.

While his uncle attempted to bend the future into an acceptable pattern on the big hologram, Johnnie kept a real-time course display in one quadrant of his visor. The youth grimaced at the situation.

The other vessel had stopped using radar when L7521 came within ten miles; passive sensors were sufficient for it to accurately track the oncoming torpedoboat. Though the ambusher quivered as its prey changed direction, the commander of the surface skimmer did not bother shifting from his hiding place in the relatively-broad Channel 19 as the torpedoboat twisted into the neighboring waterway.

Johnnie kept the twin barrels of his guns aligned with the pointing line in his visor—a vector drawn by his AI toward where the surface skimmer lurked a mile up the parallel channel. He could see only foliage, though from fifty feet or even closer there was an obvious bright diversity of other life growing in the mangroves.

"They'll sweep across a low spot with all guns blazing, then, sir?" Johnnie asked over the intercom. He spoke quietly so that his uncle could pretend not to have heard if the chart demanded his full attention.

The torpedoboat sliced through a stretch of open water so narrow that reed tops slapped the bow like gunshots. Branches wove together above them, throwing the vessel into shadow.

A thirty-pound frog leaped from a mangrove trunk and sailed a hundred feet through the air on its broad feet. Its open-mouthed course took it, like a whale swallowing plankton, into a mass of insects startled aloft by the hydrofoil.

The frog slid neatly into the water. The jaws of something far larger clopped over the amphibian in a shower of spray.

L7521 banked to port, then starboard again, as it followed the meandering waterway. The directional changes were so great that Ensign Samuels cut the hydrofoil's speed to scarcely more than that required to keep it up on the outriggers.

"No, they won't take that risk unless they have to," Dan replied. "They'll stay out of sight and pop at us with indirect fire until a shell or two gets through."

Instead of course plots, a view of the long island separating Channels 18 and 19 now filled the display. Dan's artificial intelligence overlaid bright lines across the swampy land. The individual lines ranged in color from orange through yellow to chartreuse.

"I . . . ," Johnnie said. He swallowed and squeezed tighter on the grips of the twin mount.

The channel broadened into a mirror of black water. The mangroves no longer closed the canopy above. The hydrofoil's bow wave faceted the surface into dazzling jewels.

"I wouldn't think pirates, looters, would have that kind of equipment," Johnnie said as he visualized death dropping unanswerably from the sky.

"Jack de Lessups of Flotilla Blanche is a friend of mine," Dan said calmly. "But *I* don't think he's too honorable to put me out of the way before a battle—if it could be done without anybody knowing."

The torpedoboat accelerated again as the channel straightened. Halfway through the Braids, Channel 18 ended in a marsh too shallow, even at high tide, for a hydrofoil to navigate. Until that point, it provided a deceptively open course.

Dan grinned at his nephew. "You might say that Jack respects me," he added.

Johnnie wouldn't have heard the *choonk* of the mortar firing if he hadn't been expecting it. Even then it might have been his imagination—

Until the miniature Gatling gun on the cockpit lifted like a dog raising its muzzle to sniff the air.

There was a black speck in the sky, a shell just above the zenith of its arc. The Automatic Defense System twitched, locked, and ripped the air with a burst at the frequency of a dental drill. Yellow flame stabbed out of the spinning barrels; though the rounds were caseless, propellant gas puffed from the breech mechanism and blew grit over the men in the open cockpit.

The mortar bomb exploded, a flash of orange in a splotch of filthy smoke. Fragments of hot casing shredded leaves and created a circular froth in the channel. The bits which pattered onto the torpedoboat's deck weren't heavy enough to do damage at this range.

Light winked in the sky. A camera in the nose of the shell sent television pictures down a fiber-optics line to an operator aboard the surface skimmer. The operator had planned to steer the shell's tailfins by commands sent up the same line. Now the gossamer trail of glass drifted harmlessly from the sky, writhing in the turbulence from the explosion.

The operator would be shifting his console to control one of the two further rounds which burped from the clip-fed mortar as soon as the ADS detonated the first bomb.

L7521 had been accelerating. Samuels continued pouring the coal to his thrusters, closing the range to the hidden ambusher. The Blackhorse vessel was in trouble if it came off the outriggers here, because the depth of the channel might not be enough to float the hydrofoil's main hull.

They were in trouble no matter what.

Johnnie checked for at least the tenth time to be sure that his twin mount was set to fire explosive bullets. If he got a shot at the enemy, his burst had to count. He figured his best bet was to blow gaping holes in the hovercraft's plenum chamber, disabling the craft for hours and possibly—just possibly—giving the hydrofoil a chance to run clear.

The ADS snarled like a bumblebee larger even than the jungles of Venus had spawned. One of the pair of guided shells exploded at its apex. The speck of the other continued to drop while the Gatling spun to track it, then fired again.

The blast rocked Johnnie down in his seat. Something whined angrily from the neck flare of his helmet. Water just off the torpedoboat's bow spouted six feet high where a large chunk, perhaps the nose cone, hit.

The surface skimmer was parallelling them unseen on the other side of the island to starboard. Johnnie aimed where the AI told him to, praying for a visible target.

Nothing but mangroves, tens to hundreds of yards of rippling black trunks. Too dense for sight, too dense for bullets to penetrate.

The chart in the holographic display unrolled as L7521 sped down the channel. Because of the chart's reduced scale, its movement appeared leisurely compared to that of the trees and the squawking, startled animals ducking to concealment among them.

Over the scream of wind and the thrusters, the hostile mortar went *choonk, choonk, choonk*. The enemy had fired a full clip. There wasn't a prayer that a single ADS would detonate all three of the guided rounds.

Two crewmen with set, powder-blackened faces poised on the edge of the cockpit. One held a fresh drum of ammunition for the little Gatling; the other sailor would jerk the spent drum out of the way when the gun stuttered to silence. The Automatic Defense System blazed out a hundred fléchettes per second—and the feed drum held only five hundred rounds.

A blue line unrolled across the chart display, marking a neck of land so marshy that the water stood on it. At top

speed, L7521 *might* be able to cut over that part of the
island before her outriggers ripped off and—

"Uncle Dan!" Johnnie screamed. "A mile ahead
there's—"

"Too far!" Dan shouted.

The ADS fired, blasting the first of the shells. The
Gatling turned, cracked out a single fléchette, and froze
with its ammunition supply exhausted as the two remaining
bombs bored down under the guidance of their operators.

Ensign Samuels emptied his handgun skyward as his men
struggled to reload the Automatic Defense System. Even if
the bullets chanced to hit, they didn't have enough energy to
explode the shells.

The shore to starboard sucked away from the torpedoboat. Molluscs riffled the air above a sandbar; the water in
the slough beyond was too deep for mangroves, but great
carnivorous lilies spread across its protected surface. The
land beyond the slight embayment was marked by a
yellow-green line on the chart.

Johnnie's hand curved back to his own pistol.

Dan, controlling all L7521's systems through his helmet,
fired the cage of armor-piercing missiles on the torpedoboat's stern.

The crash of the first-stage rocket motors was echoed an
instant later by a sharper *crack* as each five-inch missile
went supersonic and the ramjet sustainers ignited. The six
rounds rippled off in pairs. Their backblasts enveloped the
vegetation to port in steam and yellow scorch marks. Chips
of mangrove wood exploded from the dense growth hiding
the surface skimmer from its prey.

The missiles had sharp noses and enough velocity to
damage the armor of a battleship, an ideal combination for
penetrating brush with minimal deflection. Dan had waited
to fire the salvo until the forest between him and the
ambusher was thin as it was going to be—

At any time before shells blew L7521 to scraps and foam.

The guided bombs staggered in the air as their operators lost control. The shells dropped into the channel ten yards to either side of the torpedoboat, raising harmless columns of mud and water. Various forms of scavengers arrowed toward the circles of dead fish.

A smoke ring, then a huge waterspout rose from Channel 19. The concussion rocked the torpedoboat to port before its outriggers could compensate. It must have been a secondary explosion, shells and fuel aboard the surface skimmer, because the armor-piercing missiles didn't have warheads.

"Sometimes you get lucky," Dan said softly. He unplugged his helmet, then collapsed into the assistant gunner's seat as the flex wound back within its cradle. The display became a normal holographic gunsight again.

"First you have to be good," Johnnie said. "Sir."

"Blackhorse Three to bridge," Dan said with his eyes closed. "Your ship again, Ensign Samuels. I suggest you take us through Channel 17 when you get her turned around. Nineteen's got better clearance, but there may be somebody there still able to shoot. Three out."

"I doubt it," Johnnie said. "I doubt there's anything left the size of a matchbox. You did . . . Uncle Dan, you were perfect."

His uncle smiled. He didn't open his eyes.

They had reached the point that the chart had marked with a blue line. The channel was deeper here. Samuels slowed L7521 and dropped her onto her main hull to turn around.

Johnnie stared at what he'd thought from the display might be a connection by which they could enter Channel 19 and get a direct shot at their attacker. Though there *was* standing water, there was also a solid belt of mangroves. The youth couldn't see the far channel through them.

"We couldn't have gotten through here, after all," Johnnie admitted over the intercom.

Dan surveyed the terrain with a practiced eye, then shrugged. "We'd sure have tried if I hadn't gotten lucky with a missile," he said.

And if neither of those mortar shells had blasted us to atoms, Johnnie's mind added.

Aloud he said, "It's solid trees, Uncle Dan. They would have torn us apart if we'd hit them."

L7521 accelerated, kicking up a triple roostertail as she rose onto her foils.

Commander Cooke smiled humorlessly at his nephew. "I didn't say it was a good choice, lad," he said. "But losing is the worst choice of all."

A great, anvil-topped cloud of black smoke marked where the surface skimmer had exploded. As the hydrofoil passed that point in the parallel channel, Johnnie heard the crackle of a fuel fire across the narrow island.

8.

*They bit, they glared, gave blows like beams, a wind went with
their paws;*
*With wallowing might and stifled roar they rolled on one
another. . . .*

—Leigh Hunt

BLACKHORSE BASE WAS an atoll rather than an embayment
of one of the larger land masses. Dozens of separate islands,
most of them waving green plumage, formed a pattern like
the individual blotches of a jaguar's rosette. Even where the
connecting reef rose only occasionally above the sea, life
forms clawed at one another for light and food and the sheer
joy of slaughter.

By focusing his gunsight past one of those low spots in
the reef, Johnnie glimpsed the great gray shapes of Blackhorse dreadnoughts in the central deep-water anchorage.

With a motion more like that of an elevator than a
vehicle, L7521 slowed and settled toward the surface of the
sea. The main hull slurped down and wallowed as the
auxiliary thruster took over the load; the outriggers came
out of the water.

Johnnie blinked. Something with suckers and bright,
furious eyes stared back at him from the blade of the bow
foil. It dropped away with regret as direct sunlight baked the
plastic surface to which it clung.

How the creature had ever managed to get and hold a grip
at seventy-plus knots. . . .

"Why did we stop out here?" Johnnie asked. They were

half a mile from the nearest island, and he could see that the entrance to the central anchorage was some distance farther around the circuit of the atoll.

"Twelve knots only feels like being stopped," Dan chuckled. "And—it isn't good form to come racing up to a fleet's base. Even when it's your own and you're expected."

He pointed to the nearest of the islands which had been cleared for occupation. Railguns, dug into coral revetments, were tracking the hydrofoil.

Johnnie started to focus his gunsight for a closer look at the installations, but his uncle caught his hand. "*Real* bad idea," Dan said. "Aim your guns straight up."

L7521, now operating as a conventionally-hulled craft, puttered past an island at a safe three hundred yards from its luxuriant vegetation. Something looked out of a mangrove thicket and snarled. A machine-gunner along the starboard railing snarled back with a short burst.

The next island in the loose chain had an oddly leprous appearance. Johnnie thought he saw the shapes of heavy equipment, but there were also patches of vegetation whose green was brighter than that of the other islands.

He squinted. His uncle took a pair of flat electronic binoculars out of his breast pocket and scanned the island.

"We've only cleared three of the islands," Dan explained. "Now that the Blackhorse is expanding—thanks to the Senator—we decided we needed more room for facilities. This latest flap caught us after we'd made an initial pass on Island 4, but long before we'd gotten the soil sterilized. All available personnel are busy bringing ships up to combat standard, so the clearing operation's had to wait."

He handed the binoculars to Johnnie.

Construction equipment, including bulldozers, rock plows, and support structures which looked like stranded barges, stood as though choked by the vegetation that crawled over the machines and the ground alike. A sheep's-foot roller had eight-foot trees growing from the soil which clung to its great studded wheels, and another huge device was anonymous within a wrapper of green tentacles.

"How long has the work been abandoned?" Johnnie asked.

"Twenty-seven days," the older man said with grim amusement. "Lets you know why our ancestors decided to colonize the sea floor instead of the land, doesn't it?"

Dan touched the keypad of his helmet and said in a different voice, "L7521 to Base Control. Request permission to engage life forms on Island 4 with the twins. Over."

"Wow!" said Johnnie.

Something had just lifted its head from the prey it was devouring beside a bulldozer. As the actinic radiation bathing Venus mutated the creature's ancestral germ plasm, its legs became shorter and thicker; its body slimmed; and its wing cases shrank to vestigial nubs to be displayed during courtship rituals.

"Base to L7521," said a bored voice. "Permission denied. We've still got equipment on 4 and it's not for target practice. Over."

The creature's head and great shearing mandibles were still those of a tiger beetle.

"Base, let me rephrase that request," Dan said in a tone that suggested he had a rasp for a tongue. "Director of Planning Cooke aboard L7521 requests permission to engage life forms on Island 4 with the twins. Over."

"Base to L7521," said the voice, no longer bored. "Permission granted. Out."

Johnnie swung the powered mounts and lowered the gun barrels as part of the same movement.

"Wait one," his uncle said as he turned and waved to the hydrofoil's commanding officer in the cockpit.

"Roger, go ahead, sir," Ensign Samuels responded over the com set.

The tiger beetle's head dipped, then rose again. Its jaws were working furiously on the strip of white flesh gripped in its mandibles. The creature's eyes did not shift to follow the vessel, but the sun glinting on different sets of the faceted lenses gave the impression of movement.

Johnnie thumbed his sights to x2, then x5 when he'd acquired the target. He projected a translucent orange ghost ring. At the higher magnification, the broad ring hopped and wobbled with L7521's motion, almost unnoticed until then. Johnnie dialed in mils of elevation until the bottom of the ring no longer skipped down into the bulldozer, then locked the mount's stabilizer—

And pressed the firing tit.

Though the twin-sixties were heavy armament in Johnnie's terms, their use on a torpedoboat was more to disconcert enemies a thousand times larger than in the realistic hope of destroying an opponent. The feed drums were loaded with every other round a tracer. The guns spat a lash of glowing fireballs—a sight to make a hostile gunner flinch, even if he was behind twenty-inch armor and watching through a remote pick-up.

The guns belched two solid, pulsing lines of gold which converged at the laser-calculated range to the target. The lining of Johnnie's helmet clamped firmly over his ears like a punch to both sides of his head. The muzzle blasts slapped his face as the guns recoiled alternately.

Blinking with the double shock to his vision and skin, Johnnie lifted his thumb from the trigger.

The tiger beetle charged. It climbed over the bulldozer with a swift fluidity which suggested it had scores of legs instead of six.

The charge was blind reflex. The creature's head had vanished. The short burst of high-explosive .60-caliber bullets had blown eyes and brain to jelly in a dozen red flashes.

All the guns mounted on the starboard rail began firing. Passengers joined in with automatic rifles and even pistols. The beetle's armor sparkled with the dusting of tiny bullets exploding harmlessly across it.

While the others banged ineffectively at the headless creature, Johnnie switched his feed selector from X to S—solids instead of high-explosive. He squeezed the trigger again and held it down. His long burst halted the charging beetle, then knocked it backward.

Though the mechanism still fed from the same loading drums when the guns were set to the S position, the bursting charges in the bullets did not get the jolt of electricity necessary to prime them. Instead of exploding against the first object they struck, the bullets smashed their way through to the creature's vitals, ripping the heart and the ganglia controlling the shimmering legs.

Johnnie stopped firing. He raised the barrels of his gun and rotated them in line with the vessel's axis again.

Lubricant and powder smoke oozed out of the mechanism, filling the gun tub with their sickening mixture.

The tiger beetle lay on the island's margin. The right side of its thorax was staved in and leaking white fluid. Its legs twitched feebly, but smaller predators were already appearing from both land and water to feast on the unexpected bounty.

Uncle Dan smiled at Johnnie. "Told you I'd find you some target practice," he said.

L7521 burbled past Island 3, a mass of shops and barracks formed of concrete and stabilized earth. There were variations of style and color, but no semblance of formal art. Despite—or perhaps because of—that, the buildings made a pleasing whole and seemed in keeping with the harsh ambiance of sea and sky around them.

The net-protected entrance to the central lagoon was between Islands 3 and 2. Railgun emplacements flanked it. On the tip of either island was an openly displayed depth-charge mortar.

"Shouldn't they be in pits?" Johnnie said, nodding toward the mortars as winches drew open the outer pair of nets.

"They aren't for submarines," the Blackhorse officer explained. "Subs wouldn't get this close through the outer ring of sea-bottom sensors. But some of the local life forms are about as dangerous as a hostile sub."

The torpedoboat slid through the narrow opening, then waited at idle as men on shore made certain that nothing had entered *with* L7521. Only when security was satisfied did the inner nets part to allow the little vessel into the lagoon.

Long quays reached out from the three inhabited islands. Vessels up through the size of cruisers were moored to them, three and four deep. There were scores of submarines, their smooth black backs awash almost to the conning towers. Johnnie suspected that there were more than the ninety subs which Wenceslas' data bank credited to the Blackhorse.

The heavy ships, the dreadnoughts and the two carriers, were anchored out in the lagoon. Swarms of lighters, some of them of five hundred tons but looking like water beetles by comparison, surged between the big ships and the quays.

A railgun crashed angrily. Johnnie jumped and touched his grip controls. The shooting was just the weapon on the west end of Island 1 discouraging a visitor—perhaps another beetle—from the uncleared portion of the atoll.

Four heavy vessels were visible only as portions of superstructure poking out above the drydocks on Island 1. "New construction?" Johnnie asked, nodding.

"Two of them are," Dan agreed. "Work's stopped for now while we concentrate on the ships we'll be able to use within the next week . . . which itself may be a little optimistic on time. The other two are battle damage."

He brushed his lips with the back of his hand, a trivial gesture unless you happened to be watching his bleak eyes as he did it. His voice had gone slightly harsh as he added, "The *Catherine* may be ready in time. The *Isabella* won't be."

"The *Isabella* was your squadron flagship three months ago, wasn't she?" Johnnie said.

"Yep," said Dan. He laughed—or cackled. "But you should see the other guy."

Then he shook himself like a dog coming in from the rain; and when he met his nephew's eyes again, he was wearing his familiar, insouciant grin.

L7521 slid up to a landing stage built out from a quay on Island 2. Seamen at bow and stern belayed lines tossed from the stage, but they didn't tie them off.

Ensign Samuels cursed as his vessel slipped back from the worn rubber fender and grunched solidly against the stage. "All passengers ashore," he ordered over the cockpit loudspeaker. "And step on it. If you please. Sirs."

Uncle Dan took off the borrowed commo helmet and set it on his seat.

"Let's go, Provisional Recruit Gordon," he said with a smile. "And see if we can get Admiral Bergstrom to confirm you."

The passengers from the stern and cockpit were already hopping onto the landing stage. Captain Haynes jumped with surprising grace; looked back over his shoulder at Dan and Johnnie; and began striding down the catwalk—

Toward the Base Operations Center.

9.

The great mind knows the power of gentleness
Only tries force, because persuasion fails.

—Robert Browning

THE REFRIGERATED AIR of the Base Operations Center made
Johnnie stumble as he stepped through the door. Dan looked
at him in amusement and said, "You've acclimated quickly.
That's good. I hadn't counted on it."

"How cold do they keep it?" the younger man asked as
he looked around the entrance hall. It was dim and a little
dingy as well as being cold. Not cool, *cold*.

"Eighty degrees," Dan said. "Which is wrong—it ought
to be pegged to no more than ten degrees below the
ambient, but people like to be comfortable when they
can . . . and they don't worry about what's going to
happen in action, even on a dreadnought, when the cooling
plant takes a direct hit."

The door marked 'Commander in Chief' was open, but
that was just the outer office. The secretary/receptionist at
the central desk and electronics console wore the bars of a
senior lieutenant.

"Good morning, Commander," the lieutenant said. "Admiral Bergstrom asked if he might have a few minutes alone
with Captain Haynes before you joined them."

*Captain Haynes demanded a few minutes alone with
Admiral Bergstrom,* Johnnie translated. His face grew taut.

He remembered what his uncle had said about control, but he wasn't able to relax.

Despite all the sophisticated hardware associated with the desk, there was an acetate-covered sign-out chart on one wall of the room. It was printed with boxes in which the names and destinations of officers were written in grease pencil. On the opposite wall was a holographic seascape: pelicans banking over dunes sprinkled with sea oats, while a gentle surf foamed up the strand.

The seascape showed a memory of Earth. Nowhere on Venus was there a scene so idyllic.

"Sure, that's fine, Barton," Dan said easily. "We'll wait in the hall and keep out of your hair."

There were bulletin boards in the hall. One of them listed a handful of apartments in Wenceslas Dome. Dan nodded to it and said, "Leases that got opened up three months ago. They've been pretty well picked over by now."

"Is it going to be all right?" the younger man asked tightly. "With Haynes already there?"

"We'll make it all right, won't we?" Dan said. "Just follow my lead, is all."

He grinned in what seemed good humor and added, "You can think of it as your baptism of fire, John. Only, no matter how bad you screw up, nobody's going to die."

The expression changed minusculely. "For a while, that is."

"You know," Johnnie said, "in all the years I've known you, Uncle Dan, there's only once I've seen you really angry."

Dan chuckled. "You've seen me angry, lad? When was that?"

"Yesterday. In the Senator's office, when you told him he was a—that he didn't have any balls."

"Oh, that," the older man said. He chuckled again. "And that's why you decided your father was a coward, is it?

Well, you mustn't mistake tones for emotions. The Senator reacts very emotionally to anything involving you—that's just biology, after all. So I—"

He spread his right hand and looked critically at the nails. "—had to get his attention on the level at which he was operating."

Johnnie blinked and turned away. "Then it wasn't true?" he said, trying to keep the tremor out of his voice.

"Look at me," his uncle said. "*Look* at me."

"Yessir."

"What's true is that Mankind has a chance to survive and spread to the stars," the mercenary officer said without raising his voice. "What's true is that I'll do whatever I need to do in order to protect that chance."

Johnnie was standing rigid. Dan relaxed with a visible shudder and attempted a grin.

"One more thing and we'll drop this, John," he said. "I want you to remember. I've killed people because it was my job. I've killed people because I was scared. But I've never killed anybody because I was angry."

Johnnie nodded. "Sure," he said. He would have made the same reply if his uncle had told him it was noon, and the information would have made as much difference to him.

"Commander?" called Lieutenant Barton from the office doorway. "The Admiral will see you now."

Dan put his arm around Johnnie's shoulders. "Buck up," he said as they strode forward. " 'Forward into ba-at-tle, see our banners go!' "

"I'll be fine, Uncle Dan." He really believed it now.

"Sure you will, John," Dan replied. He settled himself and his sweat-marked uniform into the semblance of the third-ranking officer in the premier mercenary fleet on Venus. "You wouldn't be here if I weren't sure of that."

Dan motioned Johnnie through the inner doorway first.

Captain Haynes, seated in one of the two chairs in front of the Admiral's desk, snapped, "Not him."

Johnnie paused. Dan's touch moved him into the office.

"Yes, him, Captain," Dan said as he closed the door and stepped past his nephew. "Recruit Gordon's presence is necessary for this discussion."

He nodded toward Admiral Bergstrom. "But the explanation won't take very long."

Admiral Bergstrom's office was large without being spacious. It was filled with enough scrap and rusted metal to suggest a salvage yard.

One wall held a stencilled swatch of a gunboat's bow panelling. The last digit of the number, Z841–, had vanished into the hole blown by an explosive shell.

Above the panel was a hand-held rocket launcher of a pattern at least thirty years old. Beside them both was the sun-bleached, shrapnel-torn pennant of a flotilla commander; and to the right of that in the corner beside the door was the empty circular frame which had once held the condensing lens of a high-resolution display.

All four walls were similarly adorned, and larger pieces of junk took up floor-space besides.

Souvenirs of a life spent in the service of war.

Admiral Bergstrom looked like a clerk with tired, nervous eyes. His left hand was withered, though he used it to play with a miniature mobile of shrapnel chunks as he looked from one to another of his visitors.

The rumor Johnnie had overheard in conversations in his father's house was that Bergstrom had a maintenance-level drug habit. The Admiral's dilated pupils suggested the rumor might be true.

Dan sat. "Sir, it's necessary that Recruit John Gordon be given officer's rank and made my aide without the usual formalities. His background is such that he'll be a credit to the company, but—"

"That's absurd!" said Haynes, his face darkening.

Don't be sorry. Be controlled.

"But it isn't because of *that* that I make the request," Dan continued. "I presume you've realized that Recruit Gordon is my nephew . . . and Senator Gordon's son. Unfor—"

· "If there was ever a good time to provide, uh, untrained civilians with commissions," Haynes said, "it's not now when we're facing the most severe test in the Blackhorse's history."

The catch in the captain's voice suggested that he'd intended a less flattering phrase than 'untrained civilians.' Discretion, and memory of just how powerful a politician's brat Johnnie was, had bridled his tongue.

"Untrained . . . ," Dan repeated, as if savoring the word on his tongue. Then, sharply but not hostilely, "Johnnie, keep your eyes on me!"

"Yessir!"

"There's a lens frame on the wall behind you. Shoot withi—"

The double *cra-crack!* of the pistol shots surprised everyone in the office except Commander Cooke; even Johnnie, especially Johnnie, because if he'd thought of what he was doing, he'd never've been able to do it. Two rounds, and he didn't turn until the second was away, shockingly loud in a room without a sound-absorbent lining.

Johnnie thumbed the catch and replaced the partial magazine with a fresh one from his belt pouch. His fingers worked by rote. His first round had starred the concrete wall just beneath the eight-inch ring; his second had struck in the center of the target. Both of the light, high-velocity bullets had disintegrated in sprays of metal against the hard surface.

The door burst open. *"What the—"* shouted Lieutenant

Barton. His eyes widened and his hand dropped toward the
butt of the pistol he carried in a flapped service holster.

Johnnie slipped his own weapon into his cutaway holster
and turned his back on Barton. His ears rang, and the air
was cloying with the familiar odor of powder smoke.

"That won't be necessary, Lieutenant," Dan said, lifting
one leg lazily to hang it over the arm of his chair. "Everything's under control here."

The door closed. Johnnie focused his eyes on a signed
group photograph on the wall above Admiral Bergstrom's
head.

"Under control . . . ," Haynes said. "Cooke, you're
insane."

"Now that we've covered the matter of Recruit Gordon's
training," Dan said, "there's the serious matter of why—"

"There's more to training than skill with small arms,
Daniel," said the Admiral quietly. "As you know."

"As I know, sir," Dan agreed. "In everything but
hands-on experience, Recruit Gordon compares favorably
to the best of our junior lieutenants. But the reason it's
necessary that we commission him isn't that we need
another officer—useful though that may be . . . but
rather, because Senator Gordon doesn't trust us."

"What?" blurted Captain Haynes.

What? Johnnie's mind echoed in equal surprise.

"With increasing irritation the Senator has been following
our attempts to associate a supporting company," Dan
continued smoothly. "He called me to him to demand an
explanation—"

"That's not yours to give, Daniel," Admiral Bergstrom
said with an edge to the words that Johnnie hadn't thought
within the capacity of the Commander in Chief.

"I know that, sir," Dan continued, nodding. "But I know
my ex-brother-in-law also, and there was nothing to be

gained by claiming those negotiations were none of my affair, so he'd have to talk to one of you."

He dipped his head first to Bergstrom, then to Captain Haynes.

"But that's ridiculous," Haynes protested. "There've been some delays, certainly, but they weren't through any fault of ours."

"I told the Senator that, yes," Dan said, bobbing agreement.

"And in any case, now that I'm back it's just a matter of working out the last details of our agreement with Admiral Braun of the Angels," Haynes continued.

"That I *couldn't* tell the Senator," Dan said, "because as you know, I don't believe it myself."

"Right!" blazed Haynes. "You don't believe it because Admiral Braun's a friend of mine. What do you propose, Commander? Working a deal with your great good friend de Lessups in Flotilla Blanche?"

Johnnie couldn't see his uncle's face as he met Haynes' glare, but his voice seemed as calm as if he were ordering lunch as he replied, "Admiral de Lessups offered me his number two slot last year, Captain. But neither he nor I would expect the other to act dishonorably when our companies were already engaged by rival domes.

"Any more," Dan continued in a sudden, jagged snarl like that with which he had hectored the Senator, "than I'd expect your Admiral Braun to act honorably at any distance greater than pistol range!"

"Listen, you—"

"Gentlemen!"

"If Braun meant to sign, he'd already have signed!" Dan shouted.

"I needed to take care of business back at Wenceslas," Haynes retorted with a hint of defensiveness. "I'll meet him face to—"

"You had to see your wife, you mean!"

Admiral Bergstrom's right fist rang deliberately on a section of dimpled armor plate on his desktop. *"Gentlemen!"* he shouted.

Captain Haynes had jumped into a crouch. He blinked like a sow bear at her first sight of spring sunshine, then sat—or flopped—into his chair again. His right hand clenched and relaxed; and clenched again.

"Now that I'm back," Haynes resumed in a voice that was almost falsetto, "I'll go to Paradise Base and knock down the final details." He raised his eyes to meet those of the Admiral. "With your agreement, sir?"

Bergstrom grimaced. "Yes, yes," he said without enthusiasm. "I would have thought that perhaps Hackney's Wizards were a better bet, but—"

"The Angels have the big-bore throw weight that'll be crucial, sir," Haynes said earnestly.

"Yes, well," the Admiral said. "It's really too late to begin negotiations with another fleet now. And anyway, the Angels will certainly be satisfactory. Almost any company would be, given our own strength."

Almost under his breath, Bergstrom added, "I don't understand why they seem to be treating the Blackhorse as a pariah. We've always kept up the highest standards. . . ."

"Yes, *sir,*" Haynes said. He rose. "I'll take a hydrofoil to Paradise immediately."

"And you'll take Ensign Gordon with you," Dan said from his seat.

"I'll do no—"

"Because by taking Senator Gordon's trusted observer," Dan continued with icy, battle-order precision, "the Senator's spy, if you will . . . we'll be proving to him that we have nothing to hide."

Dan stood, a smooth uncoiling of his body from the seat

as graceful as the motion with which his nephew had drawn and fired behind his back. "Isn't that so, Admiral Bergstrom? We have nothing to hide."

Bergstrom grimaced again. He closed his eyes briefly, looking more than ever like an overworked bookkeeper at the end of the day.

"Yes, of course," he said at last. "You'll be taking some staff with you to Paradise Base, Captain. I don't see any reason why Ensign Gordon shouldn't be among them."

Johnnie was looking at his uncle. Commander Cooke grinned.

10.

From many a wondrous grot and secret cell
Unnumber'd and enormous polypi
Winnow with giant arms the slumbering green.

—Alfred, Lord Tennyson

THE FORWARD GUN tub was decorated with the hydrofoil's stencilled number, M4434, and a freehand rendition of her unofficial name: *Bellycutter*. There was also a cartoon of an oriental figure to explicate the name for anybody who hadn't seen the casualty rates for torpedoboats.

The lone sailor on duty behind the twin guns was dozing, but there wasn't much reason for him to be alert. They had sped from Blackhorse across open sea and through the Kanjar Straits. The run was without incident until a pair of skimmers came out of Paradise Base, inspected M4434 as she dropped off her outriggers, and howled back within the harbor at high speed.

Johnnie stood in the bow, bracing himself against the roll with a hand on the tub's armored rim. The continent of North Hell was a mass of greens and earth tones ahead of M4434, punctuated by concrete and plastic constructions on both jaws of land enveloping the Angels' fine natural harbor.

The Angels, like Flotilla Blanche and the Warcocks, were based on the periphery of the Ishtar Basin. That would make link-up between the Angels and the Blackhorse— whose atoll was in the Western Ocean—tricky, though not impossible. Even if the direct route via the Kanjar Straits was blocked, there were scores of other passages through the archipelago sweeping around the south and east of the basin.

The Angels' main installations were on the southern arm of the harbor. They were protected by a wall; beyond the wall, a fence which sparkled as high currents fried life forms attempting it; and beyond the fence, strings of flashes and explosions. Guns were firing from the wall, blowing swathes in the nearest vegetation in an attempt to knock it down before roots and branches became a threat to the inner defenses.

There were signs that the Angels had recently started to clear an area farther out so that the present barrier could be given over to expanded facilities. The attempt had been abandoned, probably for the reason Blackhorse had done the same: all available men were working to put the fleet on a war footing.

If the Angels were preparing for war, then Captain Haynes must be right. What would that do to Uncle Dan's maneuvering?

The northern landspit was defended but almost unoccupied. At its tip were heavy batteries: railguns and, for engaging enemies over the horizon, conventional artillery in massive casements. The only other installations were those facing the threat of the jungle, which on this side of the harbor was muted.

While the southern jaw had been in existence for millennia, its northern counterpart was the creation of a volcano within living memory.

The lava poured out at 4,000°. Though the pullulating life of Venus had robbed the surface of its virginal sterility even before it cooled to air temperature, the fresh rock nonetheless formed a sufficient barrier against the largest and most dangerous of the predatory vegetation.

A low electrified fence, supported by chemical sprayers and flame guns, protected the gun emplacements from surface roots and the occasional large carnivore which burst from the jungle beyond the two hundred yards of russet lava. In a century—or even a few decades—rain water and the jungle would break the raw rock into permeable soil, with disastrous results for the gun crews on duty when it happened.

But that would be another day, and the concerns of a mercenary were for the far shorter term. . . .

Except maybe for Uncle Dan.

Dan had said to observe *everything* about Paradise Base, the way he'd reflexively observed Admiral Bergstrom's office as he entered it. Bergstrom and Haynes probably thought Johnnie had been briefed on what to expect during the interview; the exhibition of shooting had impressed them, even Haynes, despite that.

But the test had been much more extreme than that. Commander Cooke had wanted to see how well his nephew's training responded to genuine field conditions. '. . . *your baptism of fire, John*. . . .'

Walcheron, the sailor manning the gun tub, suddenly snapped to alertness.

Johnnie's left hand made an instinctive grab for the rifle butt-upward beside the unoccupied assistant gunner's seat. His head rotated quickly, scanning to find the cause of alarm.

There didn't seem to be anything amiss.

A pair of gliders wheeled high in the white sky, no threat even to a torpedoboat wallowing along on its main hull. The only other vessel in sight was the Angel net-tending boat. The distance between the jaws of land was too great for the protective nets to be operated from shore, as at Blackhorse Base. Instead, a double-ended fifty-ton vessel equipped with winches accomplished the task from the center of the channel.

The net-tender was lightly armed, even by torpedoboat standards. Besides, some of the crewmen aboard her were waving cheerfully at the visitor which would break the utter boredom of their duty.

The man in the gun tub turned to Johnnie. "Your name Gordon?" he asked.

"Yes—ah, yes," Johnnie replied, catching himself barely before he, an officer, called a seaman 'sir.'

The gunner tapped his commo helmet. Johnnie hadn't been offered one—and hadn't wanted to ask—on this trip. "Cap'n Haynes wants t' see you in the stern," the seaman explained, gesturing with his thumb.

Johnnie opened his mouth to ask what he realized before speaking was a silly question.

"He wants t' tell you something private, I guess," said the sailor, giving the obvious answer anyway.

Captain Haynes had made this run (as the previous one, from Wenceslas Dome to Blackhorse Base) in the cockpit. Now he got up from his seat at the control console and made his way sternward. His stocky body rode gracefully through each chop-induced quiver of the deck.

Haynes didn't bother to look over his shoulder to see that Johnnie was obeying the command.

"Right," Johnnie said, picking his way carefully along the railing. He wasn't at all steady, though he was sure he'd learn the trick of walking along a pitching deck if he managed to avoid drowning in the near future.

"Careful, kid," warned a tobacco-chewing petty officer amidships. He reached out to steady Johnnie as the youth passed by.

The sailor was amusing himself by spitting tobacco juice onto the sea. Water boiled as predators attacked the insubstantial prey.

Johnnie wondered if Haynes would permit the torpedoboat to stop and rescue him if he fell overboard. Judging
from the way teeth instantly tore into the tobacco juice, it
probably wouldn't matter. . . .

The deck widened astern of the cockpit. Breathing hard
from the earlier portion of the forty-foot journey, Johnnie
reached the captain's side.

Haynes had drawn his heavy pistol. He was looking back
over the wake. He didn't turn around.

Johnnie curled the fingers of his left hand firmly around
the cage of ramjet penetrators. "Yes sir?" he said, uncertain
whether or not the captain knew he'd arrived.

"I've been ordered to bring you along, Ensign Gordon,"
Haynes said.

He spat. The gobbet sailed to a point six inches from the
surface of the water. A fish that was all teeth and shimmering scales curved out of the wake and snatched the spittle
from the air.

Haynes fired, blasting a waterspout just short of the
target. The explosive bullet sprayed bits of miniature
shrapnel into the fish so that it left a slick of blood as it
resubmerged.

Seconds later, the wake surged in a feeding frenzy more
violent than a grenade going off.

Johnnie relaxed. *If that was meant to impress
me* . . . he thought.

He'd almost put two rounds of his own through the head
of the fish before it went under; but he had a task to carry
out for Uncle Dan. This wasn't the time or place to show
off.

Haynes holstered his weapon without reloading and gave
Johnnie a satisfied smirk. "I'm under orders to bring you
along," he repeated, "but that doesn't mean you'll be
present during the negotiations. I'm *not* taking a chance of

some untrained kid blurting the wrong thing and putting the whole deal at risk. Do you understand?"

"Yes sir," Johnnie said. He even agreed. After all, a deal with the Angels would be the best proof possible that the Blackhorse wasn't attempting some phony game to fool Senator Gordon.

"And don't try to scare me with what your father's going to say," Haynes continued in a rising voice. "The deal I cut with Admiral Braun will *prove* that the Blackhorse has been negotiating in good faith."

"Yessir," Johnnie said. He wondered if Haynes was stupid—unlikely, given his position—or whether the captain just thought that everybody he disliked was stupid.

"There'll be bars open at Paradise Base," Haynes continued. "Or you can stay with the boat if you like. Just keep out of trouble or I *swear* it won't matter who your relatives are."

"Yessir."

Haynes strode past him, back to the cockpit.

Johnnie rubbed his right palm on his thigh. His uniform had been soaked with spray on the high-speed run, but the hammering sun dried the cloth in minutes after the M4434 dropped off her foils.

He really wished he'd showed up Haynes' clumsy marksmanship; but there'd be another time. . . .

He wiped his gunhand again and returned to the bow while the torpedoboat rocked and waited for the outer net to open. He could just as easily have waited where he was, but then somebody might have thought he was afraid to chance the narrow catwalk amidships.

Johnnie reached the bow in time to steady himself against the gun tub when the auxiliary thruster accelerated M4434 through the minimal opening which the net-tender drew for them.

Reverse thrust slowed the hydrofoil again. A derrick on

the net-tender's bow slid the folds of net forward again to
mate with the line of buoys holding up the fixed portion of
the meshes. The water was a deep blue-green, slimed with
wastes discharged from the base installations.

Something else had entered with M4434. A paddle-
tipped tentacle as big around as a pony keg curled out of the
water and wrapped itself around the net-tender.

For an instant, all the chaos and violence was of the
squid's doing. A second long tentacle encircled the little
vessel. There was a flurry of foam, and a mass of shorter
tentacles, writhing like Medusa's hair, drew six feet of the
squid's mauve body up the net-tender's starboard side.

The vessel bobbed. Waves lapped its starboard rail.

Three, then a dozen guns opened up from the hydrofoil
and the net-tender itself. Explosive bullets dimpled the sea,
the net-tender's hull, and the squid. Johnnie snatched out
the automatic rifle as the gunner spun his twin-sixties to
bear.

"Not those!" Johnnie shouted. "You'll sink them!"

When the big guns continued to rotate, the side of
Johnnie's fist slammed the sailor's helmet hard enough to
knock the man out of his seat. There was no time for
delicacy.

"Use solids!" he warned, but he didn't have a commo
helmet, so nobody could hear him over the gunfire . . .
and anyway, nobody would've listened to a young ensign-
in-name-only.

But he was right.

A young officer leaned over the net-tender's rail with a
sub-machine gun and fired most of the forty-round magazine straight down into the squid. Sparkling explosions
blew the eyes to jelly and raised a cloud of lime dust from
the huge parrot beak.

Sepia flooded the water around the squid; pigment
darkened its flesh from mauve to greenish black.

A pair of tentacles unhooked from the rail and seized the Angels' officer. A third twisted the gun from the youth's hand as skillfully as if the squid still had eyes.

Johnnie switched his rifle to solids and fired a three-shot burst between the monster's eyes. He began walking down the squid's torso with further short bursts, probing for the ganglia. Bullets that exploded on the skin couldn't possibly kill the huge invertebrate.

The creature suddenly spasmed and blushed a pinkish white color. Its tentacles went slack, though the long pair still crisscrossed the net-tender amidships.

The young officer dropped onto the squid's sagging body. Its beak closed reflexively over his waist, but his bullets had powdered the hooked tip which would otherwise have punctured his intestines and crushed his spine.

One of the net-tender's crewmen with more courage than sense jumped into the roiling water and grabbed the stunned officer. In three frog-like kicks he made it back to the vessel's side. Four pairs of hands reached over desperately to pull him and his burden back aboard.

There was a quiver of movement from deep within the water.

"Look out!" Johnnie screamed as he pointed his rifle at where the newcomer would break surface—directly under the struggling men. It was no use trying to shoot *through* the water, but the target would appear jaws-first. . . .

A net-tender crewman, bleeding from a pressure cut on his cheek and forehead, tossed something that looked like a six-pack of beer over the side.

It must have been a bundle of rocket warheads with a short time-fuze, because it went off with a blast that was still bright orange after being filtered through the water.

The gout of water slammed the two vessels apart and lifted their facing sides. Johnnie fell down, but the net-tender's crew used the surge to help them snatch their fellows safe aboard.

A fragment of the squid's tentacle floated near M4434.

The other creature must have been a fish with a swim bladder to rupture in the explosion. It sank to the bottom, unseen save for a flash of terror through the bullet-spattered water.

"Cease fire!" roared Captain Haynes over the cockpit public-address system. "Cease fire! We're not here to waste ammunition!"

Johnnie's left hand was patting the magazine well of his borrowed rifle. He had ejected the empty magazine by rote, but he didn't have a full one with which to replace it.

11.

Oh stay with company and mirth
And daylight and the air;
Too full already is the grave
Of fellows that were good and brave
And died because they were.

—A. E. Housman

"SURE YOU DON'T wanna come, sir?" said Walcheron. Instead of being angry, the sailor seemed pleased that Johnnie had knocked him down in order to save the Angels from the tender mercies of his twin-sixties. "There's an officers' club if you don't wanna . . . ?"

Johnnie forced a smile and waved. "No, I'll just wander. I—I've been in bars, but haven't had a chance to look at a fleet's base before."

"Hang on," warned the Angel driver as he engaged the torque converter of his prime mover. The flat-bed trailer, loaded with sailors from the hydrofoil in place of its more normal cargo, jerked at the end of its loose hitch toward the base cantina.

Captain Haynes and the two staff lieutenants who made up the negotiating team had already been carried two hundred yards to the Administration Building in a slightly-flossier conveyance, an air-cushion runabout. That left Johnnie and a single disconsolate sailor—the watch—alone with the M4434.

Johnnie nodded to the sailor and walked down the dock, coming as close to a saunter as the hot, humid air permitted him.

Paradise Base was a smaller, less polished version of
Blackhorse Base. The Blackhorse torpedoboat was docked
at the destroyer slip; the Angels had no hydrofoils of their
own. The next facility around the circumference of the
harbor was a drydock holding a dreadnought. The combination of concrete walls and a battleship completely hid
everything else in that direction.

Johnnie walked past, looking interested but nonchalant.
Dan had told him to observe everything, but not to make
any notes or sketches until M4434 was at sea again. Johnnie
didn't know what his uncle wanted—and he couldn't
imagine that it made any difference, since the Angels'
precise strength would become a matter of record as soon as
the deal was done.

But Johnnie had his orders, and he was going to carry
them out.

He reached the land end of the quay, facing the Admin
Building and a series of barracks. He turned left to pass the
drydock.

There were twelve destroyers in the slip. All of them
seemed to be combat ready—but that was the full extent of
the Angels' strength in the class. Though destroyers weren't
capable of surviving the fire of heavier vessels for more
than a few seconds, they provided the inner screen against
hostile torpedoboats—a particularly important mission for
the Angels, who didn't have hydrofoil gunboats of their
own.

Johnnie walked on. The drydock had been cast from
red-dyed concrete, but under the blasting sun it seemed to
glow a hazy white. Sweat soaked the sleeves of Johnnie's
cream tunic, and he could feel the skin on the back of his
hands crinkle.

One side of the quay beyond the drydock was given over
to cargo lighters hauling supplies to the dreadnoughts
anchored in mid-harbor. Traffic was heavy, and there were

several railcars backed up on the line leading to the quay from warehouses within the base area.

Two cruisers were drawn up in the slip to the other side. They were middle-sized vessels, armed with rapid-firing 5.25-inch guns rather than the heavier weapons that might have been able to damage a battleship. In effect, they were flagships for the destroyer flotillas; and the pair of them were the only vessels of their class in the company.

Mercenaries have been called the whores of war. Like many prostitutes, the Angels found specialization the best route to success.

The Angels specialized in dreadnoughts.

There were four of the mighty vessels anchored in deep water. They quivered in the sunlight like gray flaws in the jeweled liquid splendor. The ships looked as though they had just crawled from the jungle which ruled the shore encircling most of the harbor.

The most distant of the battleships, the *Holy Trinity,* was huge even by the standards of her sisters. Her armor could take a battering for as long as any vessel on the seas of Venus, and shells from her 18-inch main guns would penetrate any target they struck.

By themselves, the Angels were suicidally out of balance. The company had no scouting capacity of its own; its light forces were insufficient to screen its battleships; and the handful of submarines Johnnie saw moored to a rusting mothership might be useful to test the Angels' own antisubmarine defenses during maneuvers, but they certainly weren't a serious threat to another fleet.

None of that mattered *now:* Admiral Braun could have the deal he wanted, because the Angels' five dreadnoughts would be the margin of victory in the coming fleet action.

A man on a two-wheeled scooter—nobody at Paradise seemed to walk when out of doors—had left the cantina and raced up the quay from which Johnnie had come. Now the vehicle was back, revving high and leaned over at sixty degrees to make the corner onto the harbor road.

Johnnie stepped to the side. There was plenty of room for a truck, much less the scooter, to get around him, but he didn't trust the driver to have his mount under control.

He was probably over-sensitive. There were no personal vehicles in the domes: the slidewalks took care of individual transportation. He'd have to get used to—

The scooter broadsided to a, curving halt in front of Johnnie.

The driver jumped off, leaving his machine rocking on its automatic side-stand. He was young, Johnnie's age, but his skin was already burned a deep mahogany color by the fierce light penetrating the clouds of Venus. He wore ensign's pips on his collar and the legend '*Holy Trinity*' in Fraktur script on the talley around his red cap.

"Is your name Gordon?" the Angel ensign demanded.

"Ensign John Arthur Gordon," Johnnie said. His mind was as blank and white as the sky overhead.

We regret to inform you that your son, John Arthur Gordon, was executed as a spy. May God have mercy on . . .

The other youth smiled as broadly as a shrapnel gash and thrust out his right hand. "Right!" he said. "I'm Sal Grumio, and you just saved my brother's life!"

"Huh?"

"Tony, you know?" Sal explained as he pumped Johnnie's hand furiously. "He was in command of the *Dragger*, you know, the guard boat?"

"Oh," said Johnnie as the light dawned. "Oh, sure . . . but look, it wasn't me. One of his own people jumped in after him. That took real guts, believe—"

"Guts, fine," Sal interrupted. He waved his hands with a gesture of dismissal. "We're all brave, you bet. But *you're* the one had brains enough to use solids and kill the squid. That was you, wasn't it?"

"I, ah . . . ," Johnnie said. "Yeah, that was me."

Sal jerked a thumb in the direction of the cantina. He gestured constantly and expressively. "Yeah, that's what your gunner said in there. Said you're screamin', '*Use solids, use solids!*' and shootin' the crap outa the squid with a rifle. Tony'd've been gone without that, and hell knows how many others besides."

"Well, I . . . ," Johnnie said. "Well, I'm glad I was in the right place."

"Hey, look," Sal said with a sudden frown. "You don't want to wander around out here in the sun. Come on, I'll buy you a drink or ten."

"Well, to tell the truth . . . ," Johnnie said. "Look, I'm so new I haven't been in the Blackhorse a full day. I've never really *seen* a base or any ship but a torpedoboat. I'd just—"

"Hey, you never been aboard a dreadnought?" the Angel ensign said, grinning beatifically. "Really?"

"Never even a destroyer," Johnnie said/admitted.

"You got a treat coming, then," said Sal, "because I've got one of the *Holy Trinity*'s skimmer squadrons. Hop on and I'll give you a tour of the biggest and best battleship on Venus!"

Sal swung his leg over the saddle of his scooter and patted the pillion seat.

"Ah," said Johnnie, halting in mid-motion because he was sure Sal would take off without further discussion as soon as his passenger was aboard. "Look, Sal, is this going to be okay?"

. . . *your son, John Arthur Gordon, has been* . . .

"Hell, yes!" the other youth insisted. "Look, nothing's too good for the guy who saved Tony's life, right? And anyway—"

Johnnie sat, still doubtful. The scooter accelerated as
hard as it could against the double load.

"—you guys and us're allies now, right? *Sure* it's okay!"

12.

There is never a storm whose might can reach
Where the vast leviathan sleeps
Like a mighty thought in a mighty mind. . . .

      —John Boyle O'Reilly

"FASTEN YOUR BELT," Sal ordered, stuffing his cap in a side pocket as he dropped into the pilot's seat of the skimmer bobbing like a pumpkinseed at the end of the ferry dock.

He latched his own cross-belted seat restraints and added nonchalantly, "It won't matter if we flip—there won't be a piece of the frame left as big as your belt buckle—but at least it'll keep you from getting tossed into the harbor when we come off plane."

"Right," said Johnnie, realizing that the scooter ride had been the calm part of the trip.

The skimmer had a shallow hull with a powerful thruster, two side-by-side seats, and a belt-loaded 1-inch rocket gun mounted on a central pintle. The weapon could either be locked along the boat's axis or fired flexibly by the gunner . . . though the latter technique meant the gunner stood while the skimmer was under way.

Other recruits had learned to do that, so Johnnie figured he could if he had to. For now, it looked tricky enough just to stay aboard.

Sal touched two buttons on his panel. First the thruster began to rumble; then the bow and stern lines loosened from

the cleats on the quay and slid back aboard the skimmer as
their take-up reels whined.

"Hang on!" Sal warned unnecessarily. He cramped the
control wheel hard, then slammed it forward to the stop in
order to bring the drive up to full power.

The skimmer lifted; its bow came around in little more
than the vessel's own length. Within the first ten feet of
forward motion, almost nothing but the thruster nozzle of
the tiny craft was in the water. A huge roostertail of spray
drenched the dock behind them.

"Yee-*ha!*" Sal shrieked over the sound of the wind and
the snarling drive.

The seat back and bottom hammered Johnnie as the
skimmer—the ass-slapper—clipped over ripples in the harbor surface that would have been invisible to the eye. He
braced his palms against the armrests, letting his wrists
absorb much of the punishment and—incidentally—per-
mitting him to look forward past the vessel's rounded bow.
The *Holy Trinity* was expanding swiftly.

Johnnie knew Sal was giving him a ride as well as a
lift—but he was pretty sure that the pilot would have been
running in a similar fashion if he'd been alone. What Dan
had said about hydrofoil crewmen was true in spades about
the skimmers.

But it was true at higher levels also. The battle centers of
the great dreadnoughts were buried deep below the waterline and protected by the main armor belts. All the sensor
data—from the vessel itself and from all the other vessels in
the fleet—was funneled there.

The battle center was as good a place from which to
conduct a battle as could be found in action. The muzzle
blasts from the ship's main guns jolted the battle-center
crews like so many nearby train wrecks, but even that was
better than the hells of flash and stunning overpressure to
which the big guns subjected everyone on the upper decks.

Enemy shell-hits were a threat only if they were severe enough to endanger the entire vessel.

In the battle center, hostile warships were a pattern of phosphor dots, not a sinuous dragon of yellow flashes and shells arching down as tons of glowing steel. Friendly losses were carats in a holographic display rather than waterspouts shot with red flames and blackness in which tortured armor screamed for the voiceless hundreds of dying crewmen.

The battle center was the best place from which to direct a battle . . . but the men down in the battle centers were clerks. The commanding officers were on the bridges of their vessels, emotionally as well as physically part of the actions they were directing.

It made no sense—except in human terms.

But then, neither did war.

The *Holy Trinity*'s mottled hull swelled from large to immense behind the rainbow jewelling of sunlit spray. Part of the blurred coloration was deliberate camouflage, shades of gray—gray-green, gray-brown, and gray-blue, applied to hide the great dreadnought in an environment of smoke and steam . . . but the environment had similar notions of color. The natural stains of rust, salt, and lichen spread over even a relatively new vessel like *Holy Trinity* and provided the finishing touch that outdid human art.

They were getting *very* close. Sal heeled his pumpkin-seed over in a curve that would intersect the dreadnought's armored side at a flat angle instead of a straight-on, bug-against-the-windshield impact, then throttled back the thruster.

For a moment, the skimmer continued to slap forward over the ripples; the major difference to be felt was the absence of drive-line vibration. Then they dropped off plane and Johnnie slammed forward into his cross-belts, hard enough to raise bruises.

Sal let the reflected bow wave rock the skimmer to near stasis, then added a little throttle to edge them forward at a crawl. He was chuckling.

"How d'ye like that?" he asked Johnnie. "Are you going to specialize in ass-slappers yourself?"

"Ah, no," Johnnie said, answering the second question because he was going to have to think about the first one for a while before he was sure. "I'm supposed to be serving as aide to my uncle, so I guess that means battleships. Ah, my uncle's Commander Cooke."

Sal raised an eyebrow. "Commander *Dan* Cooke?" he asked. "I've heard of him. No wonder you're good."

Johnnie beamed with pride and pleasure.

Sal had brought the skimmer to a tall, six-foot-wide slot at the waterline, some hundred and fifty feet astern of the cutwater. For a moment, Johnnie thought the hole was either battle damage or some general maintenance project as yet uncompleted.

"Starboard skimmer launch tube," Sal explained with satisfaction. "Come to think, you don't have ass-slappers in the Blackhorse, do you?"

"Ah," said Johnnie. "I don't think we use them, no."

"Gunboats look all right," his guide said scornfully, "but what they really are is bigger targets. *This* baby—" he patted the breech of the rocket gun "—can chew up torpedoboats and spit out the pieces. And besides, they can't hit *us*."

Try me on a hydrofoil's stabilized twin mount, Johnnie thought, but it would've been rude to speak aloud. Rocket guns coupled a serious warhead with the low recoil impulse which was all a skimmer could accept, but neither their accuracy nor their rate of fire was in any way comparable to the armament of a hydrofoil gunboat. The ass-slappers made a bad second to hydrofoils for fleet protection—

But they were better than nothing, and nothing was the alternative which economy would force on the Angels.

Sal rotated the skimmer on her axis again.

Johnnie was looking up at the side of the *Holy Trinity*, expecting to see a derrick swing into view to winch them aboard. "What are we—" he started to say.

Sal accelerated the boat into the tight, unlighted confines of the tube meant for launching skimmers in the opposite direction.

The skimmer bumped violently to a halt on inclined rollers. Its wake sloshed and gurgled in the tube, spanking the light hull another inch or so inward.

Sal cut the thruster. "Anybody home?" he called. He switched on the four-inch searchlight attached to the gun mount and aimed it upward.

They were in a cave of girders and gray plating. A dozen other skimmers—eleven other skimmers—hung from a curving overhead track, like cartridges in a belt of ammunition.

"Anybody?" Sal repeated, flicking the searchlight around the large cavity in a pattern of shadows. His echoing voice was the only answer.

The skimmer magazine was in a bulge outside the battleship's armor plating. A sliding plate, now open, could be dogged across the launch tube's opening when the vessel was at speed, though neither protection nor the watertight integrity of the main hull was affected if it stayed open.

Forty feet overhead was a large, grated hatch in the forecastle deck, the opening through which the ass-slappers were meant to be recovered by derrick. There was also a man-sized hatch into the main hull. The latter looked like a vault door and was probably much sturdier.

The little boat was sliding slowly back down the launch rollers. Sal added a bit of throttle and ordered, "Grab that—"

The searchlight indicated an empty yoke on the overhead track. The skimmers already in place were hanging from similar units.

"—and bring it down to the attachment lugs. There oughta be somebody on duty down here, but they've drafted everybody and his brother from the watches to get the *St. Michael* refitted in time."

Sal grinned. "We'll get a better price from Admiral Bergstrom if we bring five dreadnoughts 'n four, right?"

"I think . . . ," said Johnnie. He stood on his seat, then jumped to grab the yoke. Its telescoping mid-section deployed under his weight, allowing him to ride it down.

"I think we'll kick the Warcocks 'n' Blanche's ass just fine with four," he went on, because he *did* think that. "But sure, more's better."

Together they locked the skimmer into its yoke; then Johnnie watched as his guide operated the winch controls to hoist the little vessel up with its sisters.

"Now," Sal said, "let's look at the best damned ship in the world!"

There was a large handwheel in the center of the personnel hatch, but a switch—covered with a waterproof cage which Sal opened—undogged and opened the massive portal electrically.

The hatch was tapered, like the breechblock of a heavy gun. It swung into the skimmer dock, so that a shell impact would drive it closed rather than open. The hatch, and the forward armor belt of which it was a part, were twelve inches thick.

"In battle," Sal explained, "all the watertight doors are controlled from the bridge. If the bridge goes out, control passes to the battle center. I guess that's a bitch if you're trying to get from one end of the ship to the other in an emergency—but it beats losing watertight integrity because somebody didn't know the next compartment was flooded."

"Everything's a trade-off," Johnnie said; agreeing, but balancing in his mind an expanding pattern of decisions. Dreadnoughts and skimmers, against fewer dreadnoughts, a carrier, and hydrofoils.

Above that, the Blackhorse on retainer to Wenceslas Dome: using the permanent arrangement to expand in power and prestige faster than rival companies . . . but facing *now* utter defeat and humiliation, because of the jealousy and fear of rivals who were no longer peers.

Above *that,* Commander Cooke and the Senator juggling war in the service of what they said was peace, would *be* peace, if. . . .

All in a pattern that took Johnnie's breath away in a gasp, though he knew that he saw only the base of it and that the superstructure rose beyond the imaginings of even his father and uncle.

"Yeah, well," Sal said as the hatch closed behind them. He grinned because he misunderstood Johnnie's sudden shock. "It's not as though it matters to *me* whether they got the door back here dogged shut."

There were lights on in the passageway behind the armor belt. Sal led the way briskly, commenting, "There's nothing much at main-deck level, just bunks, chain-lockers, and the galleys. I'll take you down t' the battle center 'n' magazines, then give you a look at the bridge."

They had turned into a much wider passage, one which could hold hundreds of men rushing for their action stations in a crisis. On one side was a barracks-style bunk room whose three double doors were open onto the passageway. On the other side of the passage was what Johnnie presumed was an identical facility, but it was closed up.

"We've got just a skeleton watch with the drafts working on *St. Michael,*" Sal explained, "and they're trying to keep the power use down so that we'll have max fuel available if the balloon goes up real sudden."

Johnnie tried to match the other ensign's knowing grin. Sal had *been* in action before. All the training in the world couldn't make Johnnie a veteran. . . .

"Anyhow, they're just running the air-conditioning to the one sleeping area—and where there's people on duty, of course, the engine room, the bridge, and the battle center."

The accommodations were spartan. Cruises of more than a week or two were exceptional for vessels of the mercenary fleets. There was no need to provide luxury aboard warships when the crews would be back at base (or on leave in a dome) within a few days.

On the other hand, *space* wasn't at a premium on a battleship. Automation permitted 350 men to accomplish tasks that would have required a crew of thousands in the days of the early dreadnoughts on Earth, but the hull still had to have enough volume to balance the enormous thickness of armor covering the ship's vitals.

Here on the *Holy Trinity,* sleeping crewmen had only a simple bed and a locker for a modicum of their personal effects—but the bunks were individual, and they were clamped to the deck at comfortable distances apart. Sleeping quarters in the domes themselves were far more cramped for any but the richest and most powerful.

Sal began clattering down a companionway. "No elevators?" Johnnie asked as his own boots doubled the racket on the slatted metal treads.

"We'll go up by the bridge lift," Sal said. "Most of 'em are shut down, like I said. . . ."

He looked back over his shoulder with his wicked smile. "Besides, I can't think anyplace I'd less like t' be than trapped in an elevator cage because the power went off when the ship was getting the daylights pounded outa her."

They'd reached the lower-deck level, but Sal kept going down. He waved at the huge, dim shapes beyond the companionway. "Generator rooms for the forward star-board railguns," he said.

The companionway ended on the platform deck. The air was dank and seemed not to have stirred for ages. Instead of a single long passageway, the corridor was broken by watertight doors every twenty feet. For the moment, they were open, but a single switch on the bridge or battle center could close them all.

"Next stop, A Turret magazine," Sal said cheerfully. "How do you like her so far?"

So far she seems dingy and brutal and no more romantic than a slidewalk installation, Johnnie thought.

"She's really impressive," he said aloud.

The armored wall of the barbette enclosing the magazine was sixteen inches thick. The mechanism opened smoothly, but it seemed an ungodly long time before the drive unit withdrew the hatch far enough that the hinges could swing the plug out of the way.

"How long does it take to open it by hand if the power's off?" Johnnie asked.

"Hey, this is a battleship, not an ass-slapper," Sal laughed. "Things take time, right?"

The powder room was circular, with spokes of sealed, side-facing pentagonal bins in double racks built inward from the walls. The two ensigns had entered one of the wedge-shaped aisles between racks. Above them was a track-mounted handling apparatus, empty at the moment.

The air had a faint, not unpleasant odor. The room could have been a linen store.

"There's a four-man crew in each powder room during action," Sal explained as he unlatched one of the bins. "If everything's going right, they just sit on their hands . . . but with the shock of the main guns firing, stuff jumps around like you wouldn't believe."

Johnnie grinned tightly. "And that's if the other guys' shells aren't landing on you, I suppose?" he said.

Within the bin—filling it to the degree a cylinder could fill a pentagonal case—was a powder charge sheathed in transparent plastic.

"The inner casing's combustible," Sal noted. "But then, if something penetrates to the magazine, you got pretty big problems already."

"It's *huge*," Johnnie said, looking at the garbage can of propellant.

"And that's a half charge," Sal said complacently. "A full charge takes two bins—over twelve hundredweight. And if you think that's something, the shells—"

He pointed at the steel floor, indicating the bilge-level shell room beneath them.

"—weigh thirty-six hundredweight apiece. How'd you like to be where *they* land?"

The center of the powder room was a ten-foot-diameter armored shaft. Waist-high hatches, big enough for men but intended for the powder charges, were positioned at the center of each aisle where they could be fed by the automatic handling apparatus—or, in an emergency, by the sweating human crew struggling with charges on a gurney.

A ladder led up from the powder magazine in a tube beside the hoist shaft. Sal strode to it and began to climb. "Come on," he directed. "This leads to the gun house."

"Isn't this hole dangerous in case the powder explodes?" Johnnie asked.

Sal laughed. "It's the blow-off vent," he explained. "The idea is, maybe it'll channel the blast up instead of blowing the sides out."

Johnnie blinked. "Will it work?" he asked. "The vent?"

"I'm just as glad I'll be a mile or so away if it comes to a test," Sal said. He laughed again, but his words were serious enough.

The vent plating was relatively light—two-inch, thick enough to redirect the powder flash which even the heaviest armor couldn't contain. Sal opened the hatch into the turret's gun house while the vent continued up its own angled path to the deck through the barbette wall.

"This," said Sal, rapping his knuckles on the barbette armor, "is a thirty-two-inch section, just like the turret face. Because it's above the main belt, you see, so it may have to take a direct hit by itself."

"Right . . . ," murmured Johnnie as he stared at the huge machines around him. He wasn't really hearing the words.

A computer program could perfectly duplicate scenes of war as plotted in a dreadnought's battle center. A man who never left the domes could become as expert in strategy and fleet tactics as the most experienced admirals of the mercenary companies. But that led to an impression of the instruments of war as being items of electronic delicacy—

And they weren't. Or they weren't entirely, at any rate. Here, in a gloom relieved only by the glowstrips that provided emergency lighting, were the triple loading cages—each of which lifted a shell weighing over two tons from the central hoist and carried it up a track into the turret above.

The loading cages rotated with the turret so that the guns could be fed in any position. A rack-and-pinion drive, powered by a massive hydraulic motor, encircled the top of the barbette. This was the apparatus that trained the guns by swinging the whole turret with the precision of a computer-controlled lathe.

Friction wasn't a factor: the turret bearings were superconducting magnets. But the sheer weight of the rotating mass must be over a thousand tons. It was inconceivable until you saw it—

And even *then* it was inconceivable.

"Pretty impressive, right?" Sal noted as he began clambering up the ladder into the turret.

"That's not the word," Johnnie said as he followed.

He wasn't sure quite what the word *was*, though. A dreadnought in action would be a foretaste of Hell.

The door at the back of the turret was open. Johnnie blinked and sneezed at the light flooding in. Powder fouling and burned lubricants gave the air a sickly tinge; all the surfaces were slimed with similiar residues.

The breeches of the 18-inch guns were closed. Their size made them look like geological occurrences, not the works of man. Johnnie tried to imagine the guns recoiling on their carriages; the breeches opening in a blast of smoke and the liquid nitrogen injected to cool and quench sparks in the powder chambers; hydraulic rammers sliding fresh thirty-six-hundredweight shells from the loading cages and into the guns as the twelve-hundredweight powder charges rose on the track behind the shells. . . .

A vision of Hell.

"Really something!" Sal noted cheerfully. "The guns can be fought from here—" he pointed to the four seats, each with a control console of its own "—if something goes wrong with the links from the bridge and battle center."

Or something goes wrong with *the bridge and battle center.* . . .

Johnnie walked to the door. The armor, even on the back of the turret, was so thick that it gave him the impression of going through a tunnel. "I'm about ready for some sunlight," he said.

It struck Johnnie that he'd never *seen* direct sunlight until the day before . . . but the carefully balanced illumination of the domes had nothing in common with the crude functionality of this huge weapon's artificial lighting. The heat and glare on deck were welcome.

The deck had a non-skid surface, but at the moment it

was under a glass-slick coating of blue and green algae. Sal spat over the side and muttered, "They need to hose this off with herbicide, but everybody's so damn busy with the *St. Michael* and loading stores that it'll maybe have t' wait till we're under way."

At the land perimeter of the base, a sort of battle had broken out between the guard force's flamethrowers and what were probably roots, though they moved as swiftly as serpents. Human weaponry created enormous evolutionary pressures on the continental life forms, ensuring that whatever lived or grew in the immediate vicinity of fleet bases was tougher and more vicious than similar forms elsewhere in the planetary hellbroth.

A tall barbette raised B Turret so that its guns could fire dead ahead, over A Turret. Just abaft and starboard of the barbette was one of the ship's four railgun batteries. Johnnie looked with interest as they walked past it.

From the outside, the installation was a fully-rotating dome whose only feature was a pair of armored slots which could open from $+90°$ to $-5°$. That spread was wide enough to permit the railguns to engage anything from a missile dropping out of orbit to a hydrofoil a pistolshot out.

The tubes themselves were too fragile to survive on the deck of a ship under fire, so the weapons were designed to accelerate their glass pellets up a helical track. That way, their overall length could be kept within an armored dome of manageable size.

Given enough time—and not a long time at that— railguns could blast through anything on the surface of Venus, whether a dreadnought or a mountain. But, though they could destroy a target in orbit, they were unable to engage anything over the horizon from them. Furthermore, the powder requirements of a railgun in operation meant that only dreadnoughts had the generator capacity to mount such weapons.

They were lethal and efficient within their limitations; but those limitations made railguns primarily defensive tools, the shield of the battleships slashing at one another with the sword of their big guns.

There was another enclosed companionway leading up the exterior of the shelter deck superstructure to the bridge whose wings flared out beyond the line of its supports. Sal opened the hatch, then paused.

"Those," he said, pointing to the railguns, "would have to be ungodly lucky to hit us in the ass-slappers."

They can hit a plunging shell, Johnnie thought, *so they could damn well hit a skimmer if they wanted to waste the ammunition.*

"And *those,*" Sal went on, indicating a turret holding twin guns of the dreadnought's secondary armament, "the five-point-two-fives, *they* couldn't hit us if they had angels riding on every shell. Sure you don't want to transfer to us and ride skimmers, Johnnie? Safest job in the fleet, I tell you!"

"Aw, my uncle's a big-ship man," Johnnie lied with a grin as the two of them began echoing up the slotted treads of the companionway.

The skimmers weren't safe even when nobody was shooting at them. The bow wave of a friendly vessel—or the back of a surfacing fish—could flip one of the little pumpkinseeds in the air like a thumbed coin. If that happened and the ass-slapper's own speed didn't kill the crew, the life teeming in the sea would finish the job in minutes if not seconds.

No, skimmers were romantic—and now that Johnnie had seen a dreadnought close up, he realized that the big ships surely were not. But battles were decided by the smashing authority of the dreadnoughts' main guns. Everything else, necessary though it might be to a successful outcome, was secondary to big-gun salvoes.

Everything but perhaps strategy was secondary to the big

guns. Uncle Dan hadn't risen to his present position simply because he knew how to press a firing switch.

Johnnie had thought he was in good shape . . . and he was, for the purposes for which he'd trained. He hadn't been running up and down staircases on the planet's surface, though. His legs were so rubbery that he used his grip on the handrail to boost him up the last few steps to the hatch marked 'Bridge/Access controlled.'

"It's closed," Sal explained as he touched the switch, "because they've got the air-conditioning on inside. Scratch a big-ship man," he added, smiling to take the sting out of the words, "and you find a pussy."

A puff of cool air spilled down the companionway as the immensely thick hatch cycled open. It revived Johnnie like a bucket of cold water. He wasn't sure that the constant change from Venus-ambient to artificially-comfortable wasn't a lot less healthy than acclimating to the natural temperature—

But for now it sure felt good.

There were six men already present on the bridge. One of them was the senior lieutenant acting as officer of the day. The armored shutters were raised so that Johnnie could look out at the harbor area through glazed slits; but it seemed to him that the banks of displays, both flat-screen and holographic, gave a better view.

The OOD was talking to a control console. He looked up and frowned as the ensigns entered the bridge. "Roger," he said as his right hand threw switches. "Roger. Out."

"Just showing a visitor the *Holy Trinity*, sir," Sal said cheerfully, before the lieutenant could ask.

"Well, keep out of the way, will you?" the senior officer said sourly. "Base wants us to help with the yard work."

"Turret Eye-Eye live, sir," said a technician at another console.

"Bring it to seventeen degrees until they give us final

corrections," the OOD instructed. "They'll pipe them in, they say. And load with incendiaries."

"That's the forward starboard five-point-two-five turret," Sal explained, though Johnnie had already figured out the reference. "There's four secondary turrets on either side amidships."

"Want me to ready Beta Battery, sir?" called a junior lieutenant from the far wing of the bridge.

"No, I do *not* want you to light the main drives, Janos," the OOD snapped. "Besides, for what they want, the secondaries'll do a better job than the railguns would."

There was a horrible squeal of dragging metal, through the fabric of the ship as well as the air. The turret's superconducting gimbals had not come up to full power before the mechanism started to turn.

"That ought to be repaired!" the OOD said.

"It has been, sir," replied the man at the gunnery board. "That mount, it always does that. I think it's the power connections to—"

"Mark!" said the OOD.

A pattern of lines overlay a map display on the active gunnery screen. They shifted suddenly without any action by the tech at the console. The ship vibrated as gears drove Turret II a few seconds of fine adjustment.

Johnnie stepped to the window. The glazed slit was eight inches high, but the thirty-two-inch bridge armor it peered through made the opening seem as narrow as the slots in a jalousie.

The *Holy Trinity* was deep within the bay and closer to the northern side than the main occupied area on the south. That was desirable for the present purpose, since the mile or more the shells had to travel would give them a chance to stabilize, thus limiting the chances of a wild round. The 5.25-inch guns were only secondary armament for a dreadnought, but their shells were big enough to cause real

problems if they landed among the base defenses they were
firing to support.

The bridge was forward of the secondary battery amidships, but holographic displays inset every two yards
beneath the viewslit showed the entire vessel—a quick
reference for purposes of damage assessment. Seven of the
eight secondary turrets were aligned with their twin guns
perpendicular to the ship's axis. The front turret on the right
side pointed just off the bow.

"Fire one," said the OOD.

The right-hand of the pair of guns in hologram flashed
and recoiled. The *Holy Trinity* rang like a railroad collision,
and a ball of orange powder gases hid the viewslit for an
instant.

*If these are the secondaries, what happens when the big
guns fire?*

The spark of the shell landing was almost lost in the
jungle beyond the gash of bare No-Man's-Land, but it
bloomed into a cloud of devouring white smoke. The
consoles twittered inaudibly with exchanges between base
control and the guard units engaged with the non-human
threat.

Johnnie turned to Sal, standing beside him, and asked,
"Are the turrets manned, then?"

"All automatic," Sal said with a shake of his head. "You
only need people if there's a problem—or if director control
goes out."

*If the superstructure is a flaming ruin, with sensors and
communications disrupted and scores of dead . . . then
the turrets could fight on alone.*

"Fire for effect," said the OOD.

For a while.

The guns began to belch flame at a rate of a shot every five
seconds, *WHANG WHANG WHANG WHANG WHANG*—

A pause.

WHANG—

"Cease fire!"

The target area was a roiling mass of smoke. A huge root burst out of the soil halfway between the jungle and the human defenses; it writhed and died before flamethrowers were able to bathe it.

"Sir, the left tube has a stoppage," announced the man at the gunnery console.

"I know it's got a bloody stoppage!" snarled the OOD. "I can bloody hear, can't I? Get a crew to clear it."

There were patterns of compression and rarefaction rippling across the algae which slimed the dreadnought's forecastle. The marks were vestiges of the muzzle blasts.

"Ah, shall I wake the off-duty watch?" the technician asked.

Something huge leaped from the jungle where the shells had landed. It was a mass of flames. A track of yellowing leaves followed it for hundreds of yards through the forest.

"No, dammit, go yourself," said the OOD. "I'll have Rassmussen send somebody from the engine room. Two of you ought to be able to handle it."

He turned to another technician. "Graves, bring up Turret Eye-Vee in case they need—"

The OOD broke off as his commo helmet spoke to him. He looked at Johnnie. "You," he said. "Are you Ensign Gordon?"

Johnnie drew himself up stiffly. "Yessir."

"Then you're about to go home," the OOD said. "They're bringing your hydrofoil alongside in a few minutes."

The man beamed. For the first time, Johnnie saw him looking cheerful.

"I think," the Angel lieutenant added, "that we've got a deal!"

13.

Venus looked on Helen's face,
*   (O Troy Town!)*
Knew far off an hour and place,
And fire lit with the heart's desire;
Laughed and said, "Thy gift hath grace!"

—Dante Gabriel Rossetti

SAL PUSHED THE hatch control. "Come on, Johnnie," he said. "You up to a fast ride down?"

"Elevators at last?" Johnnie asked. "Sure, I'm up to anything."

"Bring 'em around to the starboard quarter, Lieutenant Hammond," the Angel ensign called back to the OOD as the hatch closed behind them. "Anything it is, my friend. You're going by the skimmer winch."

They clanged down the companionway from the conning tower more easily than they'd come up it, and perhaps a little faster; but a part of Johnnie's mind kept imagining his uncle sneering, *"Arthur, your idiot son broke his neck running down stairs. . . ."*

The air was thick with powder fumes. The breeze riffling across the harbor brought with it faint hints of burned vegetation and phosphorus—though that might have been Johnnie's imagination.

Voices cursed from the forward 5.25-inch turret. The men sent to clear the stoppage began to hammer, an uncontrolled sound that struck Johnnie as a doubtful way to deal with high explosive.

Sal opened a coverplate on the starboard foredeck and

lifted up a folded, telescoping derrick. The cover was cross-dogged, but even so, Johnnie doubted that it would survive the muzzle blasts of the 18-inch guns firing above it. After a battle there would be considerable damage to all the dreadnoughts, whether or not they'd been struck by enemy shells.

Sal spread the extensions that were meant to clamp the lifting points of a skimmer. "Hop in," he said. "Your limousine awaits."

His face turned serious. "Ah—but if you think you might slip, we'll go by the regular landing stage."

M4434 had pulled away from the dock and was curving toward the *Holy Trinity*. Flotsam and the opalescent stains of oil wobbled in the hydrofoil's wake; the motion brought bright flashing teeth to life in the harbor as well.

"I'm fine," said Johnnie, setting one boot on either clamp and gripping the hinge where the arms joined. He was sure he'd be all right; and he'd rather drop into the watery killing ground below than admit to Sal he was afraid. "Lower away!"

With a loud squealing—from the winch brakes rather than the monocrystalline cable—Johnnie dropped smoothly toward the harbor. Sal waved from the control box.

As the dreadnought's gray-green hull slid past, Johnnie looked down—and rotated dizzyingly as the motion changed his center of mass. A skimmer would be held by three arms, not two and the hinge. He braced himself erect again, as though he were preparing to be shot.

"I don't want us staving our sides in with this nonsense!" Captain Haynes shouted from close by. "Be ready to fend off forward!"

Strong hands caught Johnnie by both forearms and pulled him in, over the amidships rail. "Step back, sir," said Walcheron.

Johnnie obeyed. Because the sailors were holding him,

he didn't fall back into the cockpit when his heel stubbed the coaming.

"I'm okay," he gasped, realizing as he spoke that he really was.

"Bring us around, Watkins," Haynes ordered the torpedoboat's commander. "Let's get *home*, man!"

The cable hummed its way back onto the take-up reel. Johnnie looked up. Sal was peering down past the pronounced flare that directed waves like a plowshare instead of sweeping them into the superstructure when the dreadnought was at speed.

The young Angel officer waved. Johnnie started to return the gesture, but he had to grab the rail as the M4434 accelerated in a tight turn.

"Good hunting, John!" Sal shouted past the rumble of the auxiliary thruster.

Johnnie started forward toward the gun tub.

"Ensign Gordon," Haynes ordered. "Come into the cockpit with me."

The guard boat, more than a half mile away, had already drawn back the net's inner layer. The hydrofoil headed for the gap at all the speed the hull motor alone could provide. The little vessel bucked and pitched as it crossed the vestiges of its own wake.

Johnnie swung his legs over the low bulkhead, trying not to kick any of the five men already in the small enclosure. "Yes, sir?" he said. He wondered if he ought to salute.

Haynes, seated at one of the paired control consoles, looked up at him. "Who told you to go buggering off on your own, Gordon?" he demanded. "It would've served you right if I'd just left you to find your own way back, you know."

The hydrofoil's helmsman and the commanding officer— an ensign—kept their eyes studiously on the business of running the boat, but Haynes' two staff lieutenants stared at Johnnie with sycophantic amusement.

"I—" Johnnie began, but this was a test too—life was a test—and he wasn't going to tell *this* man what directions he'd gotten from Uncle Dan.

"Sir," he resumed, "I thought this was a good opportunity to familiarize myself with the Angel operation, seeing that we may be acting in concert with them in the coming action."

"Did you think that indeed, Ensign?" the captain said with a sort of heavy playfulness. Even his initial attack had lacked the anger Johnnie would have expected to underlie the words. "That we'd be 'acting in concert' with Admiral Braun?"

"Yessir," Johnnie said.

The helmsman throttled back as the torpedoboat entered the netted lock area. Crewmen had rifles and grenade launchers ready in case there was a repetition of the excitement when they locked through from the open sea.

The guard boat's hull bore a line of fresh patches where stray bullets had raked her. All the visible members of her crew were waving.

"Well, Gordon," Haynes said, "you're right. Perhaps I shouldn't judge you by the maternal side of your family."

Johnnie kept his lips pressed together. Uncle Dan didn't need a junior ensign to defend him, and anyway—*Don't be sorry. Be controlled.*

The hydrofoil's commander muttered an order. M4434 speeded up again. The bow slapped, then rose, and the outriggers began to extend in iridescent domes of spray. Johnnie gripped the coaming behind him with both hands.

To his amazement, Captain Haynes squeezed deeper into the console and motioned Johnnie down onto the corner of the seat beside him.

"Admiral Braun is calling a company meeting right now,

Gordon," the captain said. "He and Admiral Bergstrom will handshake by radio, probably before we've gotten back to Blackhorse Base. Would you like to know how I arranged it?"

"Ah, yessir." He had to put his mouth close to be sure the captain had heard him.

"Not more money," Haynes said, gloating over his triumph and his captive audience. "That's what your uncle would have tried, but I know Admiral Braun. I offered him the chance to merge his fleet with the Blackhorse on favorable—though reasonable—terms."

Johnnie waited for more. "Yes sir?" he prompted when he saw Captain Haynes' face darken at what he was reading as dumb insolence.

"Yes . . . ," Haynes said, purring the word like a zoo-fattened lion. "Quite reasonable. All the Angel officers and men in the rank of lieutenant or below transfer with an additional ninety days in grade for the purpose of bonus distribution. That's fair, isn't it, Ensign? For an additional five battleships plus supporting units?"

"Yessir," Johnnie said. "That seems a very fair deal."

It did. Johnnie didn't see where the catch was, unless Haynes was simply preening over his success . . . and there seemed to be more in his tone than that.

The hydrofoil had risen to full speed. With a load of torpedoes aboard she would have been a few knots slower, but the additional weight might have damped some of the high-frequency vibration Johnnie noticed now that he was out of the wind's buffeting.

"And as for Admiral Braun himself," Haynes continued, "he receives the rank of captain and moves into the number three slot in the Blackhorse. Director of Planning."

"That's Uncle Dan's position." Part of Johnnie's mind was amazed by the cold lack of emotion with which his tongue had formed the words.

"It *was* Commander Cooke's position," Haynes smirked. "He'll move. I think—obviously Admiral Bergstrom and I need to work out the internal details—Commander Cooke will become Commodore of Screening Forces. . . . A position of expanded responsibility since Blackhorse is being reinforced by the Angels in that category too."

"Sir," said Johnnie's ice-cold tongue. He was speaking loudly to be heard, but he wasn't shouting; he was sure he wasn't shouting. "The Angels are heavy in capital ships, not destroyers. Their adjuncts to our screening forces are insignificant."

And the water beneath is wet and full of hungry things, Johnnie's mind gibed at him, *since we're stating the bloody obvious now.*

"Yes, well, Ensign," said Captain Haynes. "Our first duty is to our employers, Wenceslas Dome, you know. I'm sure your father could explain that to you if you don't understand it already. If some individuals have to pay a price in the accomplishment of that duty, well—soldiers have to be willing to pay the price, don't they?"

"Sir," said Johnnie. "I request permission to join Seaman Walcheron in the forward gun tub."

Haynes made a contemptuous shooing motion with the backs of his fingers. "Go on, then, Gordon," he said. "Maybe your uncle will take you with him to Flotilla Blanche—if he really has an offer from Admiral de Lessups the way he claims. *And* if there's anything left of Flotilla Blanche after we engage them!"

Johnnie sat in the assistant gunner's seat staring blankly out over the water. The sunset was fiery and brilliant, hurling the torpedoboat's distorted shadow hundreds of yards astern of the racing vessel, but the young ensign had no stomach for visions of the new surface world of which he'd become so recently a part.

Walcheron's commo helmet was hooked into the base-to-ship frequency. He heard the message sent to Captain Haynes when M4434 was only three miles from Blackhorse Base, then repeated the gist of it for Johnnie.

Heidigger and Carolina had just declared war. They had hired Flotilla Blanche and the Warcocks, as expected.

The Angels had signed with Heidigger Dome as well.

Admiral Braun had suckered Captain Haynes. There wasn't a chance now of associating another company before the Blackhorse alone faced her triple opponents.

14.

No counsel is more trustworthy than that which is given upon ships that are in peril.

—Leonardo da Vinci

CAPTAIN HAYNES WAS off M4434 and jogging toward the Base Operations Center before the hydrofoil had been secured to bollards. His pair of lieutenants hesitated, then jumped after him. They were big-ship men. The jig the torpedoboat did as the vessel rebounded from a fender made one of the aides sprawl full-length on the floodlit dock.

Johnnie's reaction to the bad news—the disastrous news that doomed the Blackhorse, Wenceslas Dome, and perhaps all of Mankind—was relief. Commander Cooke had been right all along; Captain Haynes looked a fool and an incompetent.

Johnnie knew his reaction made sense only on the emotional level, not intellectually . . .

But he was beginning to realize that most people acted on a primarily emotional level, himself included.

Johnnie jumped to solid ground. Like Haynes and his team, he was superfluous to the business of docking and shutting down the hydrofoil's systems.

Unlike Haynes, he hadn't any idea of what he ought to do next.

"Did you have a good trip, John?" called a voice from the pool of shadow at the base of one of the light standards.

Johnnie turned and blinked. "Yessir," he said.

He felt his lips rising in a cruel grin. "A better trip than Captain Haynes did, Uncle Dan. *I* carried out my mission."

Insects brought out by darkness buzzed enthusiastically around the men. The living sound almost buried the hum of the high-frequency generators in the epaulets of Blackhorse uniforms which repelled the bugs.

Johnnie slapped his cheek. *Most* of the bugs.

Dan gestured in the direction of the BOC. The two men fell in step with an ease that had nothing of training to it, in at least Johnnie's case; he and his uncle were just in synch.

"Haynes didn't let you into the negotiations, did he?" Dan asked when the dock and the men busy there were ten yards behind them.

"No sir." *Should he have insisted on being present?* "I didn't insist." *No excuses.* "I viewed the base arrangements and went aboard one of their battleships, the *Holy Trinity*."

Dan looked at him sharply. "*That* one," he said. "What's her status?"

"Combat ready. She's dirty because most of her crew's working on the *St. Michael*, but she's ready to go."

He cleared his throat. "Uncle Dan," he said, "they were going to move you to the screening forces. If the deal had gone through."

"Two birds with one stone, hey?" Dan chuckled. "That's better strategic planning than I'd have given Haynes credit for."

Johnnie's mind revolved possibilities as they marched toward the Operations Center. One of the aides opened the door for Haynes, and the trio disappeared inside.

"If we move very fast," Johnnie said carefully, "I don't think the Angels can have the *St. Michael* ready for action."

Dan pursed his lips and made a scornful *pfft*. "The *St. Michael* isn't going to turn the battle," he said. "For that matter, the *Holy Trinity* isn't going to turn the battle if it's just one more ship in the line. . . ."

The BOC's lighted facade loomed in front of them.

Johnnie rephrased the question in his mind and said, "Shall I wait in the lobby for you?"

His uncle pushed the first set of doors open. The air-conditioning and anticipation made Johnnie shudder.

"No," said Dan. "I need you. To give honest answers to any questions you're asked—"

Johnnie opened the inner doors.

"—and to cover my back if we have to shoot our way out."

Johnnie blinked. Uncle Dan was smiling.

Probably the last clause was a joke.

Lieutenant Barton and Haynes' two aides waited in Admiral Bergstrom's outer office. The Admiral's secretary smiled tightly and said, "Commander, the Admiral and Captain Haynes are waiting for you."

"Right," said Dan. "For me and Ensign Gordon."

He reached for the door latch.

"Not—" began one of Haynes' men as he rose from his chair.

Uncle Dan's eyes met the lieutenant's and spiked him. Johnnie's right hand flexed instinctively as he turned also. He no longer assumed Dan had been joking.

The lieutenant sat down heavily.

"Right," Uncle Dan repeated. He pushed open the door.

"Captain Haynes," he said even before his foot had followed his hand into the inner office, "you excluded Senator Gordon's son from the negotiations which you—"

"Cooke, what are you—" the captain blustered.

"—botched. *Botched,*" Dan continued in a rising voice as his left hand gestured Johnnie through the door beside him and let it close of its own weight. "For that reason alone it would be necessary for Ensign Gordon to be present now."

"Then I want Lieutenant Platt—"

"Walter," snapped Admiral Bergstrom, "for God's sake, *shut up!*"

The room froze.

"Gordon," the Commander in Chief resumed in a tired voice, "sit down. No trick shooting this time. Daniel, you sit down also."

He looked from one of his senior officers to the other. "We don't need to chew each other up, gentlemen," he said. "There are three very competent fleets out there—" he gestured "—ready and willing to accomplish the task."

Johnnie slid cautiously into the seat nearest the door. It was plainer than the units in his father's office, but the data bank/hologram projector linkage was state-of-the-art.

"Sorry, sir," muttered Captain Haynes. "I'm—"

He grimaced. His fingers writhed against one another. "We're all upset."

"Perhaps," Uncle Dan suggested quietly as he too sat, "Koslowski, Molp, and Randleman should be present?"

Bergstrom shook his head. "We'll need the other squadron commanders when it's time for detailed planning," he said. "But first we have to decide what to do . . . and that's a matter for the three of us, isn't it, gentlemen?"

He nodded ironically toward Johnnie. "And for Senator Gordon's representative, of course."

"There's no certainty in battle," Haynes said, speaking distinctly but toward the image in his hands. "Sure, we're outnumbered, but that doesn't mean we can't engage and win."

"If we met the others one at a time," said the Commander in Chief, "we could possibly defeat them all in detail. But—"

"If we station ourselves *in* the Kanjar Straits," Haynes

said eagerly, "if we do it right away—they can't use their full strength against us. Then—"

"Then they put out a screen of subs and light forces on the ocean side of the Straits and let us rot until our hulls are foul and we have to return to base to refuel," Uncle Dan broke in without raising his voice. "When we attempt to do that, their combined fleets sail from base—clean and fully prepared—run us down while we skirmish with their screen, and send us to the bottom."

"Are you saying we should surrender now?" Haynes demanded. "Are *you* saying that?"

Dan didn't speak. Admiral Bergstrom played with a piece of rusty shell casing on his desk, then looked directly at Haynes. "Frankly, Walter," he said, "I don't see much point in fighting a battle we're certain to lose, either. Lose badly."

"Sir," said Haynes, "honor demands we fulfill our contract to the best of our abilities."

"Honor won't win a battle against overwhelming strength," Uncle Dan said.

He ignored Johnnie completely. The other senior officers kept flicking their eyes toward the man they thought was the political envoy from Wenceslas Dome.

"Honor won't even bury us," Dan continued calmly. "Though of course that won't matter so long as the fish are on the job. I could not in good conscience recommend we engage if I didn't think we could win."

Captain Haynes opened his mouth—and closed it without speaking.

"Daniel," Admiral Bergstrom said. "This isn't a time for games."

"Sorry," Dan said; sounding for the first time in Johnnie's hearing as though he felt he'd made an error.

Dan's fingertips worked the projector controls of his chair. He cleared his throat and resumed, "My aide, Ensign

Gordon, reconnoitered Paradise Base for us during the negotiations. John, will you sketch in the location of the Angel units for us now?"

A holographic representation of Paradise Base, plucked from the BOC's data banks, glowed in the air of the office. Johnnie snapped open the cover of his own controls, slid the magenta cursor along the docks with his joystick, and began tapping a function key. The software was the same as that he'd trained on. . . .

"Twelve destroyers *here*," Johnnie said crisply. His pulse slowed and the nervous flush left his face now that he had a task to perform. "Two cruisers, bow inward, on the west side of this dock—"

He hit a different function key twice, then used his joystick to adjust the attitude of the holographic images. "They appeared to be combat ready, but I have no hard evidence on the subject. Here—"

Tap—

"—was a mother ship with five submarines. Six, actually, but one had floats attached for buoyancy and I can't imagine that she's serviceable."

"It's not their bloody subs that we're worried about," muttered Captain Haynes as he stared at his wife's picture. "I only wish it was."

"The dreadnought *St. Michael* here in drydock," Johnnie said, ignoring the comment. "Local personnel believed that she'd be combat ready shortly, perhaps as soon as twenty-four hours. The *Holy Trinity*—"

He toyed with the joystick to align the huge ship's image correctly near the harbor's jungle margin to the north.

"And three more dreadnoughts, which I believe to be the *Azrael*—"

Tap—

"—the *Spiritus Sancti*—"

Tap—

"—and the *Elijah,* though with these three I'm going by silhouette matching, not local information."

"That doesn't matter," said Uncle Dan.

"Perhaps you'd like to tell us exactly what *does* matter, Commander Cooke?" Haynes said sharply. "Where the vessels are when they form a battle line against us may be important, but—"

Uncle Dan faced his rival and said, "The *Holy Trinity* matters. I propose taking fifty men on two of our submarines and cutting her out tomorrow night. Stealing the most powerful unit in the three fleets we face."

"There's a way through the minefields and nets?" the Commander in Chief said in amazement. "You've found a path?"

"No sir," Dan said. "We'll go overland *here*—"

He slid the cursor to a jungle-clad neck of land to the north of the harbor, beyond the plug of igneous rock which protected the outpost on the tip.

"—carrying boats with us, then board our target at night. She has only a skeleton crew."

"No," said Admiral Bergstrom. "Through the jungle— that's suicide."

"I don't believe so, sir," Dan rejoined. "With proper planning—and I *have* been planning this for some time, as a contingency in the event—"

"As a plan for throwing away fifty men, there are easier ways," Haynes snapped.

"—in the event Admiral Braun behaved as *I* expected him to," Dan went on forcefully. "With proper planning, and the special skills which Ensign Gordon here brings to the endeavor, I believe we have a high likelihood of success."

He looked at Johnnie; looked at the Commander in Chief; and said, straight toward Captain Haynes with their eyes locked, "I will of course expect to lead the cutting-out expedition myself."

Johnnie's face turned toward the display, but his mind fleshed out the holographic blur with memories of the green-black Hell he'd seen from the decks of hydrofoils and the dreadnought herself.

Haynes glared at his rival. "Commander," he said, "I don't question your personal courage. But if you choose to commit suicide, there's no reason to take forty-nine other men with you. We'll need them for the battle."

"The *battle*, as you propose it, would be suicide on a much larger scale, Captain," Dan said coldly.

"You'd scuttle the *Holy Trinity* with explosives, then?" said Admiral Bergstrom. "Interesting, but surely it wouldn't require so large a force . . . would it?"

"We'll need a considerable force to fight our way through the neck of jungle," Dan explained. "I'm not pretending that this will be an easy job—only that it's possible, practical."

He cleared his throat. "And no, we won't be sinking the ship, we'll be stealing her. As I said. It's actually safer to leave the harbor with a dreadnought under us than it would be in any other fashion—"

"You can't sail a dreadnought with fifty men!" Haynes said.

"We can't *fight* a dreadnought with fifty men," Dan replied. "We won't try. We *can* sail her out of the harbor and join the rest of the Blackhorse."

Haynes stared but did not speak.

"One ship isn't going to tip the balance," Admiral Bergstrom said musingly. For the first time during the meeting, his voice had animation. "Though the *Holy Trinity* is a very large ship. . . ."

"That's part of the plan," said Uncle Dan as his fingers

sorted files from the data bank and picked one. "The other part involves the probable response by our . . ."

The image of Paradise Base vanished and was replaced by a large-scale map of the entire Ishtar Basin.

". . . the response by our opponents."

As his uncle began to lay out the details of the plan on which he proposed to venture his life and Mankind's future, Johnnie's mind filled with visions of trees stalking like dragons and great, fire-wrapped beasts crashing through the jungle toward him.

15.

"WELCOME TO THE penthouse, lad," said Uncle Dan as he unlocked the door of his suite and waved Johnnie through.

"Good evening, sir," said Sergeant Britten, "Mr. Gordon."

"Uh!" said Johnnie.

Commander Cooke's suite was on the top—third—floor of a barracks block. While it was scarcely a penthouse, the furnishings of the living area were striking in the extreme.

"I told Personnel that I'd billet you here for the night," Dan went on. "They can find you permanent quarters after you come back from tomorrow's operation. Assuming that you do, of course."

His familiar grin didn't change the truth of what he'd just said.

The table and chairs of the combined living/dining area on which the door opened were of good quality but ordinary design. All four of the walls, however, were hidden within changing holographic vistas.

Johnnie glanced back at the door by which he'd entered. It was now a shop entrance in a good district of Wenceslas Dome. Pedestrians hurried past, chatting silently and looking at window displays. He couldn't be sure how long the hologram loop ran, but it didn't repeat during the time his eyes followed it.

The wall in front of which Sergeant Britten stood, smiling imperturbably, was the seascape that had made Johnnie gasp.

Seascape—not a beach scene. It showed the green-gold water ten feet below the surface, probably in a lagoon like that around which Blackhorse Base was constructed. A mass of silvery fish, none of them more than a finger long, flicked into sight like magnesium raining from a star shell.

The school of fish vanished as abruptly as they had appeared, with and perhaps because of the appearance of something with spines, tentacles, and nodes that could be either eyes or the receptors of a vegetable life form. It slid just over the bottom, raising curls of sand. Johnnie thought the newcomer was the ugliest thing he'd ever seen in his life—

Until a section of bottom the size of a bedsheet roused itself and wrapped the spiny creature in a flurry of blood and bubbles.

"I like my surroundings to remind me that there are alternatives," Dan said drily. "It helps prevent me from becoming too rigid . . . Or it may be that I'm just a little weird."

As before, the smile didn't affect the truth of the statement.

The wall on Johnnie's right was jungle. At first glance it seemed relatively static. A closer examination showed that one of the strangler vines crawling up a massive trunk was in turn being attacked by a swarm of ants.

Worker ants were hacking through the cortex with their pincers and bringing up globules of sap which they loaded on their backs. Tendrils curled from the flanks of the vine, but a cordon of warrior ants, twice the one-inch length of the workers, was burning back the vegetable defenses with squirts of acid from the tips of their abdomens.

A gray-white shadow like a mass of ash swept across the scene, then vanished upward into the canopy again with a snap of its ghostly wings. The ants, workers and warriors alike, were gone. There was a deep semi-circular gouge missing from the vine where they had been.

Swarms of flying insects arrowed to the vast well of sap now that the ants were no longer present to fend them off.

Across from the wall of jungle was an image that Johnnie couldn't place. Mountains in the middle distance thrust up into a sky that was an unfamiliar streaky mixture of white and blue, like partly-mixed paint. Closer by were rutted white fields across which meandered black streaks like the tracks of giant slugs. The foreground—the portion of the scene that Johnnie could have touched were it not a hologram—appeared to be water, but there were chunks of white rock floating in it.

"Recognize it?" Uncle Dan said, waving toward the image on which the younger man's eyes were focused. He was smiling, but he almost always smiled; and this was not an expression of real humor.

"No, I don't," Johnnie said. "Where is it?"

"It's one of the outlet glaciers of Vatnajökull," his uncle explained. "On Earth. Before."

Johnnie looked hard at the scene. Ice, then; sliding across the land and carrying streaks of dirt and crushed rock with it to the sea. Hard to imagine such a volume of water cold enough to freeze—and under an open sky, as here. . . .

But that had been Earth.

"I like," Dan repeated softly, "to be reminded that there are alternatives. This particular view reminds me that some alternatives are closed off forever, because of what men like me did or failed to do a very long time ago."

"Ah," said Johnnie. "It's disconcerting, I guess. To me, at least."

He forced a smile. "But maybe that's good."

"Come into the office with me," Dan said, stepping toward the wall of jungle. "I want to go over the table of equipment for the operation—unless you're too tired? I was going to have Britten make up a bunk for you in the office after we'd finished, but you can have my bed if you'd like."

His hand swung back a door which seemed to be part of the trunk of a fallen giant. A pack of mutated slime molds now slithered their way through the foliage, leaving gray, burned patches behind them. The section of office visible through the opening was even more dissonant than the lines along the corners where the holographic images joined.

"I'm fine," Johnnie said. "I—look, I'm doing fine, but I couldn't sleep now anyway, Uncle Dan."

"Nothing wrong with living on your nerves, John," the older man said with a chuckle as he led Johnnie into the office. "Myself, I've been doing it for years. Britten, why don't you get us all something to eat?"

The sergeant's face split in a grin. "Hearty meals for the condemned, you mean, sir?" he said.

"Don't laugh, boyo," Dan called back through the closing door. "You're going too, you know."

"Indeed I am, sir," Britten said in a muffled voice.

Britten sounded cheerful; Johnnie was scared.

Not scared of the jungle, exactly, though his view of their likelihood of success in reaching the harbor by the back way was nowhere near as sanguine as the one Uncle Dan had polished in Admiral Bergstrom's office. . . . And not scared about the risks involved in first capturing a dreadnought, then sailing away in it while pursued by at least three other battleships. Johnnie hadn't been able to think that far ahead.

He wasn't afraid the operation would fail: he was afraid it would fail because of *him*.

"Are you sure you're all right, John?" his uncle said.

"I don't want to mess up, Uncle Dan."

"Join the club," the older man replied; and again, there was very little humor in his smile.

The office was smaller than the Senator's—Commander Cooke had no need to impress anyone here. The walls were cream-colored, enlivened neither with real windows nor by holographic views as the living room was.

The desk was double-sided. A light-pen lay in front of the identical consoles which faced one another; a similar pen was in its holder at the other station. Three visicubes aligned with the long axis of the slate-colored expanse were the only other ornamentation.

"Well, sit down," Dan said as he slid into one of the consoles. "I didn't really figure the Admiral would agree to fifty men—the second submarine doubles that aspect of the risk, after all—but I think thirty will be sufficient for what we need to do."

The senior officer's right hand played over the keypad while his left removed the pen from its holder. Columns of names and figures, the Blackhorse personnel roster, glowed in the air between them. The holograms shifted as they began to sort themselves according to skills and efficiency ratings.

Johnnie was staring at the visicubes.

"You won't know the men, of course," Dan said, "but—"

He looked at his nephew and paused.

"I'm sorry," Johnnie blurted in embarrassment, raising his eyes.

"Oh, they're worth looking at, lad," his uncle said with an honest laugh.

Each cube held the image of a different woman: a blonde,

a redhead, and a brunette with white skin and almond eyes. The blonde was a statuesque beauty; the redhead was heavier than some men's taste, though Titian would have painted her as Venus; and the brunette was bone-thin.

Their expressions were equally alluring, even frozen in the visicubes.

"Go ahead, touch them," Dan said.

"Are they all your . . ."

"Friends?"

"Wives, I meant," Johnnie said.

His index finger tapped the touch-sensitive patch at the bottom of the first cube. The blonde's face suddenly brightened in a smile. Her voice, lilting despite the limits of the reproduction medium, said, "Hello, Dan. I'm really looking forward to seeing you again, so don't do anything foolish. All right?"

The image blew a kiss.

"Companions, yes," his uncle agreed without expression.

Johnnie touched the second cube, as much as anything so that he had something to look at instead of the older man. "Do they . . . know about each other?"

"Dan," said the plump redhead, "you don't want to hear how much I love you . . . but when you come home, I'll make you as happy as a woman can make a man."

"They'd almost have to, wouldn't they, lad?" Dan said coolly. "I don't volunteer any information, and they don't ask me. But sure, I assume they know, all three of them."

The dark-haired woman lifted an eyebrow, then adjusted the scooped neckline of her violet blouse. She grinned, but the image did not speak.

"Don't they care?" Johnnie said. He looked up. "Don't they *care*?"

"Johnnie," said his uncle, "life isn't simple. I don't put any restrictions on them that I wouldn't keep myself. They find that acceptable, I suppose, or they'd find someone else."

He licked his dry lips. "But that's me, and them. We're individuals. And my sister—your mother—is an individual too, living her own sort of life. With men and women, there aren't certainties for everybody. Not the way your father thought there ought to be; and not the way I live my life, either."

Dan reached out and squeezed the younger man's hand against the desktop.

"Sorry," Johnnie said. He twisted his hand palm-up and returned the grip.

Uncle Dan grinned impishly. "These cubes can be programmed to take a double message, you know?" he said. "And keyed to a particular fingerprint as to which they play."

He touched the third visicube with the little finger of his right hand. The brunette pulled the puff sleeves of her blouse down to display her breasts. They were well defined though small, and the areolae were almost black.

"Dan, darling, dearest Dan," the image said in a husky voice, "I wish you were here with me now so that you could kiss my nipples, so that you could *bite* my nipples the way you do, because that's ecstasy for me. . . ."

Johnnie stared at the wall. His face felt hot and he was sure that he was blushing.

"Everybody's different, lad," Dan said with a chuckle as the visicube returned to its innocent static state. "Figure out how you want to live your own life and don't worry about other people. Especially about relatives."

The door opened. Sergeant Britten, carrying a platter with two place settings, a dish of chicken and dumplings, and a visicube, stood silhouetted against the glacial scene on the opposite wall.

"Ready now, sir?" he asked.

"Ready for raw Pomeranian," Dan said, patting his flat stomach. "Set it right down here."

"When I unpacked," Britten said as he doled out the plates and flatware with the skill of a croupier, "I found this, sir. I didn't know where you wanted it placed."

'This' was a visicube containing the image of a plumpish, attractive woman of middle age—Beryl Haynes.

"Umm, yes," said Dan. "I had one of our techs make it up for me back at the dome. It's by way of being a gift for Captain Haynes . . . but I'd rather he didn't know about it. Since you know Greider, his batman . . . can you get it into his quarters to replace the cube he usually keeps in his combat uniform?"

Sergeant Britten grinned. "With what Greider owes me from poker last month? You know I can! I can get you Haynes' desk and Greider'll help me carry it."

Dan began spooning out the savory dish onto his plate and Johnnie's both. "You're a jewel, Britten," he said. "Try to come back from this operation, will you?"

"No fear," snorted the sergeant as he left the office with the cube and the empty platter. "If *you* buy it, try to get swallowed whole, will you? I don't want to have to carry a—"

The door closed. Vaguely through it: "—bloody corpse back."

16.

If the red slayer think he slays,
Or if the slain think he is slain. . . . .

    —Ralph Waldo Emerson

VIEWED THROUGH THE image intensifier in Johnnie's visor, the water at the creek-mouth boiled with life.

And death.

The jungle glimpsed from a fleet's base or in the holographic environs of a simulator seemed to be the army of Nature arrayed against Man. Here the battle was just as intense and Man was not even an incident. The varied factions of Nature were too busy fighting one another to notice the beached submarine.

"For God's sake, hurry with that chute!" said the submarine's commander, Lieutenant van Diemann.

As though the words had flown straight to heaven from his lips, there was a hiss from the bulky apparatus four of the party were deploying from a cylinder welded to the sub's deck. A tube two meters in diameter, stiffened by a glass-plate floor, began to extend slowly in the direction of the shore. Sergeant Britten, carrying a flamethrower, rode the tip of the protective chute.

"You may have to edge a little closer," said Commander Cooke. "I'm not sure the hundred feet will be quite enough."

"I can't!" van Diemann snapped. "We're already aground!"

Dan turned with the easy motion of a marksman and said, "I know you're aground, Lieutenant. I said you might have to edge a little closer to shore through the bottom muck. If you're incapable of carrying out the maneuver, I'm sure it's within the capacity of Ensign Gordon here."

Uncle Dan is scared, and he's taking it out on other people . . . who are scared too.

Something huge had died or been washed up at the creek-mouth; Johnnie couldn't be sure whether the creature had come from the jungle or the sea to begin with. Now the corpse was a Debatable Land for scavengers and things which preyed upon scavengers . . . and those who devoured them in turn.

Crabs a foot across the carapace backed together to form iron rings which rotated slowly across the carrion. One large pincer tore the flesh into strips of a size that the mandibles could worry loose, but the other pincer was always raised to threaten any creature that moved nearby.

Occasionally something with a long beak or armored paws would pluck at the defensive circles, but for the most part the crabs were safe—

Unless two groups collided. When that happened, the rings flattened against one another and all thought of food or defense was lost in a ravening urge to slay their closest kin—and therefore closest rivals. Other predators coldly picked their victims from behind or simply waited for crushed and fractioned debris to be flung away by other crabs.

"Sorry, sir," said van Diemann. "But we—I mean, a stranded sub would be a dead giveaway to an Angel reconnaissance flight, wouldn't it?"

"If you weren't the best submarine commander in the Blackhorse, Ted," Uncle Dan said, "I'd've picked somebody else for the mission. You're good enough to work her loose before daylight and the thermals."

"Shall I . . . ?" The lieutenant offered.

Dan shook his head. "The chute's going to reach. I was nervous, and you say things when you're nervous."

Something slithered from the sea, dripping with soft phosphorescence. Johnnie thought it was a root or a tentacle, but it bore jaws that slashed a chunk from the carcase. The whole creature vanished back the way it had come with a bulge of meat working its way down the throat. Moments later the fish was back for another piece, but this time an insect as large as the lid of a garbage can slid across the water's surface and stabbed.

There was a flurry like the explosion of a depth charge. As much as ten yards of the fish writhed to the surface at one time, but the insect kept its grip with suicidal intensity until both combatants were lost in the roiling water.

Life on Venus was a constant round of struggle and slaughter, meaningless except perhaps in some greater framework hidden from the participants. The humans on the surface of the planet—the mercenary companies— conformed to the same paradigm.

"Ready the lead element," snapped Sergeant Britten as the inflating tube neared the shore at the speed of a staggering walk.

"Lead element report," Johnnie ordered, letting the artificial intelligence in his helmet route the request to the men of his team. A block in the upper right corner of his visor glowed yellow, then went green in nine quick incre- ments as the lead element reported ready.

The lead element. The forlorn hope.

"Lead element ready," Johnnie said crisply.

Long, trailing branches swayed toward the carrion from the canopy as if carried by a breeze, but the air was still.

One of the tendrils curled vaguely in the direction of the beached submarine.

"Watch tha—" Johnnie said, butting his rifle to his shoulder.

As he spoke, a spark that the troops' visors blanked to save their vision slapped between the bare tips of two of the hanging branches. A squadron of crabs and hundreds of the lesser creatures crawling around them froze in varied attitudes of death. The tendrils began to twine around the quantity of freshly-electrocuted meat, ignoring the carrion.

Johnnie fired with the flash. His explosive bullet whacked the base of the branch questing toward the men. It dangled from a strip of bark for an instant, then fell into the water where a boil of teeth met it.

Others of the men on the cramped deck jerked around in surprise to look at the young ensign.

"You'd think," said Commander Cooke, removing all question about the propriety of the shot, "that the jungle would let us come to it . . . but I suppose it's a case of the early bird and the worm."

"The worm's got teeth," said Lieutenant van Diemann, who was about twenty-five years old. "Nice shot, kid."

"Send the lead element forward," said Sergeant Britten's voice in the helmet earphones. Johnnie, as head of the lead element, was part of the command net.

"Lead element forward," Uncle Dan—Commander Cooke—ordered.

"Lead element, follow me," said Johnnie as he slipped the magazine with one round fired into the pouch from which he'd just taken the fresh reload. He stepped into the tube; and, as soon as the protective walls were around him, began to jog from eagerness and a desire to release tension.

The chute was a standard design which most of the free companies used for fire-fighting and expanding their bases into the jungle. The walls were woven of fine-spun quartz monofilament, refractory in themselves and interlaid with bands of beryllium which could be electrified if necessary. Mounting one on the deck of a submarine was awkward, but that was nowhere near as difficult as most of this operation.

The chute would take the expedition to the edge of the jungle in safety. For the rest of the way they were on their own.

For a moment, Johnnie's boots echoed alone on the walkway; then the chute rocked in a multiplying rhythm as the members of his lead element clambered out the submarine's hatch and joined him.

Three of the men carried flamethrowers—Red Section; three of them carried reload tanks for the flamethrowers—Blue Section; and the remaining three men of Green Section had quad-packs of armor-piercing rockets. Many of the men were half again Johnnie's age; all of them had vastly more experience than Johnnie did—

And the raw ensign was leading the force because nobody knew as much about the jungle as the simulator had taught him. The Blackhorse fought nature only as an incident to fighting men.

The block of light in Johnnie's visor was still solid green. He could have asked his helmet for a remote view from any or all the men in the lead element, but they weren't going to get lost—and the jungle ahead needed his full attention.

Johnnie paused at the edge of the chute beside Sergeant Britten, aiming his weapon—outward, not at a specific target, for there was none. He projected a compass bearing in his visor, then moved back a half step to make room for the section leader who was supposed to be immediately behind him.

"Red One," he said. Johnnie didn't know the names of the members of his section, but their military job descriptions were all that mattered now.

He indicated an arc by moving his left hand beneath the

barrel of his rifle/grenade launcher combination. "Sweep
twenty degrees with a three-second shot."

Red One braced himself behind the nozzle of his
flamethrower, but he didn't fire. "What am I aiming at?" he
asked.

"Red One, you're relieved!" Johnnie shouted. "Report to
the center element for assignment. Sergeant Britten, take
over Red Section."

Britten's flamethrower snarled like a dragon waking. A
pencil-thin rod spat from the nozzle in a flat arc. The fuel
was magnesium-enriched; its flame was almost as bright as
the electrical discharge from the tree a moment before.
Foliage curled and crackled as the sergeant walked his lethal
torch waist-high across *precisely* twenty degrees in *precisely* three seconds.

Johnnie's helmet visor automatically blanked the high-
intensity core of the flame, but the reflections—from water,
leaves, and even the smooth bark of some trees—made a
dazzling pattern all around him. Something screamed horribly over the roar of the flame; he wasn't sure whether it
was an animal or steam escaping from the trunk of a dying
tree.

The white flame and its soul-searing noise cut off.
Orange sparks puffed and showered; occasionally one of
them flew against the breeze in a vain attempt to escape the
destruction it carried. A wide section approximately fifty
yards into the jungle was either clear or too stunned to pose
an immediate threat to the expedition.

"Good work, Britten," Johnnie said. "Lead element,
follow me."

He hadn't been sure of exactly what was in the section the
flamethrower swept, but he knew that where the jungle met
a beach or stream bank, the flux meant that the nearest life
forms were particularly savage and determined. Once the

team had penetrated the immediate wall, they had a chance with the jungle's ordinary denizens.

"What?" blurted Red One, who hadn't understood—and hadn't understood that orders must be carried out *instantly* if they were any of them to survive. "Wha . . . ?"

"Force Prime to all personnel," said Uncle Dan's voice over the earphones, "Lead Prime, your orders transferring Red One and Force Two are approved. Red One, trade weapons with Force Two so that he's got the full bottle. And *move out!*"

John Gordon, ensign in the Blackhorse for a matter of days, stepped forward as point man in an operation that was at least as dangerous as anything the veterans behind him had ever attempted in their years of service.

It felt good.

17.

LIGHT ENHANCEMENT GAVE Johnnie a good view of outlines, but he switched his visor to thermal imaging as he stepped out of the chute's protection. Sensors in his helmet mapped the temperature gradients around him down to variations of a half degree. His AI fitted the blotches of heat into patterns which it highlighted on the visor when required.

Vines were at air temperature. The stick insect, poised vertically along a tree bole near the course Johnnie planned, was several degrees warmer. Though 'cold-blooded,' the insect had warmed itself by muscle contractions so it could strike with maximum speed and suppleness when the line of men passed beside it.

Johnnie switched back to light-enhanced vision and aimed, using the lower set of sights.

"Sir, what're you—" Sergeant Britten said in a low voice.

The grenade launcher beneath the rifle barrel went *bloonk!* The heavy recoil jarred Johnnie's shoulder, even though he let it rock him back instead of trying to fight it.

The grenade detonated with a bright green flash, blowing the insect's head to pulp and throwing the fifty feet of body into furious motion as dangerous as that of a runaway bulldozer. Medium-sized trees crashed as the not-yet-corpse careened through the jungle in a series of jointed motions.

"God almighty!" said Sergeant Britten.

"Right, let's move," Johnnie said as he stepped into the reality of a forty-pound pack that he hadn't worn in the simulator. Some food, some medical stores. . . .

Mostly ammunition. For his rifle, grenade launcher, and the little pistol on his hip. The raiders couldn't shut off the jungle just because they'd emptied their magazines, and Nature's scoring program had very tough sanctions for losers. . . .

Twenty yards away, a patch of ground quivered in the midst of the ash and embers. Leaves lay on it, but the sheen of mud was bright around their edges.

"Watch it," Johnnie whispered, facing his first real test. "That looks like a swamp-chopper burrow. I'll move close and when it rises I'll—"

"Excuse me, sir," said Sergeant Britten blandly. He held the nozzle of his flamethrower in his left hand so that his right was free to unhook a heavy grenade from his belt. "Let's try it my way first."

The veteran lobbed the grenade like a shot put, putting his upper body behind the throw with a grunt. The missile arched down and entered the soft ground with a sullen *plop*. The explosion that followed was a mere burp of sound, more a quiver through Johnnie's boot soles than a blast.

A column of mud and water shot ten feet into the air, then subsided. Bubbles with a sheen of blood rose and burst for thirty seconds more.

"I thought that might be simpler, sir," Britten said. "No . . . extra credit for neatness here, you see."

"Right," Johnnie said, tight-lipped. "Thanks." He set off past the lair, now harmless.

There was a trail near the end of the burned wedge, worn by God-knew-what and headed in something close to the planned bearing. Johnnie decided to follow it, since the ground was likely firmer than that of most of this low-lying area. They'd still have creeks to cross, and there *wasn't* a safe way to do that.

But then, there wasn't a safe way to fight any war—unless you were a politician.

The lead element proceeded several hundred yards without incident. Johnnie was on point, and his men were spaced at six-foot intervals behind him—tighter than would be safe against human enemies. He moved slowly, looking in all directions and switching his visor repeatedly between modes of vision.

"Don't forget the canopy," he warned on the general net. "Keep looking up. That's where the real bad ones'll be."

Some of the real bad ones.

The hot, saturated air felt like a bucket of molasses as he slogged through it, and the broad straps of his pack were knives. He *couldn't* let discomfort affect his alertness, but he didn't see how he could avoid that happening.

Too little light penetrated the forest canopy for there to be a heavy growth of green plants at ground level, but masses of fungus in a variety of forms made up for the lack.

Johnnie paused. Thermal mapping told him that the figure crouching beside the trail wasn't the lizard it seemed to be. It was a toadstool, a Trojan Horse fungus, which had grown into a distorted shape that would attract rather than repel larger, hungry predators. Therefore—

"Red Section," he ordered, pointing. "Together on my count of three, hit that. One, t—"

A member of Blue Section fired off the magazine of the automatic rifle he carried in addition to a flamethrower reload. The surface of the lizard-form puffed out yellow spores launched by chambers of compressed gas within.

"Flame!" Johnnie shouted, knowing it was too late even though Sergeant Britten had anticipated the order by triggering his flamethrower. Helmet filters clamped over Johnnie's nostrils; he squeezed his lips shut against the urge to suck in air through his mouth when his nostrils were constricted.

The white dazzle of Britten's flame-rod touched the fungus and turned it into a soft gush of light as its methane chambers exploded. A second flamethrower intersected with the sergeant's.

The third member of Red Section didn't fire. He lay on his back, arching in convulsions. Either the man had sucked spores in through his mouth, or he'd gone into anaphylactic shock from mere skin contact.

His tongue was black, and there was no life behind his bulging eyes.

The bare backs of Johnnie's hands prickled.

"Right," said Johnnie. He felt cold, as though he'd just stepped into ice water, but that was merely his sweat. "Force Prime, lead element has one fatal. Force Two, take the fresh flamethrower. Blue Two—" the man who'd fired his rifle "—carry the sergeant's flamethrower besides your own equipment."

"Hey, I can't carry—" the man said.

Johnnie slapped the side of the man's helmet with his rifle butt.

"You dickhead!" he screamed. "You just killed him, don't you see? That toadstool was waiting to be attacked so its spores would have first crack at fresh meat to grow on! And that's just what you gave them! Your buddy!"

The dead man's face was entirely black now, but the color was more than chemical reaction. Tiny fingers of fungus were already reaching up from the skin, speeded by the warmth of the flesh and the violent struggle for place through which life here had evolved.

"Oh," said the rifleman. He took the heavy flamethrower Sergeant Britten held out to him. "Oh."

Johnnie turned and vomited off the side of the trail.

"Lead element, are you able to proceed?" Uncle Dan demanded from his position back with the rear guard.

Johnnie spat, then wiped his mouth and swallowed. "Roger, lead element proceeding," he said in a voice he didn't recognize as his own.

That was the first time he'd seen a man die.

It wouldn't be the last.

Dawn was a blaze of heat and enough additional light that the enhancement circuitry in the helmet visors was no longer necessary. Colors became real—and therefore more boringly uniform, black/green/gray, than the computer had made them for the sake of contrast.

The expedition was making very slow progress; but they *had* time, since there was nothing they could do when they reached the harbor shore except wait until midnight.

The trail met a creek, black with tannin and decay products. Track and watercourse together twisted off to the southeast, away from the harbor. The shallow banks were less than ten feet apart, an easy jump for the men if they hadn't been carrying their loads of weapons and equipment.

"Force Prime," Johnnie said as he eyed the water. It didn't look very deep, but they were going to have to check that before they entered it. "We've reached a stream. We'll need fencing."

The heavy equipment—the three boats, the mats for soft ground, and the fences to block a safe pathway through running water—were in the relatively-safe center element. Those burdened troops were almost defenseless, but their two unladen guards needed to watch only the flanks.

"Roger, I'll send some forward," Uncle Dan replied calmly . . . as calmly as Lead Prime, Johnnie himself. "What width do you—"

There was a roar and screams, audible through the air as

well as over the helmet radios. Rifles ripped out their
magazines in single, barrel-melting bursts. A pair of back-
pack rockets added their *whack-SLAP!* sounds to the jungle-
muffled din.

Johnnie's men spun around, staring vainly through the
undergrowth. A few of them started to move toward the
sound of the guns.

"Lead element, circle around Lead Prime!" Johnnie
ordered sharply. "The sound will bring—"

And it did, sweeping like a flying carpet ten feet high
above the water of the creek: head grotesquely small against
the forty-foot expanse of flattened ribs on which it glided,
but still wide enough to swallow a man whole.

It was genetically a snake, but the skill with which
evolution had molded its body into an airfoil permitted it to
fly for more than a mile if it found a tall enough tree from
which to launch its attack.

Johnnie fired a grenade, but the creature banked and
presented its body edge-on as he did so. The projectile
sailed harmlessly above it and detonated in a mass of
vegetation which hid even the flash.

The snake wasn't heading for the lead element but rather
for the commotion which had caught its attention. Sergeant
Britten raised and swung his flamethrower, but the weapon
was too heavy to track at the speed of the flying target.

Johnnie sighted on the saffron scales of the snake's
underside and slid an embroidery of three-shot bursts along
them, working from mid-section to head as the target
flashed past. The creature suddenly buckled in the air,
braking its flight just long enough for Britten to whack the
flat body in half with his rod of ravening flame.

The pieces fell separately, one to either side of the
stream. As they did so, Green One punched a rocket
through the front half.

"God almighty . . . ," Sergeant Britten muttered

again. He took his right hand from the flamethrower's grip and waggled it in the air. The fine hairs were singed off the back of his fingers. The weapon's nozzle glowed orange from the long stream he'd fed through it.

"Keep watching the front and sides," Johnnie ordered in a pale, distant voice. "Somebody else will take care of what's behind us."

He fumbled with the fresh magazine. He'd gripped the rifle so hard that his fingers were almost numb.

The roars from the following elements had died away. It took repeated orders from Force Prime before the shooting there stopped, however.

"Lead Prime," Uncle Dan reported, "the fence is coming forward now. We won't be able to recover all of it, so try not to cross any more creeks, okay?"

Johnnie could hear men panting up the trail toward him. "Ah . . . Force Prime, what's the problem with the fencing?" he asked.

"No problem with the fence," his uncle said bluntly. "We just don't have the men to carry it any more."

Sergeant Britten had fitted his flamethrower nozzle to a full container of fuel. The container he'd used, completely empty, lay on the ground beside him. Rootlets were beginning to explore it for the possibility of food.

Two men of center element, uninjured but with harrowed looks on their faces, struggled forward with their loads of electronic fencing.

"What happened back there?" a rocketeer demanded.

Johnnie opened his mouth to tell the questioner to do his job and leave center section to its personnel—

But the rocketeer had already taken one end of the bundled fence; and anyway, Johnnie wanted to hear the answer as badly as his men did.

"It was a spider," the other bearer muttered. "I didn't see

anything, it just . . . somebody shot, and it knocked me down like, like, I don' know. . . ."

"The rest a you, keep watching," Sergeant Britten ordered gruffly. "We're maybe going to get more company."

There was a post in the center of each roll of fencing. The troops set them in the soft ground of the creek bank, about six feet apart. The bearers—engineering techs—unfastened the small control pods atop the posts.

"It grabbed Bodo and Taylor, both of them," the first tech amplified. "I tried to . . . I tried to hit it with the boat—"

"You were carrying the fence, weren't you?" Blue Three objected.

"Watch the trees!" snapped Britten.

"Bodo here had fence, Taylor 'n' me, we had the boat," the bearer corrected in a voice without emotion. He depressed a button. The post rotated. The free end of the fencing began to extend itself through the water like a sliding door of fine mesh. His partner at the other post did the same.

"They hit it with rockets, but it didn't stop," the second tech said, resuming the story. "Only it turned and grabbed the rocketeer instead."

"Saved my life," said the first bearer. "Saved *my* life."

The three rocketeers of Green Section shied. They darted their eyes across the waste of fungus and trees with new alertness.

The fences were hung from jointed drive rods. They reached the far bank and crept up it a few feet in two roughly-parallel lines. Their metallic fabric was flexible enough to follow the contours of the muddy ground. There was a bright spark from within the stream; a bubble of steam burst to the surface.

"They hit it with a flamethrower," the first tech said.

"The hair, it was burning all over it, burning and stinking . . . but it kept sucking on Taylor and he just sagged like a balloon going flat. . . ."

"Let's go," said Johnnie.

"Just a moment, sir," Britten said as he unhooked another grenade, this time an incendiary, from his belt. He armed it and tossed it into the fenced portion of the stream. "You guys better get back."

"Yeah, we gotta get the boat," one of the techs said. They stumbled off together, oblivious of the grenade fuze sizzling in the creek behind them.

The main charge went off with a roar of colored steam. Globules of fire darted from the haze and vanished. Dark water, drawn from both up- and downstream, surged through the net and set off further sparks as creatures were electrocuted.

The fence combined a battery of sensors with a sophisticated control system—and a high-voltage power pack in its anchor. Water did not short the current paths—as it would have done without the computer control. When the sensors detected contact with an object which had an electrical field of its own—a living object, whether plant or animal, large or small—a surge fried the interloper.

The grenade burned out. Water continued to splutter and roil for several seconds longer.

"Mighta been safe before, sir," Britten said. "But again, that mighta been just the wrong stretch of bottom between the fences. I figure it's clear now, though."

"Lead element, follow me," Johnnie said as he stepped into the bubbling water. His trousers were moisture-sealed, but the fabric felt hot and clammy as it pressed against him.

He knew more about the jungle and its threats than the others did; but the veteran sergeant knew the importance of using all the firepower you had available. In war—with men or nature—no force was excessive if you were the one still standing at the end. . . .

The two men in front of the column with powered brush saws waited while Johnnie compared the relief map projected on his visor against his hand-carried inertial locator. Machines—even (especially) the most sophisticated machines—fail. When something as important as the expedition's precise position in a lethal jungle was involved, an ounce of redundancy was more than justified.

"We're almost there," he said. He'd settled his pack on the ground while he took the bearings. The release of weight felt like a long rest. "Well, almost to where we'll wait for, for . . . to go off tonight. Another three hundred yards."

Thunder boomed a regular drumbeat in the middle distance, its direction diffused by the surrounding leaves and branches.

"Whazzat?" demanded a rocketeer, spinning in an attempt to face all directions during the time something could reach him. Green Section had been windy ever since they'd heard what happened in center element.

"That's the Angels shelling some tree," Sergeant Britten replied with cool scorn as he continued to examine the arc of jungle he'd assigned himself to cover. "Normal base maintenance. Don't get your bowels in 'n uproar, huh?"

Johnnie bent and thrust his arms through the packstraps again. He held his rifle upright between his knees. "There's more Trojan Horse fungus ahead to the right," he said. "Give it a wide—"

A thirty-foot-long iguana—its ancestors had been iguanas—poked its head through a mass of reeds. It clamped shut the flaps over its nostrils, then came on at a rush. Green Prime was staring straight at the creature when it began its charge.

Some plant-eating forms had evolved into carnivores on Venus, but the iguanas remained vegetarians. Fronds of brush dangled from the corners of the creature's mouth, then fell away as it bleated a challenge.

The bulls and rhinoceroses of Earth had been vegetarians also. That meant they attacked out of ill-temper and territoriality rather than from need for food; a distinction without a difference for the corpses they left behind them.

Green Prime knelt and aimed his weapons pod. Johnnie, struggling to free himself from his pack, saw the four rocket nozzles staring back at him. He flung himself to the side, abandoning his rifle.

"Watch it, you damned—" shouted Sergeant Britten.

Green Prime's first rocket ignited. The man who'd been beside Johnnie hadn't moved. The backblast caught him, and his flamethrower reload exploded.

The scream and white-hot glare of fuel threw the rocketeer off. The remainder of his ripple-fired pod raked foliage to the side of the intended target.

The first missile had struck the bony scutes protecting the iguana's skull. If the range had been slightly longer—if the rocket had reached terminal velocity—it could have drilled straight through a comparable thickness of armor plate. The difference of a second's burn-time (the disadvantage of a rocket compared to a gun) was the difference between life and death for Green Prime.

His missile glanced from the lizard. The impact staggered the beast. That was not enough to keep it from clamping its jaws over the rocketeer's torso, then spewing out the remains in a froth of blood as the creature twisted for another victim.

Sergeant Britten's flamethrower licked across the blunt head at point-blank range. A ruff of red, orange, and blue flame enveloped the iguana as horny skin burned and colored its white destroyer. The creature lashed out in blind pain, flinging Britten in one direction and his flamethrower in another.

Johnnie rolled as though driven by the ball of fire incinerating his pack and the man beside it. The brush-cutting team had dropped their saws and were firing rifles. Explosive bullets glittered across the iguana's flank; even solids would have been useless against a creature of such bulk and armor.

Johnnie's pistol was useless also. He fired anyway, aiming at the back of the creature's knees as it strode forward. The splayed legs of the lizard's ancestors had been modified into a graviportal stance suitable for the giant's elephantine bulk.

The iguana—eyeless, lipless, and terrible—turned.

Something clasped Johnnie's nose. He screamed and tried to lash free of the grip while the lizard lumbered toward him.

Nothing was holding him. His filters had just closed for protection. Sergeant Britten, moving feebly, had collapsed the clump of Trojan Horse fungus when he landed. The lethal spores were drifting out in their broad-spreading trajectory.

One of the brush cutters threw down his rifle and ran. The other tried to reload but dropped one, then another, full magazine.

The iguana doubled itself in a sideways arc, then sprang straight again and flopped over on its spiny back. Its right legs kicked violently, but the left pair were frozen.

A rocketeer walked his load up the iguana's rib cage. The third and fourth missiles were close enough to terminal velocity that they exited from the far side of the animal, sucking with them a puree of the creature's heart and lungs.

"Cease fire," Johnnie ordered. He forced his numb lips to blow out the words while he breathed only through his filters. "Cease fire, it's dead. Cease fire."

Under normal circumstances the iguana would have been invulnerable to the spores of the Trojan Horse, but Sergeant Britten's flame had burned off the lizard's nostril flaps. Black, questing streaks of fungus were already taking possession of the giant corpse.

"Lead Prime, report!" Uncle Dan's voice demanded in Johnnie's ears. "Any lead-element personnel, report!"

Sergeant Britten had risen to his knees. He crawled some distance away from the crumpled fruiting body before he got fully to his feet.

"Force Prime," Johnnie wheezed, "this is Lead Prime. Hold in place for a few minutes. We're ahead of schedule. Just keep off our backs for a while, okay?"

His filters opened so that he could breathe freely again. He didn't stand up until he'd finished reloading his pistol.

The expedition's twenty-two survivors set up a tight perimeter, just within the strand of Paradise Harbor. By extending a fiber-optics periscope through the jungle, Commander Cooke and Ensign Gordon could view their target and the remainder of the Angel installations without risk of being observed themselves.

Shortly after dusk, the boom of gunfire from the *Azrael* and *Holy Trinity* ceased. Either the jungle had gone to sleep when the high-energy actinics no longer drove its motion, or the perimeter guards had drawn back for their own safety until daybreak.

The expedition members were physically and mentally exhausted. Half of them at any one time were detailed to watch, but the off-duty men were permitted to sleep if they could manage it.

Johnnie wondered if any of them really slept. For his own part, he found he was afraid to close his eyes.

18.

Then honor, my Jeany, must plead my excuse;
Since honor commands me, how can I refuse?

—Allan Ramsay

"HOLD IT," SAID Johnnie, poised in the lead with a power saw in his hands. The clear patch of beach was the obvious point from which to launch the boats—

But there was a reason for the mud to be clear.

The image intensifier in his visor caught the ripple an instant before the anemone broke surface. Johnnie lunged, his finger on the saw's trigger, trusting that no one on the ships could hear the high-pitched whine over the night-sounds of the jungle and the vessels' own mechanical systems.

The cutting-bar sparked on the anemone's sting-clad arms before squelching through the support tube. Bits splashed Johnnie and an arc twenty feet out in the harbor.

The tube, now harmless, sucked back under the water. The head and fragments of severed arms writhed on the mud—still dangerous to a bare hand but unable to crawl high enough to strike above boot level.

"Is it safe now?" demanded a tech, understandably nervous with both hands gripping the boat.

"It's safe," snapped Uncle Dan, "unless you wait long enough for something to move into the area that the worm—"

It was an anemone, not a worm, Johnnie thought—
"—kept clear for you!"

The techs set the first collapsible boat onto the harbor strand and hooked up its pump and generator. Sergeant Britten marshalled the squad of men who waded gingerly to the edge of the shore and knelt, knives out and peering through visors to spot any serious threat moving toward them through the water.

Johnnie, holding his saw, stepped onto the end of the line opposite Britten. The water was too good a heat conductor for thermal imaging to be of much use, but color-highlighted ripple patterns would/might be enough warning.

The boat made a slurping sound, then clicked as the segments locked into place. The inner material became a colloid and expanded 300-fold when it contacted water. The colloid provided the core and stiffening for the boat, while microns-thick panels of vitril hardened the surfaces to create a practical vessel.

One of the nervous men on guard gasped and stamped his feet. What he'd thought was an attacker was only the sucking mud. "Wish we were bloody aboard!" he grunted.

"*I* wish we were back in Wenceslas Dome for the victory celebration," said Britten. The sergeant had a concussion grenade in either hand for an emergency. No one else was permitted to use explosives at this stage of the operation. "But we ain't."

"Boat's ready," murmured the tech.

There was a general sloshing movement as most of the men in the water and a few of those watching the jungle behind started to slide the boat deeper into the harbor. The man beside Johnnie tried to clamber over the gunwales. Johnnie grabbed him by the shoulder and held him till the moment of panic had passed.

Men from the rear guard boarded, according to the plan. Uncle Dan was the last aboard.

"Sorry, sir," muttered the sailor.

The first boat moved a few feet out from the shore with a muted burble from its underwater thruster. More techs dropped the second boat into the place of the first and got quickly to work. The last of the little vessels had been abandoned when it became obvious that there wouldn't be enough survivors to require all three.

"We're not exactly headed for a tea party, you know," Johnnie said to the man beside him as they both looked for trouble. Years of human occupation and entrance nets must have thinned out—maybe eliminated—really large forms from the harbor.

"Sir, I *know* ships," the sailor replied. "But I been shit-scared ever since I stepped outa the submarine."

Eliminated. Dream on.

The saw whirred like a nervous cat. Johnnie's fingers had tightened more than he'd intended.

"Boat's ready," said a tech as he twisted over the side. He lifted his feet high against the chance of something making a late grab at him.

Half the waiting men lurched into the boat while the others slid the hull toward deeper water. The technique worked well enough, but it was completely spontaneous.

This time the man who'd jumped early waited, shivering with fear or anticipation, until Johnnie clapped him on the back and said, "Go! Go on!"

Light winked on the deck of the *Holy Trinity*. Someone had opened a hatch and spilled some of the interior illumination.

Coming or going? Someone headed in to his bunk, or out onto the rail from which he'd be able to raise the alarm . . . ?

"Sir?" grunted Sergeant Britten. "*Sir*. C'mon!"

Johnnie had been walking outward at the bow of the boat. He was waist-deep in the water. He tried to lift himself over the gunwale. Britten caught him beneath the armpit and pulled hard. "Throw that damned—"

Johnnie dropped the saw, no longer necessary.

"—saw away!" the sergeant growled.

Johnnie flopped into the boat. It was already full beyond its designed capacity.

There was a flurry from the water as something struck the tool and rose with it, thrashing violently. Johnnie looked back over his hips, but the creature and its frustrating prey had sunk again.

"Quiet back there!" snapped the earphones in the voice of Uncle Dan, who must have thought the fish was part of the second boat's boarding process.

The collapsible boats started across the harbor. Johnnie was in the bow of the second. He could barely see the other vessel, twenty feet ahead of him. When Sergeant Britten completed raising the heat/light/radar-absorbent camouflage net, the second boat became equally hard to spot, even to someone expecting it.

The camouflage nets blinded the boats' crews as completely as they did outside observers. The coxswains steered by the images projected in their visors—constructs from the helmets' data banks and inertial navigation equipment.

The boats slid across the water at less than a walking pace. The wake of the leader rocked the following vessel less than the slight harbor chop. The dreadnought that was their target grew slowly in Johnnie's visor, but knowing that he saw an image rather than the actual guns and hull somehow robbed the vision of its reality.

Although: the *Holy Trinity* was real, and the hologram projected into the helmet visor was as much the object as sky glow reflected from the gray armor onto Johnnie's retinas would have been.

The dreadnought lay at an angle to the boats; they were

approaching its port side. "Force Prime," Johnnie warned, "the skimmer port on the starboard bow—the right side of the bow—" *How did you say 'port port' without being confusing?* "—is open. I'm not sure the one on this side is."

The first boat slowed. The careful computer simulation in Johnnie's helmet showed the wake travelling on ahead as the boat dropped to a crawl. Johnnie rocked as his coxswain cut power to keep station.

"Lead Prime, this is Force Prime," said Uncle Dan's voice. "Take over the lead. Bring us in, John."

"Coxswain," Johnnie said, "take us around the bow. The port we're looking for's about a hundred fifty feet back."

The thruster wound up, a hum through the hull instead of a sound. Men swung to and fro again, their heavy packs emphasizing the gentle acceleration.

"Coxswain," Johnnie snapped, "we're not in a hurry."

But they were, all of them were; in a hurry to make something happen themselves. All they could do now was wait for a burst of automatic gunfire to gut their boats and a few men, leaving the remainder to splash for a while as they provided food and entertainment for the harbor life.

The simulated bows of the *Holy Trinity* loomed above them. The boat was beneath the bow flare, invisible to anyone on the dreadnought's deck. Sergeant Britten ripped back the netting—not before time, because they were headed for the chain of the bow anchor.

The coxswain saw the obstacle without need for the warning and curses from the men in the bow, but it had been a near thing. The software controlling the simulation needed a little tinkering. . . .

The skimmer port was a black rectangle against slate gray. Water gurgled doubtfully through it. The coxswain throttled back still further.

"Easy . . . ," breathed Sergeant Britten, as much to himself as to the coxswain.

Johnnie stood up in the bow. He wasn't afraid. He didn't have leisure to be afraid.

"Here, sir," Britten murmured.

The grip of a sub-machine gun touched Johnnie's right hand from behind.

He'd been about to attack a superdreadnought with nothing but a .30-caliber pistol.

"Right," said Johnnie. He quickly snapped the weapon's sling into his epaulet, then paused. The collapsible boat was slightly broader than the opening. Johnnie braced his arms onto the armor while his feet thrust back, preventing the little vessel from crunching into the huge one. Then he jumped aboard the *Holy Trinity*.

There was no guard in the skimmer magazine. All twelve of the water-stained pumpkinseeds hung from their davits, swaying gently. Johnnie caught the line Britten threw him and made it fast to the rail so that the boat would hold its station. The remainder of the assault force followed him, splashing awkwardly on the water-covered rollers and cursing. Sergeant Britten was the last man—

As expected.

The boat gurgled as the sergeant stepped out of it; he'd pulled the scuttling strip, opening a six-by-thirty-inch hole in the bottom. They didn't want the boats floating in the harbor and perhaps arousing suspicion, but it was still disquieting to see the transport which had brought them this far slipping beneath the black water.

Britten reached for the line. Johnnie had already cut it with the diamond saw which formed the back edge of his fighting knife. A metal edge wouldn't have worked its way through the monocrystalline cord until dawn broke. . . .

The second boat slid to the mouth of the opening.

Commander Cooke tossed Johnnie another line and clanged aboard himself. His men followed him.

"Have you opened the hatch yet?" Uncle Dan demanded.

"Ah, no, I—" Johnnie said.

"Out of the way," his uncle ordered brusquely.

Dan pushed past Johnnie and clambered over the railing to where the first boatload already waited. He pulled a suction cup on a line of thin flex from his helmet and stuck it onto the wall. "Team leaders report," his mushy voice ordered.

"One."

"Two!"

"Three present!" There was a bang as the leader of section three slipped on the rollers as he hastened to board.

"Four."

Ordinary helmet communications were only useful at line of sight for this operation, since the massive armor walls of the *Holy Trinity* blocked spread-frequency radio as effectively as they did incoming shells. The leaders of the various sections—bridge, bow, stern, and engine room— reported via radio since they were all in the same room, but in action they would use the same system Uncle Dan had just tested.

The transmitter in the suction cup fed the signal through the fabric of the ship itself. It could be received directly through the helmets, but replies would have to be made with the men's similar units.

A squish and a gurgle marked the scuttling of the second boat. Johnnie cut the line. Sergeant Britten reached over the railing and helped the young ensign up to the front of the assault force.

Johnnie charged his sub-machine gun. There were similar *clack*s throughout the compartment as all the men readied their weapons to fire.

"Remember," said Uncle Dan calmly, "if we don't have

to fire a shot, then we've done a perfect job. But if there's trouble, finish it *fast*. We don't have any margin for error."

He touched a button. The hatch whined and slowly cranked its way outward.

19.

Up the close and down the stair,
Out and in with Burke and Hare.

—Anonymous

THE TEAMS SEPARATED immediately. The eight men picked
to capture the engine room, and the pair who would cut
the stern cable, went directly aft on the platform deck. The
remainder, the bridge assault team and the two men for the
bow and bow anchor, took the companionway up two levels
to the main deck before dividing again.

The dreadnought's off-duty crewmen should be sleeping
peacefully in the air-conditioned comfort of their lower-
deck quarters, but none of the assault force would be on that
level to chance a meeting.

The bridge team, with Dan, Johnnie, and Sergeant
Britten attached as supernumeraries, was officially led by
Turret Captain Reiss, a senior warrant officer. As a practical
matter, when Commander Cooke was present, Commander
Cooke was in charge—

And when Ensign Gordon was present, he was jogging
forward on point, his eyes wide open to catch movement at
their peripheries and the borrowed sub-machine gun ready
to end that movement before the victim knew what had hit
him.

There was no cover in the dreadnought's empty, drab-
painted corridors. Somebody could step out of a compart-

. any time and see the Blackhorse assault force, ned to the teeth. There was no reason a member of the *Holy Trinity*'s crew *should* be here . . . but there was no law of nature forbidding them, either.

Training had made Johnnie good at this sort of business. Now he realized that success required that he—that they—also be lucky, or at least not unlucky.

Of course, the most immediate bad luck if the raiders were discovered would be that of the Angel crewman, smashed into a bulkhead by Johnnie's burst of explosive bullets.

The armored curve of A Turret barbette bulged into the corridor. Visible beyond it was the barbette supporting B Turret. Johnnie broke stride, trying to remember the layout of a dreadnought from schematics studied at leisure and the brief glimpse he'd had of the *Holy Trinity*'s armored reality as he followed Sal Grumio.

"Sir, should we—"

—enter the barbette and go up to the shelter deck through the turret? he would have concluded if Uncle Dan, a rifleman faceless behind his reflective visor, had not broken in with, "No, the next compartment forward should be the lower conning room. We'll take the access ladder straight from there to the bridge."

"And take it *easy* when we're in the ladderway," Sergeant Britten added in a low-voiced snarl. "Remember, even if they're all half asleep, they're going to wonder if it sounds like there's a soccer crowd stampeding toward the bridge."

The lower conn was well within the main armor belt, so the compartment's bulkheads were thin, barely splinterproof. Even so, the hatch cycled slowly and unwillingly, a minor mechanical fault that Maintenance hadn't gotten around to correcting.

Johnnie took a deep breath in the enforced pause. His body shivered with reaction.

"Let's go," Dan said, leading through the hatchway.

Lights went on as soon as the presence of humans tripped a circuit. Johnnie crouched to spray the first movement, but the lower conn was empty save for the Blackhorse raiders. The hatch to the ladderway was open, for ventilation or from the sheer lazy disinterest of the last man through.

"Sorry, sir," Johnnie muttered to his uncle.

"Nothing to be sorry about," Dan said as he entered the armored staircase behind the muzzle of his rifle.

The helical treads of the ladderway were barely wide enough for men to pass in opposite directions, and there was no way that ten booted humans could climb them without sending a mass of vibrant echoes through the narrow confines. Johnnie reminded himself that the constant flexing of the dreadnought's whole tens of thousands of tons was loud enough to conceal the ringing footsteps from the bridge watch, but there was no emotional comfort in what he knew intellectually was true.

Dan paused briefly on the landing outside the conning tower, directly below the bridge. Again the hatch was open and the compartment empty. Vision slits, presently unshuttered, gave a shadowy view forward over B Turret.

"Force Prime," muttered the command channel in Sergeant Britten's voice, "*I* ought to be leading."

"No sir," Johnnie gasped. Because of the weight of his pack and the monotony of the steps, he'd had to make a conscious effort to keep his eyes lifted above the next tread. "*I* should."

"Both of you, shut—" Commander Cooke snarled.

The *tak-tak-tak* of gunfire, not loud but penetrating because it was the sound they all feared, cut him off.

A fuzzy voice over the intra-ship channel crackled, ". . . *at the accommodation la . . .*" and blurred off as the sound of another burst rattled the night. It was impossible to pinpoint the direction of the echoing sound; from the words, the stern team had run into guards at the accommodation ladder raised along the dreadnought's aft rail.

Johnnie plucked the transmitter cup from his helmet.

"*Forget that!*" bellowed Uncle Dan. "Come on!"

The massive bridge hatch was opening. An enlisted man, slinging a sub-machine gun and looking back over his shoulder to hear a shouted order, was halfway through the opening when Dan's rifle blew him back in a sparkle of explosive bullets. Muzzle blasts in the confined space stung Johnnie's bare hands and chin.

Dan jumped through the hatchway, firing. The hatch staggered, then began to close. Johnnie brushed both the hatch and its jamb as he followed his uncle into the bright-lit interior.

A junior lieutenant lay against a bulkhead painted with his blood. He'd been reaching for his pistol, but his outstretched left hand had already thrown the master switch that closed and dogged all the bridge hatches.

Dan fired. His shots blasted a console and the bulkhead beyond the ducking officer of the day.

Johnnie killed three techs still at their consoles, two of them scrabbling for pistols and the third—the dangerous one—shouting into his communicator.

Training held. A pair of explosive bullets hit each man in the head. One of the techs leaped to his feet and sprang across the bridge, caroming between consoles and bulkheads and spraying blood in a fountain. The officer of the day jumped up, screaming in horror at the sight.

This time Dan's bullets stitched him across the chest.

Somebody fired a pistol from the far wing of the bridge. The bullet was a solid which ricocheted off the armored roof, as dangerous to surviving Angels as it was to the attacking force.

"Get the hatch control!" Johnnie shouted to his uncle as he charged the gunman.

The muzzle of the pistol poked cautiously up from behind a console. Johnnie jumped to the top of the unit, surrounded by a flare of holographic movement triggered by his boot soles.

A pair of Angel technicians huddled on the other side. One had his hands folded over his head and his face against the decking; the other held his pistol as though it were a crucifix and Johnnie was Satan himself.

Not Satan but Death. The explosive bullets splashed bits of the man's terrified face in a three-foot circle.

"Get up!" Johnnie shouted to the remaining technician, the only survivor of the bridge watch.

The man moaned. Johnnie jumped down and kicked the fellow. "Get up!" he repeated. He continued prodding the prisoner with his boot until the man obeyed, still hiding his face with his hands.

The air-conditioning made Johnnie shiver. His pack was suddenly an unbearable weight. He'd meant to take it off just before the attack, but there hadn't been time. . . .

He shrugged off the load of equipment and ammunition— a dead man's load replacing the one he'd lost in the jungle—and let it thump to the bloody deck. He turned.

Uncle Dan was bent over an undamaged console. He snapped switches with his hands while he spoke through the intra-ship transmitter flexed to his helmet. Muted queries rasped through the *Holy Trinity*'s own intercom.

The bridge hatch hadn't closed completely because of the corpse slumped in it, but it had only cycled a body's width open by the time Johnnie looked around. Sergeant Britten rushed through with his rifle poised—locked onto the two figures standing at the far wing of the bridge—

"Don't!" Johnnie screamed as he flattened.

Britten's rifle slammed the prisoner into the armored bulkhead and held him there in an explosive dazzle until the magazine was empty. When the Angel technician finally fell, there was almost nothing left of his body from beltline to collar.

"Don't shoot!" Johnnie called. He lifted the butt of his sub-machine gun a hand's breadth above the console. *"Don't shoot!"*

"Omigodsir!"

Johnnie raised his head. Sergeant Britten had frozen with the empty rifle still at his shoulder. Now he flung it down as though it had bitten him. Its barrel glowed white from the long burst. The rest of the assault team had stopped behind the sergeant.

"Omigodsir!"

"Fayette," ordered Uncle Dan without looking up from what he was doing. "Take over here while I try to raise Team Two. Benns and Forrest, reinforce Team Three. They've captured the engine room, but they're a couple men short because of things breaking early."

Nobody moved.

Uncle Dan raised his head. "For God's sake!" he shouted. "Did you think this was going to be a picnic? Get *moving,* you men!"

The Blackhorse raiders shuddered back into action. Two men disappeared back down the ladderway to replace casualties from the attack on the engine room. A tech slid into the seat the commander vacated to finish locking a selection of the dreadnought's watertight doors. The console's holographic display showed that the crucial hatches, to the battle center and to the crew's quarters forward, were already sealed beyond the capacity of those within to countermand.

A pair of men, unordered, began shifting the corpses of

the bridge watch to a corner where they would be out of the way and not particularly visible.

Uncle Dan looked around somberly. "Believe me," he said, "you're going to see worse before this is over."

20.

"Good speed!" cried the watch, as the gate bolts undrew;
"Speed!" echoed the wall to us galloping through. . . .

—Robert Browning

JOHNNIE TOOK A deep breath. He was one of several members of the raiding party who were gawking like spectators, and there wasn't time for that now.

"U—ah, sir?" he said. "I'll bring up the weapon systems. I can do that."

Dan gestured brusquely toward a console. He touched the mute on the helmet through which he'd been talking to the survivor of Team Two. That sailor was now waiting to blow the cable of the bow anchor. "Get to it, then, Gordon," he said.

He looked up almost at once. "Ignore the eighteens—and whatever you do, don't switch the railguns live until you're ordered to. The overload will shut down the power boards and then we're screwed for good 'n' all."

Having delivered the necessary information with the same crisp skill he would have spent on a computer keypad, Uncle Dan went back to his business.

Johnnie lowered himself halfway into the seat, then grimaced and shifted to the console next to that one. There was a pool of congealing blood and brains on the first.

The layout of the *Holy Trinity*'s bridge consoles differed from those in the training program Johnnie had used—but as a practical matter, every ship differed from the next, even those laid down as sisters in the same stocks. Bridge consoles did the same job, and an ensign who couldn't figure out the idiosyncrasies of a new layout had no business in the Blackhorse.

The system was already live. An Angel tech had spent the last moments of his life checking the vessel's fresh-water supply. Johnnie switched screens blindly twice, then got hold of himself and found a menu. He cut quickly to the armament-status panel.

"Engine room secured," said a voice over the *Holy Trinity*'s own communications system. "We've unlocked all the boards." The man speaking wasn't Freisner, the warrant officer who'd led Team Three before the shooting started.

"Acknowledged," Dan responded as his fingers whisked across the control panel. "Send two men forward and check the status of the battle center, will you? I want to make sure that they stay sealed up until all this is over."

"Ah, Force Prime . . . ," said the man in the engine room.

"Team Three?" Dan said sharply. "Are you too short-handed? Shall I—"

"Negative, negative. We'll take care of it, you just get us the hell outa here."

Johnnie began opening circuits to the *Holy Trinity*'s profusion of weapon systems. Uncle Dan lit the three engines, cold while the dreadnought was at anchor, and brought up the fourth to full drive capacity. Fayette closed watertight doors, both as protection against Angels who might be loose in the ship and because the *Holy Trinity* was likely to need all the buoyancy she could get. Another technician busied himself with the cameras of the ship's damage assessment/internal security system.

There was a distant ringing sound from forward as the crewmen sealed into their sleeping quarters hammered on bulkheads. The internal divisions of the ship weren't comparable to the thirty-two-inch main belt—but even so, the two-inch bulkheads would hold despite anything unarmed personnel could bring against them in the next century.

The huge vessel sighed as she came to life. Multiple levels of vibration quivered through her fabric; but the change, so evident to those aboard her, was lost in the sounds of human pleasure and the jungle, so far as the residents of Paradise Base were concerned.

The top overlay on the armament board was the 18-inch turrets, but Johnnie knew to ignore them even if Uncle Dan hadn't made that a direct order. The minuscule Blackhorse crew was barely enough to operate one of the big turrets, quite apart from the more important tasks involved in getting the *Holy Trinity* out of Paradise Base. He touched a key and shifted to the secondary turrets.

There were manual interlocks on the 5.25-inch guns, but the legend for Turrets II and IV—those nearest the bow on the starboard side—said READY on Johnnie's display. Those were the guns which had been firing in support of the base perimeter. Though they should have been locked down again when firing was complete, nobody had bothered to do so.

Johnnie powered up the turrets one by one, so as not to overload the boards with a surge before the main drives were operating at full capacity. That was a once-in-a-million event to occur from just the power requirements of the secondary batteries—but it only had to happen once to scuttle the mission.

As the 5.25s came up in sequence, Johnnie checked the railguns. The four domed batteries, one on each corner of the superstructure, were on yellow, STANDBY, status. That meant that although they were shut down, the permanent self-testing procedure indicated that they would operate normally as soon as the correct switches were thrown.

with a group of other men; what must it be like to crouch on the stern of a hostile warship, unsure whether the next sound would be an order from your distant leader—or the challenge of a party of heavily-armed Angels?

"Full starboard rudder, sir," said Fayette before he was asked.

"All right, gentlemen," Dan said. "Then let's do it." He slid a control forward. "Teams Two and Four, fire your charges."

Johnnie looked forward, out the unshuttered viewslit. There was a bright white flash as the ribbon charge which was coiled around the anchor cable went off. The noise was sharp but, for the men on the bridge, almost hidden by vibration from the drive shafts Dan had just engaged.

The *Holy Trinity* gave a double lurch as both the bow and stern lines parted.

The raiders could have hoisted the anchors easily, but that process was both time-consuming and extremely noisy. The quick and dirty method was the only way this operation was going to work.

Johnnie thought of the Angels' bridge watch, bit his tongue; and thought about the crisp holographic display in front of him instead.

"Base to *Holy Trinity,*" said the ship-to-shore link in a voice which combined boredom and petulance. "Report your status. Did you have an explosion aboard? Over."

"*Holy Trinity* to Base," Dan answered calmly. "Everything here is nominal. Over."

Lights on the shore were moving noticeably through the viewslit. The two engaged drive shafts were turning at only a handful of rpm, but the torque of the huge screws was enough to swing the dreadnought even at that slow speed.

"Base to *Holy Trinity,*" the voice said, no longer quite so bored. "Are you drifting? Over."

"Negative, Paradise Base," Dan said in a voice too

sullenly emotionless to trip any warning bells in a listener's mind. "Our position hasn't changed in a month and a half. Suggest you check your database. Over."

Not only did the dreadnought move in relation to the fixed lights of the land, the bow was curving closer to the harbor's southern shore. On the holographic plot, the stern of the docked *St. Michael* stuck out dangerously far. Johnnie remembered the helmsman's doubts about whether they would be able to clear the shore installations.

"*Holy Trinity,*" ordered the duty officer on shore, no longer in the least bored, "put the officer of the day on at once. At once!"

"Base," said Dan, "the Oh-Oh-Dee's in the head and—"

A raucous klaxon sounded from the center of Paradise Base. Jungle beasts echoed what they took for a challenge.

"Fuck your mother with a spade," said Dan very distinctly.

Johnnie clicked his light-pen, waiting all this time.

"Starboard screws astern," said Fayette. "She wallows like a pig! *Astern starboard!*"

Uncle Dan slammed back one of the slide switches he'd configured as a throttle. Johnnie moved his pen, poised, and clicked it again. The *Holy Trinity* exploded in glare, smoke, and racket as all her automatic weapons fired at once.

Johnnie didn't bother to aim individual tubs; that wasn't the point. He was just trying to create confusion with guns that were too small to do serious damage.

And at the moment, confusion was the most serious damage the Blackhorse raiders *could* do.

Some of the bullets arched into the wilderness, shredding foliage in a minor sideshow to the destruction the jungle regularly wreaked upon itself. A few rounds hit the other dreadnoughts anchored in mid-harbor, scarring paint or even starting minor fires.

A plurality of the streaming tracers, randomly aimed but

as heavy as the first rush of a rainstorm, raked the Angel shore installations. Lamp standards went down, windows blew out; concrete walls cracked and cratered under the wild shooting.

Smoke from the multiple machine guns wreathed the *Holy Trinity,* fogging the muzzle blasts and turning the tracers into fingers of lightning which reached from a stormcloud. Minutes of constant operation caused one weapon after another to jam and drop out of the fusillade. The barrels of those still firing glowed an orange which verged on yellow.

Johnnie looked from the forward viewslit, toward the plot in front of the helmsman; then back again. The reality of the great drydock growing before their bow was more vivid than the hologram, but they both indicated the same thing: *Holy Trinity* would collide with a mass of concrete and steel through which not even her own size and power could carry her.

There was a long, shuddering tremor as the outer starboard propeller began to bite the water in reverse while the port screws continued to drive forward. The bow swung sideways, like the head of a horse fighting a hand jerking its reins.

They were clear.

There was a puff of powdered concrete as the dreadnought's swelling port side ticked the end of the drydock— tens of thousands of tons slipping past one another on either side, touching in a lovetap that could be repaired with a bucket of paint, if anybody cared.

The *Holy Trinity* headed for the harbor mouth, answering to her rudder alone. Uncle Dan shifted all four drive-shaft controls into their full-forward position, but it would be many minutes before the inertia of the huge screws and the mass of water they churned permitted a response.

Most of the automatic weapons were silent, choked by

feeding jams or chambers so hot that rounds had exploded within before the breeches were closed. Johnnie shut down the few remaining guns. A pall of powder smoke drifted like an amoeba above the harbor.

Audible across the bridge in the relative silence, Dan spoke into a handset coupled to the dreadnought's radio, "Six, this is Three. The situation is Able, I say again, Able."

Sergeant Britten hovered behind the commander. He winced as he heard the words and warned, "Sir, sir—we don't have compatible code sets aboard this bitch. You're broadcasting in clear."

Beyond the *Holy Trinity*'s cutwater, the running lights of the *Dragger*, guarding the harbor mouth, spread from a single blob to individual points. There was a series of red flashes from the tender's deck, then a stream of machine-gun tracers. If the bullets struck the dreadnought at all, their impacts were indistinguishable in the noise of the ship working.

"Six," Dan continued, "we will rendezvous at Reference Point K, I say—"

"*Sir!*" Sergeant Britten blurted.

"—again, Reference Point K. Three out."

He laid down the handset and met Britten's eyes.

The sergeant was wringing his hand. "Sir," he mumbled, "oh, sir, we're screwed. Two years ago we were operating with the Warcocks and they *know* Reference Point K is the Kanjar Straits. They'll cut us off to the west, and Flotilla Blanche'll come tearing through to block the Straits for our main fleet."

The *Holy Trinity*'s vibration lessened somewhat. The starboard screws had slowly accelerated, so that Fayette was able to lessen the amount of rudder needed to keep the vessel on a straight course.

"They'll try, at least," Uncle Dan said calmly.

A bullet from the *Dragger* struck the viewslit and blotched the armor glass with gray metal.

"Sir, they'll *do* it!" Britten cried. "Even if our ships're already in the Straits—"

"They're not in the Straits," Dan interrupted crisply. He swept his cold eyes around the faces of the other men on the bridge, all of them staring at him. "There's just a submarine surfaced fifty miles back in the ocean, broadcasting as if it was Blackhorse Command."

He took a deep breath. "That'll work until morning, when they can get up a full complement of gliders on the thermals. The real fleet has entered Ishtar Basin from the southeast, in the direction the Warcocks are going to force us to turn. And then—"

The *Holy Trinity* staggered as she cut the heavy cable supporting the inner net across Paradise Harbor. The guardship vanished beneath the dreadnought's bow. Moments later there was a barely perceptible crunch. The white froth of the bow wave was speckled with debris, fragments of the *Dragger* and her crew as they slid back inexorably toward the churning propellers.

"—we'll have another surprise for them," Dan continued.

For a moment, his mask of calm slipped into something equally quiet but much more bleak. "Assuming that the Angels don't take care of us themselves before then," he said.

The *Holy Trinity,* accelerating with the ponderous grace of an elephant, crashed through the outer cable as well. There was a metallic scream astern as something—net, cable, or a portion of the shattered guardship—fouled one of the dreadnought's screws.

But they were out of the harbor—and out of the series of events they could control. Whatever happened next was a matter for others—and for God.

21.

An' now the hugly bullets come peckin' through the dust,
An' no one wants to face 'em, but every beggar must. . . .

—Rudyard Kipling

THE PORT OUTER drive shaft was shut down. The length of cable, caught in the free-spinning screw and streaming back in the wake, still twisted the *Holy Trinity* with a rhythmic vibration.

An hour and a half of the jolting, with no real work to take Johnnie's mind off it, was putting him to sleep.

His head jerked up an instant before it touched the console. His skin was flushed and his head buzzed. He looked around quickly to see who might have noticed his lapse, but all the faces he saw were drawn and focused on their own internal fears.

Even Uncle Dan.

". . . glider activity," one of the technicians was reporting earnestly to the commander, "and the masts of destroyers are already on the horizon."

"The battleships must be under way by now," Fayette chipped in gloomily. "I can't get this pig above twenty-three knots with a fouled screw. No way. Sir."

"We're here to draw them, aren't we?" Dan said. The words were nonchalant, but there was nothing light in either his tone or his expression. "We're just doing a better job than we'd counted on."

"We ain't going to run as far southeast as planned, neither," somebody muttered.

Dan had connected the main radio to the ship's internal communications system, so that the scattered Blackhorse parties would know as much about the situation as he did himself. As a result, the message from Blackhorse Command, broken oddly by static because of the nature of frequency-hopping transmission, came through the public-address speaker in the center of the bridge.

"Three," said the emotionless voice, "this is Six. There is heavy enemy activity to your north and west. The plan is inoperative. I say again, the plan is inoperative. Six over."

Everyone looked at Dan. He licked his lips and said, "Six, this is Three. What are your orders? Three over."

During the perceptible pause before the response came, Sergeant Britten removed the magazine from his rifle, checked it, and reloaded his weapon. There were beads of sweat on his face.

"Three, this is Six," said the distant voice. "Use your own initiative. I have no orders for you. Six out."

"Six, what do you *mean*?" Uncle Dan shouted into the pick-up wand. "We don't have any initiative! One of the props is fouled. Six, what are your orders? Three over!"

"Three, this is Six," Headquarters repeated. "I say again, we have no orders for you. Save what you can. Six *out*."

Dan put down the wand. "Fayette," he said calmly, "bring us onto a course of one-twenty-three degrees. Flank speed."

He grinned. His face looked like a skull stained dark by oxides. "Or as close as we can get to flank speed, with three screws and a sea anchor," he added.

The helmsman made a series of quick control changes. The *Holy Trinity* was too big to react suddenly to anything, but Johnnie felt the ship slowly heel as she started to come around in the severe course change.

"Hey, cheer up, guys," Dan said brightly. "That was all an act for the other side. *You* know that."

Johnnie tried to smile. He *did* know that the exchange of messages had been scripted.

The words still felt real when he heard them delivered; and for that matter, the *Holy Trinity*'s situation was just as bad as if the whole thing were exactly as their allied enemies were intended to think.

"The destroyer bearing three-four-zero degrees absolute," said a worried technician, "is pinging us with his laser rangefinder."

"John, that was good work," Uncle Dan said. "With the machine guns."

"Thank you, sir."

"Not a cloud in the sky," Fayette muttered as he stared at the unsympathetic prop-revolution read-outs. "We need a bloody storm, and we get the best weather I've seen in seven years on the surface."

Dan touched a control on his console. "I'll take over gunnery now, Gordon," he said as his display duplicated the holograms before Johnnie.

The commander's finger tapped a key in a short, repetitive motion. At each downstroke, the *Holy Trinity* staggered as her generators accepted the demands of the railguns' warming coils. READY/READY/READY/READY replaced the STANDBY legends on Johnnie's display.

Johnnie was redundant now.

"The destroyers aren't closing, but they're moving up on either quarter," said the tech who was running the surveillance boards. "I think they're trying to get us in a scissors for a torpedo attack."

"Right," said Uncle Dan, throwing another switch. "Britten, take Lajoie from the bow and man the forward starboard five-two-five turret. If there's a jam—"

"I'll go with him," Johnnie interrupted. "Sir."

Dan looked at his nephew. There was nothing in his eyes but calculation. "Right," he said again. "If you can't clear a problem fast, just shift back to the next turret."

"Yessir!" Sergeant Britten said, starting for the hatch before the commander finished speaking.

Johnnie was only a step behind him.

"Good luck!" Uncle Dan called to their backs; and he certainly meant the words, but Johnnie knew the wish wasn't the most important thing on Commander Cooke's mind just now.

The ladderway amplified vibration from the fouled drive shaft into a high-frequency buzz. Sergeant Britten had both hands free. He hopped three steps at a time, guiding himself by the handrail. Johnnie's sub-machine gun was slung over his right shoulder, where it clanged against the curving bulkhead as he followed.

If they ran into Angel crewmen still loose, Britten might regret abandoning his rifle on the bridge . . . but that was probably the wrong thing to worry about.

The hatch from the ladderway out onto the shelter deck was open. Reiss and Mertoh must have left it that way when they passed through on their way to unlock the port 5.25-inch turrets. Johnnie wasn't sure that was a good idea with the ship going into action—but it speeded him and Britten now, and he didn't take the time to close it himself.

There was a lengthy whine and a series of clanks from above them. Johnnie skidded, unslinging his sub-machine gun as he looked upward to find the cause. There was nothing to see on the superstructure looming against the gray sky.

"Forget it, kid!" Sergeant Britten shouted as he disappeared into Turret II. Interior lights went on, turning the hatchway into a rectangle with rounded corners. The sergeant's voice resumed, blurry and dull with echoes, "They're just shuttering the bridge viewslits."

Johnnie took a final look at the horizon astern. He could see nothing, but he had no doubt that destroyers maneuvered there like hunting dogs preparing to cut out a wildebeest.

Turret II made a keening noise as its magnetic gimbals raised it from the barbette. Johnnie jumped through the hatch just as the turret began to rotate its guns sternward.

The turret was being operated from the bridge. Sergeant Britten bent over a control panel, but that was to set the holographic remotes from the magazine and lift tube.

The personnel hatch in the turret floor was closed and dogged. Johnnie doubted that it would be worthwhile trying to clear a malfunction below, but standard operating procedure required that the turret crews keep in touch with all portions of the operation.

There wasn't much standard about this operation.

"Secondaries report," ordered a crackly voice from the speaker in the roof.

The breeches rotated an eighth of a turn to unlock the interrupted-screw locking mechanism, then drew back. The 5.25-inch bores looked incredibly small against the thick tubes of metal encircling them.

"Forward port ready," said Reiss' voice from the speaker.

Cased rounds—not separate shells and powder charges as with the 18-inch main guns—moved up the lift tube and into the paired loading cages. The cages paused for a moment, then ratcheted forward to ram the shells home ahead of the closing breeches.

Britten threw a switch. A panoramic display quivered to life on the turret face above the guns. It showed the horizon with a speck that swelled into the blurred image of a warship's superstructure as the sergeant turned a control.

"Turret Eye-Eye ready," he reported with satisfaction.

"Stand by," warned the bridge.

"For swattin' destroyers," Britten said to Johnnie, "these—"

He pointed to the 5.25s just as the breeches lowered to elevate the muzzles from their rest position. The guns were poised like hounds, waiting for the gunnery controller to slip their electronic leashes. "These're better'n the big mothers, the eighteens. Now, with only two turrets live, we might have a problem if the Angels had a decent destroyer force, which they—"

The guns slammed, one and the other. The breeches spewed out the empty cases as the rammers fed fresh rounds into the smoking bores and the lift tube raised the next sequence for the loading cages to grip. Ten seconds after the first shots, the next salvo was on the way and the third was loading.

Johnnie's helmet protected his ears, but the floor jumped and the blasts echoing through the open hatch behind them were punishing blows. The air was a hazy gray from smoke. When his nose filters clamped down, Johnnie opened his mouth. Though he only breathed through his nostrils, caustic gases seared the membranes at the back of his throat.

Hammers struck the *Holy Trinity*, in time with the recoiling guns of Turret II but syncopating them. Turret I on the other side of the superstructure was firing at another of the shadowing destroyers.

There were rhythmic red flashes from the ship on the display. For a moment Johnnie thought he was watching their own shells hit, but it was too soon for impacts on a distant target.

The flashes came in threes—bow, bow, and stern—while Turret II salvoed shells in pairs. He was watching the muzzle flashes of the destroyer's own guns.

Aimed at him.

Sergeant Britten pointed and grinned. "Don't sweat that,

kid," he shouted over the deafening pulse of the 5.25s. "Torpedoes can hurt us, but—"

The center of the destroyer's image disappeared behind a waterspout—a near miss, short. By the dreadnought's standards, the 5.25s were small guns, but the explosion of one of their shells lifted *tons* of water.

There was another spout on the far side of the target. The fire director had straddled the destroyer with the first salvo.

The second, third, and fourth pairs of shells landed before the destroyer's captain could even start to maneuver out of the killing zone. The bursting charges were a deeper red than the muzzle flashes with which they mingled, and their sullen light was dirtied further by tendrils of the black smoke from which they erupted.

A shell casing stuck in the breech of the left-hand gun, just as the deck rippled with a *clang!* that knocked Johnnie off balance. He grabbed a stanchion while two more Angel shells rang against the dreadnought's hull.

"Come on, kid!" Sergeant Britten shouted. There was a toolrack welded to the side of the turret. Britten snatched a pry-bar from it and leaped to the jammed gun.

The right-hand tube continued to cycle at ten-second intervals, but the left was frozen in the full-recoil position. The breech stood open, but the empty case was jammed into the threads deep in the cavity.

Johnnie reached for another pry-bar but seized a maul instead when the ship quivered to another shock. He didn't know what he was supposed to do anyway, so one tool was as good as another.

He staggered across to join the sergeant. He was suddenly terrified that he'd stumble into the path of the recoiling gun and be crushed like a bug on a windshield.

The destroyer they had been engaging sheered away. Her superstructure glowed orange, and flames licked above her

mast peaks. Pairs of shells still in the lethal circuit continued to strike and smash, fanning the blaze.

Turret I had ceased firing, but the *clang!* of a hostile shell
hitting astern echoed through the *Holy Trinity*.

The sergeant thrust the point of his bar into the breech
opening and levered fiercely to free the stuck case. His bare
arms were black with powder fouling except where drops of
sweat jewelled the skin.

The image of the burning destroyer dropped over the
horizon. A pillar of spark-shot smoke trailed back along the
crippled vessel's course.

A huge orange bubble swelled into the display, then
shrank back. The destroyer's bow and stern lifted momentarily as if they were vertical brackets enclosing the space of
the explosion.

The right-hand gun ceased firing, though shells already
on the way continued to lift columns of spray and debris on
the far horizon.

In the silence of the gun turret, Johnnie thought he heard
the screams of men burning, men cartwheeling toward the
jaws rising from the waves to meet them. But the cries were
only in his mind.

22.

When he turn'd at bay in the leafy gloom,
In the emerald gloom where the brook ran deep
He heard in the distance the rollers boom,
And he saw in a vision of peaceful sleep,
*   In a wonderful vision of sleep. . . .*

—John Davidson

"KID!" BRITTEN SHOUTED as he turned his head. When the sergeant saw that Johnnie was already at his shoulder, holding a maul, anger cleared from his expression.

"Right!" he said. "Hit it! Right here!"

Britten tapped a thick finger on the curved hook of his pry-bar. The point was deep in one of the eight slots across the breech threads, but the strength of the sergeant's arm alone was not enough to break the deformed casing free and extract it.

Johnnie hammered the end of the bar.

"Harder!" the sergeant shouted. "Put 'cher back—"

Johnnie slammed his maul into the bar, making the shaft spring back with a belling sound. The tool vibrated out of Britten's grasp, but the shell case slid loose also and rattled onto the turret floor. Foul gases curled from the case mouth. They smeared like grease when they touched solid objects.

"Bloody hell!" the sergeant muttered as he stepped backward and flopped into a pull-down seat beside the hatch. "Bloody hell."

They could feel the gear-driven vibration of one or more of the port 5.25-inch turrets rotating, but all the *Holy Trinity*'s guns were silent. No hostile shells were falling aboard the dreadnought, either, though by this time the remaining Angel battleships should have had time to catch up with their fleeing consort.

"Now our course is right across the Ishtar Basin," the sergeant said as if idly. "That's deep water, twenty thousand feet some of it."

He glanced sidelong at Johnnie, then looked away quickly when he realized the young officer was watching him.

"You can drown in two inches," Johnnie said, answering what he thought was his companion's concern. *Or be eaten by what lives in the wrong two inches.*

"Naw, not that," Britten said scornfully. "I mean it's deep enough water t' hide our subs. They could come up to combat depth when the Angel screen was past and give the dreadnoughts something to think about besides us."

He looked at Johnnie. "If they was there?" he prodded.

"Sergeant . . . ," Johnnie said, trying to match the two images of the man beside him: the burly, competent veteran; and the enlisted man of moderate intelligence, who had to trust his officer superiors to balance risks that *he* wouldn't understand even if they were laid out before him in meticulous detail.

"Sergeant," Johnnie continued, "we need to draw them on. Not just the Angels. The Warcocks and Flotilla Blanche besides, because if just *those* two have time to choose where and how they'll fight us, we lose. The Blackhorse loses. Ambushing the Angels wouldn't help."

"Except," said Britten, "it'd save *our* butts." The expression on the sergeant's scarred, blackened face did not appear to be anger, but neither had it any sign of compromise offered to superior rank.

"I don't think that's at the top of anybody's priority list, Sergeant," Johnnie said as coolly as he could manage.

Britten shrugged and looked at the open breeches, almost clear of smoke by now. "Naw," he said, "I don't guess it oughta be, even. But it gripes my soul to think how Cap'n Haynes'll laugh if Cookie bites the big one on this."

The squawk box in the turret roof suddenly cleared its electronic throat, then piped in an unfamiliar voice saying, "*Holy Trinity,* this is Angel Command. Come in, *Holy Trinity,* over."

"Why are *they* calling us?" Johnnie muttered.

He didn't realize he'd spoken aloud until he glanced to his side. Sergeant Britten's eyes had widened at proof that the officers didn't know what was going on, either.

"Blackhorse Dreadnought *Holy Trinity* to Angel Command," rasped Uncle Dan's reply. "I hope you're calling to offer your surrender, Admiral Braun, because we don't have anything else to discuss. Over."

"Hoo, Cookie's in great form t'night!" Britten crowed. He sounded as though he had forgotten that 'Cookie's' nephew sat beside him, and that the most likely result of Commander Cooke's baiting would be a sheaf of large-caliber shells.

Of course, the shells would come soon enough anyway.

"*Holy Trinity,*" said Admiral Braun. The words were slurred as if Braun had a speech impediment, but that might be because the Angel leader was choking with anger. "You've made your point. Now it's time to talk. You're cut off from, from your own fleet by overwhelming forces. We know they've abandoned you—"

"We haven't been abandoned, Braun!" Dan said, ignoring transmission lag in the knowledge that his words would step on those of the enemy commander.

"Listen to me!" Admiral Braun snarled. "The Blackhorse fleet is blocked at the Kanjar Straits! They've *told* you you're on your own, you fool! The only thing you can do now is die in vain if you refuse to listen to reason."

Braun didn't sign a transmission break, but he paused as if to give his opponent a chance to respond.

"S' long as they talk," murmured Sergeant Britten, "they're not shootin' our asses off. Which suits me."

He frowned. "Course," he added, "they maybe ain't in range yet. Quite."

"*Holy Trinity*," the Angel admiral resumed in attempted calm, "come about now. We'll take your vessel out of service for the duration of the war. All—"

"Bingo," said Johnnie. "They're talking because they don't want to—"

"—of your party will be returned to Blackhorse—"

"—lose the *Holy Trinity*. They're willing to do just about—" said Johnnie.

"—Base immediately, free to fight. We're not—"

"—anything to keep from pulling the plug—" said Johnnie.

"—asking for your paroles. And you—"

"—on their own best ship!" said Johnnie.

"—must have injured personnel. We'll provide full medical treatment for them. Angel Command over."

Silence from Uncle Dan.

"This is better than a fair offer, Blackhorse," Admiral Braun concluded in desperation. "This is a complete victory for your party! Over."

"Gun crews," muttered a different voice, one of the technicians on the dreadnought's bridge. "Stand by."

"No rest for the wicked," Britten grumbled, but there was a cruel smile on his face as he stood. He was holding the pry-bar. Johnnie noticed with surprise that his own hands still gripped the hammer.

"Braun," said Dan with the harsh anger Johnnie had heard his uncle use on Senator Gordon, "this is Commander Dan Cooke. This is my offer. You surrender all your forces immediately. That means when the war is over, you'll get them back as is, including the *Holy Trinity*. You'll still be in business . . . which you won't, if you push things to conclusions. What d'ye say, Braun? Blackhorse Three over."

The turret's panoramic display showed the masts of a ship on the horizon again. Hydraulic rammers whined, sliding the waiting 5.25-inch rounds into the tubes and withdrawing as the breeches screwed closed. The sudden activity made both men jump, but the guns did not yet fire.

"Commander Cooke," Braun said in a voice that stuck to his throat. "Dan. Dan, you know we can't do that. We've got a contract with Heidigger Dome that—"

"Listen to *me*, Braun," Dan broke in. His words buzzed like a rattlesnake's tail. "It isn't some sucker like Haynes you're dealing with this time. You know me, and you know I'll do what I say. You can take my offer, or you can rest assured I'll ram it up your ass. *Capisce?* Blackhorse Three over."

Turret II turned slightly. The motion was barely noticeable against the thumping background of the dreadnought's fouled drive. The guns elevated a few degrees, then stabilized.

"Have it your way, you bastard!" snarled Admiral Braun.

The interior of the turret brightened, lighted by the panoramic display. The image of the horizon had gone orange-red with the muzzle flashes of the three pursuing dreadnoughts.

"For what we are about to receive," Sergeant Britten murmured blasphemously, "the Lord—"

The paired 5.25s fired in close sequence, aiming not at the invisible battleships but at one of the destroyers which plotted the fall of the battleships' heavy shells. Johnnie flinched instinctively, but the concussion of the secondary armament was almost lost in the hideous sound of the railguns, firing to raise a defensive envelope above the *Holy Trinity*.

As the big shells lifted toward their target, the four domed railgun batteries sought them with bursts of hypervelocity slugs which turned metal gaseous on impact. Not even the armor-piercing noses of rounds from a dreadnought's main guns were proof against hosing streams of projectiles which had been accelerated to astronomical velocities.

Shells with bursting charges detonated, blowing themselves apart harmlessly. One of the pursuing battleships was firing solid 16-inch shot. Even those dense projectiles melted under the impacts. They tumbled off trajectory, streaming glowing clouds behind them.

The buzz of the railguns' coils energizing was marrow deep, more penetrating than a mere noise could ever be. When the guns discharged in rapid succession, the ballistic crack of a slug accelerated to thirty thousand feet per second in a few yards shattered the air like nearby lightning.

The *Holy Trinity* mounted four railgun installations. The pursuing dreadnoughts carried a total of thirty-three 16-inch guns, each of which was capable of a higher rate of fire than the *Holy Trinity*'s big 18-inch tubes. The mathematics were as simple and inexorable as statistics on aging and death.

Johnnie could *see* shells approaching in the panoramic display: three smears of red, glowing from their passage through the air. They hung almost motionless, swelling, because they were dropping directly toward the pick-up feeding the display.

"—make us thankful," Sergeant Britten concluded as the shrieking railguns detonated one of the shells so close that the flash reflected through the hatch of Turret II.

A waterspout, colored fluorescent yellow by marker dye, rose over the *Holy Trinity* and sucked the huge dreadnought sideways. The other shell hit with a rending crash. The sound went on and on while Johnnie screamed.

The turret lights dimmed, and for a terrifying instant the railguns stopped firing. In the relative silence between shots from the 5.25s, Johnnie heard a distant, overwhelming rumble. It was not thunder, any more than the red glow on the horizon was lightning. He was hearing the sound of guns which reached for his life from twenty miles away.

The railguns took up their defensive snarl again, but the timbre had changed. The port-side stern installation, Gamma Battery, was no longer part of the mix of ravening noise.

"Watch it!" Britten mouthed as he leaped for the lift tube. The round that had just presented itself to a loading cage was skewed in its cradle. The *Holy Trinity* had flexed when the big shell hit, and the motion had jounced the rounds in the loading sequence.

Britten tried to force down the nose of the shell. The left tube's loading cage pivoted and grabbed the round, still at an angle; the sergeant jerked his hands away just in time to save them.

Johnnie ducked under the swing of the right loading cage, reaching for its next shell, and seized the rim of the skewed round's casing. He lifted desperately.

The shell dropped into alignment just as the rammer shoved it into the 5.25's breech.

Three 16-inch shells hit the *Holy Trinity,* two and then one. The turret floor bucked and threw Johnnie into a backward somersault. His head rang on steel. The shock dazed him despite his helmet.

The left-hand loading cage offered itself empty to the gun tube. The rammer and breech mechanism cycled as though the intended load hadn't been thrown out of the cage by the dreadnought's pitching. A fully-loaded 5.25-inch round was bouncing around the turret with Johnnie, the sergeant, and all the tools thrown from the rack.

The shell wasn't likely to explode. The primer was electrical, not impact, and the shell's own base fuze was activated by the violent spin it got in the rifling of the gun barrel.

But it weighed almost a hundred pounds. When it caromed into Johnnie's hips as he started to rise, it knocked him back down with a sharp pain he prayed didn't mean a broken pelvis.

Only one railgun installation was firing. The high-voltage, high-frequency pulses turned the driving cones of its slugs into glowing plasma that hung along the *Holy Trinity*'s course like the track of a snail. The sea beneath boiled with the dreadnought's wake and gurgling, fluorescent calderas blown by shells the railguns had not stopped.

Shells roared overhead, deafening even compared with everything else going on. Fayette had made a minuscule adjustment to the *Holy Trinity*'s course, and the three-ship salvo missed—short and over, ahead and astern.

Waterspouts drenched the *Holy Trinity*, sloshing Johnnie through the turret hatch. Only the yellow emergency lighting was on. No railguns were firing.

The right-hand loading cage picked up the next round. It was aligned correctly, but the tortured lift tube had presented it back to front.

Johnnie lurched to his feet. His hip supported him.

"*Run!*" Sergeant Britten screamed, pushing the younger man aside.

Three shells hit the *Holy Trinity* simultaneously. The ship writhed, throwing Britten into the empty toolrack and tumbling Johnnie out the open hatch.

Johnnie braced himself against an exterior bulkhead. Small fish, flung onto the deck by near misses, snapped and writhed beside him in the algal slime.

The sky above was a map of Hell.

For an instant, Sergeant Britten was silhouetted against the turret lighting. He groped for the hatch opening. He'd lost his helmet, and his face was a mask of blood from a cut scalp.

Johnnie started to rise to help him just as the rammer thrust a 5.25-inch round backward into the breech. The casing crumpled, heating and compressing the powder charge. It ignited in something between a fire and an explosion while the breech mechanism was still open.

The first blast set off the remaining rounds in the loading sequence. Orange flame enveloped Sergeant Britten, incinerating the back half of his powerful body and driving the remainder against Johnnie as a mist of blood and tissue.

Johnnie lay against the bulkhead. His eyes were open. He was, so far as he could tell, unharmed.

Above him, the sky roared and blazed. The fish on deck were making furious efforts to swallow one another down, even as air dried their gills and inexorably slew them all.

After an uncertain length of time, Johnnie got up and headed for the ladderway to the bridge.

23.

The pirate Genoese
Hell-raked them till they rolled
Blood, water, fruit, and corpses up the hold.

—James Elroy Flecker

NONE OF THE *Holy Trinity*'s guns were firing. B Turret had taken a direct hit which wrecked the roof-mounted fire director and must have penetrated the gun house, because one of the 18-inch tubes pointed skyward at a crazy angle.

Because the guns were not being worked, the turret and barbette were nothing but armored boxes, as safe a target for incoming shells as any on the dreadnought. If the turret *had* been in operation, one or more of the twelve-hundredweight powder charges in the loading cycle would have burned, sending flames a thousand feet high through the punctured roof.

If the charges had flashed back into the magazine through the loading tube, the whole forward portion of the *Holy Trinity* would have vanished in a cataclysmic explosion.

Johnnie wondered what it felt like to be dead. Did Sergeant Britten care?

He tried to wipe his face, but his hands weren't clean, either.

There was a fire on the shelter deck, just aft of the second funnel. Sparks rose in swirling clouds, sometimes lifting sections of lifeboats and wardroom furnishings with them.

There must have been explosions among the flames, but their sound was lost in the greater chaos around them.

Johnnie reached the ladderway to the bridge. The hatch was missing. While it stood open, the shock of an explosion had caught it and wrenched it from its hinges.

Three shells hit the *Holy Trinity,* throwing Johnnie to the deck again. One landed among the flames amidships. A huge fireball lifted into the air, separating from the ship to hang above them like the sun on the day of judgment.

As suddenly as it had formed, the globe of fire sucked inward and vanished. The *Holy Trinity* was alone again with the Hell-lit night.

The dreadnought twisted under hammering shells as the iguana had done when Sergeant Britten's flamethrower bathed it. A shell had pierced the starboard main-belt armor, close beneath where Johnnie pulled himself to his feet. He could not have seen the hole, even if he leaned over the rail, but the fire at its heart threw a bright orange fan across the waves.

The light swept over a mass of writhing tentacles. Squid were battling for the bodies of fish killed by concussion.

Johnnie reached the ladderway again. He clung to the railing, gasping breaths of fiery air in through his mouth because the filters restricted his nostrils.

More shells hit. Johnnie bounced like the clapper in a bell, but he retained his grip on the rail.

If the shell that pierced the main belt had landed ten feet forward and ten feet higher, it would have struck B Turret magazine instead. Perhaps the barbette would have withstood the impact, but its armor was no thicker than that of the belt which failed.

It would have been quick. Oblivion would be better than this, and even Hell could be no worse.

"You on the bridge ladder!" growled a demon's buzzing voice. "Identify yourself!"

Johnnie shook his head. It seemed a lifetime since he last heard human speech. Words didn't belong in a universe of shock waves that flung men to and fro like the disks of a castanet. The helmet protected his ears, but it couldn't save his soul from the pummeling.

"Awright, sucker—" buzzed the voice.

He was being challenged over the intra-ship communicator. A Blackhorse seaman waited on a dark landing above him, preparing to fire at the figure silhouetted against the firelit hatch.

"—you had your—"

"No!" Johnnie shouted, flinging himself to the side. The shadows might conceal him, though they wouldn't stop a sheaf of ricocheting bullets. "I'm Johnnie Gordon! Ensign Gordon!"

He didn't have time to unclip his ship-structure transmitter, but for this purpose ordinary helmet radio was better anyway. Johnnie and the guard were within a few feet of one another, and the armored ladderway surrounding them acted as a wave guide.

He'd lost his sub-machine gun somewhere. Left it in Turret II, he supposed, though he couldn't remember unslinging the weapon with all that had gone on since he left the bridge.

Johnnie's pistol was in his hand, pointed toward the swatch of darkness which most probably concealed the guard. He'd drawn the gun in an instinctive response to his training, but he didn't think he would shoot even if a blast of shots lit the ladderway's interior.

The Angels' 16-inch shells were killing them fast enough. The Blackhorse team didn't need to join in the job of its own destruction.

"Ensign?" buzzed the guard. "Sir? Geez, you shoulda said something!"

Johnnie got up and holstered his pistol. The stair treads

would have been some protection, at least if the guard was firing explosive bullets.

Enough glow leaked into the armored shaft for the light-amplifying visor to work at short distance. The guard—Johnnie recognized him, though he didn't know the sailor's name—squatted in the conning tower. He'd smashed the light fixtures to keep them from going on automatically at a human's presence. He was waiting with his rifle aimed through the part-open hatch.

"What the hell's going on?" Johnnie demanded of the man who'd been about to kill him. "What're you—"

The *Holy Trinity* staggered as another shell hit her and the remainder of a large salvo landed close aboard. Metal screamed.

The ship's whipping motion was magnified because Johnnie was a deck higher than he had been before. He wondered how long the dreadnought could endure the unanswerable pounding her enemies were inflicting.

"It's the Angels, sir," the guard explained sheepishly. When the man stood up to greet Johnnie, he disengaged his flexed transmitter, so his words were relatively clear over ordinary intercom. "Bulkheads sprung when the shells hit forward, so the off-duty crew's loose now."

He frowned as his mind sought accuracy. "What survived the shells're loose. Cookie, he figures they may try to take over the bridge."

Even though the two men were face to face, neither could have heard the other's unaided voice over the bedlam of a battleship dying.

"Right," said Johnnie. If the Angels recaptured the bridge, they would radio their fellows and stop the rain of shells. Somebody aboard the *Holy Trinity* might survive then.

"Well, carry on," Johnnie muttered as he started climbing the last flight of steps to the bridge. He had to pause

midway as the treads rang and jounced beneath him in
response to a fresh salvo.

Johnnie stepped through the bridge hatch and staggered
because the deck was momentarily stable. Dan, Fayette,
and another technician were the only living humans present.
They did not notice his arrival.

Several of the consoles showed holographic displays of
the *Holy Trinity*'s interior. Fires filled compartments, lend-
ing their hellish radiance to the as-yet undamaged bridge.

"Uncle Dan!" Johnnie blurted. "Sergeant Britten's
dead!"

The three men at the consoles reacted. Fayette ducked,
the other technician snatched clumsily for his shouldered
pistol—

And Commander Cooke had the rifle from across his lap
pointed at Johnnie's chest before his eyes told his brain not
to take up the last pressure on the trigger.

Dan lowered the rifle. Johnnie let out his breath.

Sergeant Britten was dead. The entire Angels' bridge
watch was dead. Many of the Blackhorse raiders whose
packs and equipment littered the deck between the consoles
were dead, trying to accomplish whatever final tasks
Commander Cooke had set them.

Very shortly, everyone aboard the *Holy Trinity* would be
dead. A few minutes one way or the other wouldn't really
have mattered to Johnnie.

"Right," said Uncle Dan. He shifted his grip to the
balance point of the rifle and tossed the weapon to his
nephew. "Watch the hatch here, Gordon. We've got Caleif
below in the conn room, but we don't need another surprise
like you just gave us."

He turned back to his console. It was set to a damage-
control schematic with symbols rather than grim analogue
realities to show the hammering the battleship had received.
Fayette resumed speaking to someone in the engine room.

The other technician continued a program of controlled portside flooding to balance the amount of sea they'd taken in through shell holes at the starboard waterline.

The *Holy Trinity* bucked and shuddered at the heart of a fluorescent maelstrom. Salvoes from all three of the pursuing dreadnoughts arrived simultaneously. Waterspouts dyed red, blue, and yellow sprang up around the stricken vessel, and at least six more of the shells smashed home.

A 16-inch shell landed on the roof of the bridge.

Johnnie felt himself suspended in black air. Every working piece of electronics in the big room shorted as the concussion pulverized insulation and fractured matrixes. The regular lighting went out. The emergency glowstrips which replaced it had to struggle through a suspension of thick dust.

He didn't remember being thrown to the deck, but that was where he found himself lying when the world ceased to vibrate and the dust settled enough for him to see again.

The overhead armor had held. The shutters had been blown away from the viewslit, so another hit on the bridge would surely kill them all. One of the consoles muttered to itself as it melted around the blue flames at its core.

Fayette bawled something unintelligible and bolted through the hatch. A burst of explosive bullets up the ladderway hurled his corpse back onto the bridge.

"Angels!" Johnnie shouted as he fired an explosive placeholder over the body. He knew bullets fired from this angle couldn't hit anyone when they burst in the ladderway, but he hoped the sleet of zinging, stinging fragments would make the desperate Angels hesitate while Johnnie's thumb switched his feed to solid projectiles that would ricochet.

"Get out of—" screamed someone behind as Johnnie thrust his rifle into the hatch opening, tilted the muzzle down, and triggered a one-handed burst which left as much of his body as possible behind the steel bulkhead.

"—the way!" Dan finished as his body slammed against the same hope of cover Johnnie was using.

Dan fired a flamethrower through the hatch.

Johnnie's helmet visor blacked out the direct line of the magnesium-enriched fuel, but its white streak flooded the bridge like the reflection of an arc lamp. The flamethrower's nozzle tried to lift in the commander's hands, but he kept it aimed down in a perfect three-cushion shot along the shaft's inner surface.

There were only a few seconds' worth of fuel remaining in the bottle. The flame died abruptly. The yellow flash of a secondary explosion in the ladderway, grenades or ammunition, was dull by comparison.

There were still screams.

Johnnie strode through the hatch. Glowing metal walls provided light for his visor to amplify.

Caleif and three Angels sprawled below. Another Angel whose uniform was on fire clawed blindly at the conning room bulkhead.

The living figure turned. Both eyes were gone, and the flesh had melted away from the left half of his face.

Johnnie fired instinctively, sending the screaming remains of Ensign Sal Grumio to join his brother and the rest of the *Dragger*'s crew.

Nothing else moved. Johnnie stepped back onto the bridge.

Uncle Dan and the surviving technician stared at him. None of the three men spoke.

The deck was tilted at a noticeable angle. Fires were visible across most of the 270° panorama of the unshuttered viewslit. The slime forward had baked dry in the heat of the deck beneath it. The algae now burned with its own smoky flame.

The *Holy Trinity*'s bow dipped toward the sea, but the

dreadnought no longer had enough way on to sweep waves across the sullen fire.

No shells had fallen since the horrendous triple salvo.

"Look!" croaked the technician as he pointed to the southwestern sky. *"Look!"*

The horizon brightened as though the red gates of Hell had been thrown open.

Dan was kneading the singed back of his left hand with the fingers of his right. His face was terrible. "Bloody well about time," he snarled.

Patterns of red specks roared high overhead. They were full salvoes from the seventeen battle-ready dreadnoughts of Blackhorse Fleet, slamming Commander Cooke's trap closed on the Angels.

24.

Rather the scorned—the rejected—the men hemmed in with the
spears;
The men of the tattered battalion which fights till it dies,
Dazed with the dust of the battle, the din and the cries,
The men with the broken heads and the blood running into their
eyes.

—John Masefield

THERE WERE TEN of them still alive.

Two of the Blackhorse raiders, men from the engine room, were so badly burned that they had to shuffle along with their arms supported by their comrades' shoulders. Johnnie arranged the makeshift harness of packstraps around them with as much care as possible, but the wounded men still moaned and shuddered through their fog of drugs and toxins.

The gunboat D1528–*Murderer* according to the legend painted across the turret of the 2-inch Gatling gun on its foredeck—bobbed in swells reflected from the side of the *Holy Trinity.* Three of the crew used rifle butts as fenders to prevent the gunboat from being smashed into the side of the sinking dreadnought; others received each member of the raiding party as he came down the skimmer winch and passed the shaken men to such comfort and medical treatment as a hydrofoil could provide.

The sea was lighted for miles by torrents of sparks spewing from the *Holy Trinity*'s stern. Flames glinted from waves, from debris, and from the eyes of things which had learned the chaos of war meant a source of abundant food.

The hydrofoil's crew was clearly nervous. The little craft depended on speed and concealment to survive. Here, stopped dead alongside the brightest beacon in the Ishtar Basin, they had neither, but they were carrying out their orders without complaint.

As the men of the raiding party themselves had done; and had, for the most part, died doing.

Men on the gunboat's deck released the second of the wounded raiders and passed him gently to their fellows in the cockpit. Dan winched up the whining cable at the highest speed of which the drum was capable.

It didn't have far to come. The skimmer port was long underwater, and the gunboat's railing was now only ten feet below that of the sinking battleship. At any time in the past five years, that would have been an easy jump for Johnnie, even onto the bobbing deck of a hydrofoil.

At any time but now.

"Go ahead," Johnnie said. "I'll winch you down."

His uncle shook his head. "I'm the captain," he said. "I leave last. Hop in."

He pointed to the harness.

Johnnie wasn't sure whether or not the words were a joke, but he knew that he didn't want to argue—with anyone, about anything. He gripped the cable, intending to ride the clamps down without bothering about the harness.

He swayed and almost blacked out. He'd been all right so long as he had the other crewmen to worry about, to fasten into the jury-rigged harness. . . .

Dan caught him. "That's all right, John," the older man murmured. His right arm was as firm as an iron strap. "Here, we'll ride it together."

The slung rifle slid off Johnnie's shoulder. Dan tossed it to the deck and said, "We won't need that now."

The youth opened his eyes. He saw everything around him with a new clarity. "Right," he said in a voice he could not have recognized as his own. "Leave it for some poor bastard to blow his brains out before he drowns or the fish eat him."

The winch began to unreel at a low setting. Dan supported him, but Johnnie's limbs had their strength back again. Hands reached up from the gunboat's deck to receive them.

The Blackhorse line of battle was in sight, approaching from the southwest. The dreadnoughts' main guns spewed bottle-shaped flames which reflected from the cloud cover. Johnnie had never seen anything like it, even when he was hallucinating from a high fever.

The seventeen battleships were proceeding in a modified line-abreast formation. Admiral Bergstrom kept his fleet's heading at forty-five degrees to their targets beyond the horizon, so that the Blackhorse vessels could fire full broadsides instead of engaging with their forward turrets alone.

"For God's sake!" Dan muttered scornfully. "The Angels only *have* three battleships. What's he afraid of?"

No incoming shells disturbed the perfect Blackhorse formation. The dreadnoughts' railgun domes were live, trailing faint streamers of ionized air, but they fired only occasional skyward volleys. The Angels had been battered to the point they had scarcely any guns capable of replying to the ships destroying them.

"Got 'em!" shouted one of the crewmen who grabbed Dan and Johnnie. "All clear!"

The hydrofoil's drive was churning a roostertail even before the winch cable had swung back against the *Holy Trinity*'s side.

The Blackhorse fleet was almost upon the burning dreadnought. The nearest of the battleships would pass within two hundred yards. The wake of the massive vessel, proceeding at flank speed, would have crushed D1528 against the *Holy Trinity* as so much flotsam had the gunboat not gotten under way in time.

Johnnie wondered who had set the fleet's course . . . though subtlety of that sort didn't seem in character for Captain Haynes.

Flames from the *Holy Trinity* picked out details on the hull and superstructure of the oncoming dreadnought, washing three shades of gray camouflage into one. Johnnie thought the vessel was the *Catherine of Aragon*, but his mind was too dull for certainty and it didn't matter anyway.

The dreadnought's twelve 16-inch guns were now silent, but there were squeals as the secondary batteries clustered along her mid-section rotated to track the hydrofoil as the little vessel turned desperately to bring her bow into the oncoming wake. The paired 5-inch guns glared at D1528 like the eyes of attack dogs, straining at the leashes.

"Bastards!" snarled the ensign commanding the gunboat as he lifted Johnnie over the cockpit coaming. "*They* probably think it's a joke!"

D1528 rode over the wake with a snarl and a lurch. The ensign used the drop on the far side to deploy the gunboat's outriggers thirty seconds before her forward motion alone would have permitted it.

Dan swung himself into the cockpit. The motion was smooth and athletic. He seemed as fit as he had been two days before in Admiral Bergstrom's office.

Unless you looked carefully at his eyes.

"Nice job, Stocker," Dan said to the ensign.

Johnnie blinked. The name stencilled on the gunboat officer's helmet was worn and illegible in this light. Did Uncle Dan know all the Blackhorse officers by sight?

Stocker looked up from the horizontal plotting screen. "Thank you, sir!" he said.

D1528 was beating up to speed. Lifted on her foils, the

gunboat was amazingly stable even though cross-cutting wakes corrugated the sea.

"Where are you supposed to take us?" Dan asked, as if idly.

He was using helmet intercom. A red bead in Johnnie's visor indicated that Dan had chosen a command channel that the gunboat's enlisted crew couldn't overhear.

The hydrofoil was headed in the opposite direction from the battleships. The big ships were almost hull-down, their locations on the northeastern horizon marked primarily by the glowing discharges from railguns on alert status.

All the guns had ceased firing. The Angels must have surrendered—whatever was left of them—and the War-cocks were not yet in range.

Ensign Stocker looked up from the plot again. This time a guarded expression had replaced the earlier pleasure. "Ah, well, I'm to carry you to the cruiser *Clinton,*" he said. "She's the command ship for the rear screen. Plenty of room aboard her and, you know, first-rate medical facilities."

Stocker nodded toward the hydrofoil's electronics bay. One of the wounded raiders sat in the open hatchway, babbling to himself while the gunboat crewman tried to comfort him.

"Admiral Bergstrom is aboard the *Semiramis*?" Dan asked.

Stocker nodded cautiously. "Yes . . . ," he said. "Sir."

"Take us to the *Semiramis,* Ensign," Dan said.

The cockpit was cramped. Commander Cooke and the two ensigns were within arm's length of one another, but for an instant there was a cold crystal wall between Stocker and the others.

"Sir, Captain Haynes specifically ordered . . . ," the gunboat officer began.

Dan grinned at him.

Stocker braced to attention. "Aye-aye, *sir!*" he said crisply. He turned to the plotting table, then began snapping orders to his helmsman over an intra-ship push.

There was a pair of jumpseats against the back wall of the cockpit. Dan pulled one down for Johnnie, then sat in the other himself.

D1528 came about in a wide arc, banking on her outriggers. The only certain marker in the sea, the flaming pyre that had been the *Holy Trinity,* began to slide back across the western horizon as the gunboat reversed course to pursue the battle line.

"Unc-ah . . . ," Johnnie said. "I mean, sir?"

Uncle Dan put an arm around the younger man's shoulders and squeezed him.

"Uncle Dan, was it worth it? Was it worth—"

Johnnie closed his eyes, but he couldn't close out the crowding memories.

"Ask me when it's over, John," his uncle said. He leaned his head close to Johnnie's so that they could speak without using their helmet radios.

The dreadnoughts were coming in sight again. Rather, the combing bow-waves kicked up by huge vessels moving at speed reflected the sky glow on the horizon.

"You mean, after we've beat the Warcocks and Flotilla Blanche?" Johnnie said. "If we beat them."

"Oh, we'll beat *them,*" Dan said. "This war's as good as won; or will be as soon as I'm on the bridge of the *Semiramis* to make sure Haynes and the Admiral don't throw it away from too much caution.

"But what I meant," he continued, "is we won't know if it's worthwhile until there's a united government on Venus and Mankind is at peace."

Johnnie turned from the horizon beyond the cockpit windscreen and stared at his uncle. "*We* won't live to see that," he said. "Will we?"

Dan shook his head. He smiled. His face was as gentle as Johnnie had ever seen it, but the expression was without humor.

"We won't—Man won't—win in our lifetime," he said. "But we might live long enough to see us all lose. Long enough to see Venus turned into a fireball, and the last tomb of Mankind in the universe."

Johnnie nodded, but his mind was too tired to visualize Mankind as an entity.

Besides, his last glimpses of Sergeant Britten and Sal Grumio kept getting in the way.

25.

From a find to a check, from a check to a view,
From a view to a death in the morning.

—John Woodcock Graves

THE HYDROFOIL STRAINED forward like a horse whirling a sulky down the home stretch.

The jumpseats weren't fitted with terminals, but there were data feeds in the flimsy bulkhead behind them. Johnnie uncoiled one against the tension of its take-up spring and plugged it into the input jack of his helmet. After his AI sorted through the options, he settled on viewing the forward gunsight image on the left side of his visor.

The dreadnought filling that magnified picture had her port secondary batteries and at least forty small-caliber Gatling guns trained on D1528. Any one of the Gatlings—much less a single shell from the 6-inch secondaries—could reduce the gunboat to pieces small enough to fit in a matchbox.

"We're being queried by *Semiramis*," said Ensign Stocker.

"I'll take it," said Uncle Dan. He rose, then slid into the command console as Stocker vacated it.

"Kinda hoped you might, sir," the ensign said with a grin.

Johnnie shook his head in wonder at the other young officer. Stocker had decided he was going to have fun with the situation—even though he knew he was being used as a pawn in a high-stakes game between his superiors.

Courage wasn't limited to the willingness to ride a flimsy hydrofoil into battle.

Dan entered his personal code, then authenticated it with his brainwave patterns transmitted by his helmet. "Blackhorse Six," he said, "this is Blackhorse Three aboard the D1528. I need to come aboard the flagship."

Unlike the raiders' transmissions from the *Holy Trinity*, there were compatible code sets on both vessels. It wasn't impossible that Warcock intelligence personnel would intercept the exchange—even though it was low-power, tight-beam, and sent in tiny snippets over a broad spread of frequencies. The conversation could never be decrypted in time to have tactical effect, however.

Johnnie couldn't hear the response. He knew the message had been received on the flagship's bridge because the *Semiramis*' Gatling guns all lifted like the arms of troops saluting on the parade ground.

The officer in charge of the anti-hydrofoil batteries had overheard the request. He'd made the instant decision that *he* didn't want to answer questions about why he'd threatened to blow away Commander Cooke.

The 6-inch turrets moved only to track, D1528 as the little vessel closed. An officer at another console had made a different decision. Probably a decision involving Captain Haynes' likely reaction.

"Negative, Pedr," Uncle Dan said. He was speaking forcefully, though he called Admiral Bergstrom by his first name. "The *Semiramis* needn't stop or even slow. Order the port accommodation ladder lowered, and my aide and I'll come aboard."

Johnnie felt too decoupled from his surroundings to be afraid. He looked at his uncle.

The *Semiramis* alone could manage about thirty-two

knots, but the speed of the battle line as a whole would be slightly slower. The ships would still be travelling fast enough that if someone slipped while hopping from the hydrofoil's deck to the spray-slick surface of the dread-nought's accommodation ladder, impact with the water would be stunning if not fatal.

The creatures in the water would be certainly fatal.

But it really didn't matter.

Ensign Stocker called an order to his helmsman and throttled back. He looked worried. The unspoken basis of Commander Cooke's offer was that Stocker could match the gunboat's speed perfectly to that of the battleship, despite the turbulence of the huge ship's passage through the sea.

"No sir," Dan said, "I can't discuss this by radio. We *must* come aboard."

They were now so close to the *Semiramis* that the 6-inch guns couldn't depress enough in their mountings to bear on the hydrofoil. The turrets continued to track, however, as though hoping that the gunboat would somehow leap high enough in the air to be disintegrated by a salvo of hundred-pound shells.

Powder smoke still drifted from the eight 18-inch guns to surround the *Semiramis* like a sickly-sweet aura.

"I appreciate that, Pedr," Dan said. "And the sooner we come aboard, the sooner Ensign Stocker here can carry the rest of my team back to the *Clinton* for that medical treatment."

Stocker looked at Commander Cooke, then toward the shuddering, whimpering man in the electronics bay. His face was without expression.

The helmsman held D1528 thirty feet off the dread-nought's port quarter. Throttled back to the larger vessel's best speed, the hydrofoil felt sluggish. It had a tendency to follow the corrugations of the sea's surface rather than slicing at the even keel maintained by the telescoping outriggers.

The accommodation ladder hanging from the *Semiramis'* port quarter began to lower toward the water. A pair of sailors rode the stage down, ready to catch the transferring officers as they jumped across.

Dan stood up, swaying slightly with the hydrofoil's motion. "Right," he said. "Take over, Ensign Stocker. Do your usual excellent job and I won't forget you."

Stocker slid into his console and looked up at the superior officer. "Same for me, huh, sir? Cream their ass."

The ensign's words could have referred to the fleets allied against the Blackhorse, but Johnnie doubted it. He was Senator Gordon's son. He'd seen enough politics in his life to recognize them, even when they were being conducted in uniform.

Johnnie unplugged the data feed and rose as the thread-thin optical fiber coiled back onto its spool.

His uncle looked at him sharply. "Are you up to this, John?" he asked. "Because if you're not . . . ?"

"Sure, I'm fine," Johnnie said. He wasn't sure if that was true. He saw everything around him with unusual clarity, but he seemed to be hovering over his body.

It didn't matter.

He followed Dan to the starboard rail. He felt steady; which was a matter of vague intellectual interest to him, because he knew that the deck underfoot was vibrating badly. The drive motors were being run at well below their optimum rate.

Stocker and his helmsman brought the D1528 in smoothly. The accommodation ladder now hung about eight feet above the average level of the sea, but occasional swells surged dangerously near the platform's underside. At thirty knots, the stage would tear loose if it touched the water.

"Go," said Dan, and Johnnie stepped across the six-inch gap.

A dreadnought sailor was ready to grab him, but Johnnie waved the man away. The gunboat was so precisely controlled that there was less relative motion between the disparate vessels than there would have been in getting off a slidewalk.

Dan followed and continued striding toward the steps leading up to the deck. "Come on, lad," he snapped. "Time's a-wasting."

"They'll winch us up, sir!" called one of the sailors.

Dan gestured brusquely, dismissively, without turning around.

"What is it that we've got to tell the Admiral, ah, sir?" Johnnie asked as he pounded up the perforated alloy treads behind his uncle.

The gunboat, freed of its shackling need to keep station, curved away from the accommodation ladder in a roar of thrusters coming up to speed.

"I want to make sure they don't throw the battle away," Dan said. "I told you that."

There were splotches of algae on the *Semiramis'* side, but not a solid coating as had been the case with the *Holy Trinity*. This was just the growth since the battleship slipped out of port the day before.

"*I* don't have anything to add," Johnnie said emotionlessly.

Dan had reached the battleship's deck. A section of rail pivoted to form a gate. He turned and looked back at his nephew.

"Oh, you have something to add, John," he said. His lips were firm as the jaws of a vise. "I didn't lie to the Senator about that."

He strode toward a hatch in the dreadnought's superstructure. X and Y Turrets' huge 18-inch guns had blackened the deck and lifted up a sheet of the plastic covering, then plastered it against the railing.

"But *what*?" Johnnie demanded.

A staircase—a ladderway—lay behind the hatch. "In good time, lad," said Dan's echo-thickened voice as his boots clanged upward. "If not tonight, then later. . . . But I think tonight."

As Johnnie closed the hatch behind him, he heard the squeal of the 6-inch turrets. The secondary batteries were returning to the ready position now that they had tracked D1528 out of sight.

26.

*The sea is Death's garden, and he sows
    dead men in the loam. . . .*

                    —Francis Marion Crawford

A HELMETED GUNNER raised his head from one of the
Quad-Gatling tubs on the shelter deck as Commander
Cooke and his aide strode forward to the bridge.

Johnnie started. The equivalent installations on the *Holy
Trinity* had been empty. He'd never been aboard a dreadnought with a full crew.

There were crewmen where Johnnie's subconscious expected only the heat-warped barrels he'd burned out as the
raiders escaped from Paradise Harbor. He thought of
corpses rising in their coffins.

Corpses didn't do that. But neither did the corpses in
Johnnie's mind sleep.

The bridge hatch was open but guarded by a heavily-
armed senior petty officer.

"Come along, sir!" the man urged. "We don't none of us
want to be out here when the big bastards cut loose again,
do we?"

There was the sound of distant gunfire and an occasional
flicker of light on the horizon, but for the moment action
was limited to the screening forces.

Action. Thick armor cracking, perforating. Hell erupting

to spew out over the sea, winking from waves and the eyes within the waves.

The hatch ratcheted shut, closing them within the climate-controlled fastness of the bridge. Johnnie trembled because of what was in his heart, not the drop in air temperature.

The bridge of the *Semiramis* was very like Wenceslas Dome's governmental accounting office. The differences were that the warship's bridge crew was uniformed and that its personnel seemed far more alert.

Of course, accountants would be on their toes if they knew that an 18-inch shell might land in their midst at any moment.

The center of the enclosed bridge was a huge plotting table. In the air above it hung a vertical holographic projection of the same data. The hologram was monochrome, but the air projection aligned itself to appear perpendicular to someone viewing it from any point on the bridge.

The console built into the plotting table was vacant. Uncle Dan slid into it and began keying up data.

"Ah, sir?" said a lieutenant Johnnie had never seen. "That's Captain Haynes' station. He's on his way up from the battle center now."

Dan snorted. "When he heard I was coming aboard, you mean? Don't worry, Bailey. When the captain arrives, I'll vacate."

He unbuckled his equipment belt and hung it, the holstered pistol on one side balanced by loaded magazines on the other, from the seat's armrest. Then he resumed his work.

Admiral Bergstrom was at a console with no visual display up but six separate data feeds plugged into his helmet. He turned, looking like a man whose brain was

being devoured by wire-thin worms, and peered at Dan in
the seat behind him.

"Commander?" Bergstrom said. "Commander. You had
crucial information for us, you said?"

"Right," said Dan, one eye on his console display and
the other on the plotting table itself. His fingers danced on
the keys. "Have you released the subs yet, sir?"

Johnnie looked over his uncle's shoulder. Strung rag-
gedly along the western edge, barely within the confines of
the plotting table at its current scale, were two hollow
yellow circles and a yellow X: the electronic remains of the
Angel dreadnoughts, sinking and sunk respectively, which
had pursued the *Holy Trinity*.

One of the technicians had the last moments of the X
marker up on his display. There were more important things
for Blackhorse personnel to be considering at the moment,
but Johnnie could understand the tech's fascination with the
looped image.

Almost anything was more important than that particular
ship now.

The vessel had been the *Azrael*, easily identified because
it carried its main battery in three quadruple turrets forward.
The unusual layout meant that the thick belt protecting the
main magazines and shell rooms was relatively short,
saving weight without giving up protection.

It also meant that most of the explosives aboard the
battleship were concentrated in a small area.

The holographic image was a sixty-degree oblique,
transmitted to the *Semiramis* by a glider which had risked
the night winds to spot the fall of shot. The *Azrael* was
making a course correction, perhaps to bring her heavy guns
to bear on the unexpected threat from the main Blackhorse
fleet. Her railgun installations blazed blue-white, and her
curving wake shivered with phosphorescent life.

The glider's imaging system picked up the dull red

streaks of shells plunging down—not by pairs and triplets as Johnnie remembered from the *Holy Trinity,* but thirty or forty at a time. The *Azrael* was the simultaneous target for half a dozen Blackhorse dreadnoughts; there was nothing the victim's railgun batteries could do to affect the result.

"Flotilla Blanche isn't in the killing zone yet, Commander," Admiral Bergstrom said. "Ah—Commander, what is it that had to be explained face to face?"

Great mushrooms of water bloomed on all sides of the *Azrael,* distorting the wake and twisting the bow as they hollowed the surface into which the cutwater then slid.

A few of the shells which landed aboard the *Azrael* burst with bright orange flashes because their fuzes were oversensitive. The dangerous hits merely sparked on the surface of the armor and detonated far within the dreadnought's guts.

The stricken vessel's bow lifted as though she were a flying fish making a desperate attempt to escape. The explosion that engulfed her forequarters was black, streaked with a red as deep as the devil's eye sockets. C Turret sprang fifty feet into the air, shedding hundred-ton fragments like so many bits of confetti.

"We don't *need* the submarines to finish Flotilla Blanche," Dan said as he shuffled quickly through data on his console. "Or the Warcocks, for that matter. We can do that with gunfire easily enough—if we slow down the Warcocks with our subs so that we catch them before the two fleets join."

He tapped the execute key with a chopping stroke of his finger. The display quivered, then blanked. "With your permission, sir," Dan said, "I'll send the wolfpacks in now."

A thousand feet above the fiery cauldron, the column of smoke topped out in a ragged anvil. The stern half of the *Azrael* was sucked into the crater of white water. It bobbed as the sea closed over itself, then vanished with scarcely an additional ripple.

The recorded images ended with a blur of incandescent light.

The loop began again. Johnnie forced his eyes away with difficulty; the technician continued to watch the repeated horror.

There but for the grace of God. . . .

"I *don't* think . . . ," Admiral Bergstrom began, but his glare turned to a grimace.

The ultra-low-frequency pod beneath the *Semiramis'* keel began to transmit orders to the Blackhorse submarine fleet at a frequency of between ten and a hundred hertz. Johnnie's bowels quivered.

Due to the sluggish transmission frequency, there was time to abort the command before it reached the submarines lurking on the bottom three miles down. Instead, Bergstrom said, "Oh . . . Yes, I suppose you're right."

The submarines were beneath the thermocline, a differential of temperature and salinity in the deep sea which blocked both active and passive sonar. That helped conceal them from the Warcocks, but the subs' best protection was a matter of psychology rather than physics.

The Angel fleet had run the same course without interference. The Warcocks and Flotilla Blanche, now desperately trying to join forces in the northwest quadrant of the Ishtar Basin, assumed the only dangers they need fear were the Blackhorse surface ships which had reduced the Angels to blazing wreckage in a matter of minutes.

The petty officer, alerted by a message through his helmet, activated the control of the hatch he guarded.

"Right," said Dan. He started to get up.

Johnnie's face was still. His mind visualized a pair of raiders wearing Angel khaki as they burst through the hatchway with a cataclysm of rifle and sub-machine gun fire.

Consoles sparking around stray bullets; the chests of neat cream uniforms exploding in blood and smoldering cloth; fingers which were accustomed to stroke keys flailing wildly for pistols almost forgotten beneath polished holster-flaps.

The stink of gunsmoke, and the greater stink of feces when fear and death voided men's bowels.

Captain Haynes squeezed through the hatch before it was really open enough to pass a man of his solid bulk.

Haynes was panting. He must have walked—run—all the way from the deep-buried battle center rather than chance an elevator when any instant could bring a shell and a power failure.

His face was livid, but that was more from anger than from exercise. His left hand was clenched so hard that his knuckles were mottled.

"Commander Cooke," Haynes said in a voice like millstones, "you're at my station—"

Though by the time the words came out, Uncle Dan had moved to an ordinary console nearby. A quick gesture—a twist of his index finger as though it were a boning knife—sent the technician there scrambling out of his seat.

Johnnie followed as if he were his uncle's shadow. He was drifting through this ambiance like a thistle seed in a zephyr. He felt nothing, but his senses were sharper than he ever remembered them being.

Captain Haynes seated himself with the swaggering certainty of a dog staking out its territory. He glanced at the visicube of his wife on the plotting table before him. "Sir," he said to Admiral Bergstrom, "I felt the ULF communicator activate while I was on the way here. What—"

"Pedr thought," Dan broke in, "that unless we slow the Warcocks⁺ withdrawal, they'll be able to join Flotilla

Blanche before we bring them to battle. If they have to zigzag because of submarine attack—"

"Let them join!" Haynes snapped. "Then our subs take care of both of them!"

The Warcocks' ten battleships were in a straggling line-ahead on the plotting table. The new emergency had further disturbed a formation that had been rough to begin with.

The Warcocks left their base in a rush to block the *Holy Trinity* from the presumed destination of the Blackhorse fleet at the Kanjar Straits to the northwest. When the stolen dreadnought turned southwest, Admiral Helwig had thrown his Warcocks into the pursuit—as though the Angels' own three battleships would not be sufficient.

Now they were racing back to the northwest again, hoping to join Flotilla Blanche as it streamed from the position it had taken at the mouth of the Straits.

The light forces of Flotilla Blanche speckled the upper edge of the plotting table. The Warcock screen of cruisers and destroyers formed a broad arc between their dreadnoughts and the oncoming Blackhorse fleet. They were well positioned to block torpedo attack by Blackhorse hydrofoils, but they could do nothing to stop the one- and two-ton shells from the dreadnoughts which would rumble overhead as soon as the range closed to thirty miles or so.

They weren't in a good position to defend against the submarine ambush the Warcocks had blundered into the center of, either.

"Subs can't *destroy* them," Dan said, speaking loudly enough to be heard by everyone on the bridge. "These are good outfits, both of them. We can just cause confusion, as we decided in the planning—"

"The Admiral and I—" Haynes shouted.

Admiral Bergstrom's face was suffused with the frustrated pain of a child listening to his parents quarrel. He must have been a decisive man at one time, but age and his rumored drug habit had rotted away the hard core of his personality.

"—changed the plan, Commander, while you were off having your fun playing soldiers!"

"Oh, God!" muttered a lieutenant commander, who then buried his face in his display. Everyone, even Captain Haynes, looked embarrassed.

Everyone but Dan and Johnnie. Their burned, bloodied, torn fatigues left them immune to embarrassment by any of the clean-uniformed personnel on *Semiramis'* bridge.

Besides, there was no room in Johnnie's eyes for embarrassment or any other emotion.

The starboard secondaries opened fire. The enclosed bridge damped the shock of the muzzle blasts, but the hull belled as the guns' thick steel breeches expanded from the pressures they contained.

"Torpedoboat attack in sector A-12," explained a lieutenant loudly.

Any of the bridge personnel could have learned that data from their own consoles, but the statement served its real purpose of breaking the vicious argument between two of the fleet's most senior officers. Admiral Bergstrom gave the lieutenant a look of gratitude. The emotional temperature of the big room dropped to normal human levels.

"All right," muttered Captain Haynes as he twisted his face toward the plotting table. "We've got a battle to fight, let's not forget."

Dan's fingers worked his keypad, though he continued to watch the side of Haynes' determinedly-averted face for some moments longer. A distant—blurry despite being computer-enhanced—view of the Warcock line appeared on his console.

The display above the plotting table showed sudden chaos within the hostile battlefleet. None of the ship symbols indicated damage, but the dreadnoughts had started to curvet like theater-goers after someone noticed smoke.

"Revised estimate of time to engagement," said the public-address speaker in the mechanical voice of the battle center computer. "Three minutes thirty seconds for leading El Paso elements; sixteen to seventeen minutes for all El Paso elements."

Captain Haynes opened his mouth and reached for the transmit key of his console.

"I'll take care of this, Captain," Admiral Bergstrom said coolly. He pressed his own transmitter and said, "Black-horse Six to all El Paso elements. You may fire as you bear, gentlemen. Blackhorse Six out."

For this operation, 'El Paso' was the code name for the dreadnoughts.

An ensign at the far end of the bridge shouted, "Yippee!"

27.

Then suddenly the tune went false,
The dancers wearied of the waltz,
The shadows ceased to wheel and whirl. . . .

—Oscar Wilde

ON UNCLE DAN'S display, the second ship from the rear of the Warcock line suddenly wreathed itself in flame and powder smoke. She had opened fire with her main guns. A moment later, all the other battleships visible from the glider joined in.

The Warcocks certainly knew that they were still out of range.

They also knew that they were shit outa luck.

"Ah, sir . . . ?" said Captain Haynes as his left hand touched the image of his wife. "Do you think it might be better to delay firing until we can overwhelm them with a full fleet salvo?"

"No," said Admiral Bergstrom without turning to face his executive officer. "I do not."

"We'll be eating them up piecemeal, Captain," Dan said. He glanced from his display and then back. "Their formation's strung out for nearly five miles."

Johnnie nodded, professionally impressed by the way his uncle managed to keep his tone along the thin neutral path between insulting and conciliatory.

"We'll have plenty of concentration on the rear of their line," Dan continued blandly as he examined the desperate

Warcock dreadnoughts, "even if only the eighteens can fire
for the first ten minutes."

Haynes' face was a thundercloud, ready to burst in a
storm of invective unmerited by anything that had happened
in the past few minutes. As his mouth opened to snarl, the
port-side Gatlings blazed in a sudden fury whose rate of fire
made the enveloping armor sing.

Johnnie's training held, though his intellect was dissoci-
ated from control of his actions. He reached reflexively for
the keypad of the console behind which he stood. The only
reason his fingers did not shift the display to the gunnery
board and echo the Gatlings' target information—

Was that Uncle Dan's fingers were already doing so.

The ship-shivering burst ended three seconds after it
began. There was nothing on the targeting display except a
froth where over a thousand 1-inch projectiles had ripped a
piece of flotsam.

"Omigod, sorry, sorry," muttered the junior lieutenant
whose console was the primary director for the Gatlings. "I
thought, I mean. . . ."

He caught himself. His face hardened. "No target," he
said crisply. "All clear. No target."

The *Semiramis'* main fire director rippled off a salvo
from A and B Turrets, four 18-inch guns. The dreadnought
shook herself like a dog coming in from the wet. The air of
the bridge was suddenly hazy because finely-divided dust
had vibrated out of every crack and fabric.

The thirty-inch armor covering the bridge flexed noticeably with the waves of compression and rarefaction.
Johnnie could not imagine how the sailors manning the
open gun tubs survived the muzzle blasts.

Dan switched back his display. The dreadnoughts had
ceased cavorting in wild attempts to avoid torpedoes from
Blackhorse submarines. The Warcock line re-formed and
resumed shaping to the northwest. Anti-submarine missiles

from the dreadnoughts and their screen were forcing the
subs to concentrate on evasion rather than attack—or to
press on and die pointlessly.

Yellow symbols on the plotting-table hologram indicated
that two of the Warcock battleships had been hit, but they
were still keeping station. Half a dozen red symbols marked
the destruction of attacking submarines.

Johnnie's face did not change. Ships and shells and men;
all were expendable.

The rearmost of the Warcock battleships had been the
leaders in the pursuit. They were the fastest and generally
the most modern members of the fleet, and two of them
mounted 18-inch guns.

Semiramis' six railgun batteries began to tear the universe
apart, dwarfing the racket of the Gatlings a minute before.
Railgun discharges brightened the images of the Warcock
vessels as well, but a splotch of white water beside the last
ship marked a shell that had gotten through the defensive
barrage.

The rising banshee moan of a dropping shell became a
background to the crackling of hypervelocity slugs.
Johnnie's face did not change, but his body began to
shudder uncontrollably. The youth's deep-buried lizard
brain remembered that sound. Conscious courage—
conscious fatalism—could do nothing to quell the tremors.

The shell burst with a dull *crump,* thousands of feet short
of its intended target.

". . . oboats in . . . ," the ceiling speaker said during
the brief interval the railguns were silent.

If Johnnie cared to hear the details of the report, he could
have flexed his helmet to the console, but the information
didn't matter except to the men at the gunnery boards. The
6-inch batteries were firing, both port and starboard; a
moment later, the Gatlings added their sharp-tongued chant.

Three shells burst directly above the second ship from the

rear of the Warcock line, so close that the red-orange flashes and the blots of filthy smoke they left behind were visible in the image transmitted to Dan's console.

Most of the salvo screaming in a few seconds later struck on or around the dreadnought.

The forward superstructure, including the bridge, warped and shredded. There was a glowing pockmark where armor of particular thickness had been heated white-hot by a 16-inch shell.

A shell penetrated X Turret magazine. Instead of an explosion, a yellow flash hundreds of feet high blazed from every interstice of the turret and rear hull. As the initial glare sucked itself back within the blackened armor, the Y Turret magazine flashed over and burned with identical fury.

Johnnie keyed intercom mode on his helmet, the channel reserved for members of the raiding party. Him and his uncle; no one else within range . . . and scarcely anyone else alive.

"They're screwing up," he said flatly. "Their railguns are on automatic mode, but then they only react to direct threats. The poor bastards at the end of the line are on their own."

Like we were in the Holy Trinity.

Dan made a quick series of keystrokes without bothering to check whether or not the input was necessary. "Blackhorse Three to El Paso elements," he said to his console. "Your railguns are now firing on Sector Defense Mode. You will not switch them to Local Defense without orders from the flagship or an acting flagship. Out."

He turned to look up at his nephew. The 18-inch guns boomed out another salvo just then, but Johnnie could see his lips forming, ". . . *safe than sorry.*"

The third and fourth ships from the rear of the Warcock formation winked amidst waterspouts. The second had fallen out of line, her whole stern a mass of flames ignited by the powder flash.

The final vessel seemed to bear a charmed life with no shells falling near it, but her course had begun to diverge from that of the remaining dreadnoughts. Carats on the plotting-table display indicated that several torpedoes had gotten home and had jammed the ship's rudder.

"Sir," said Uncle Dan, "with your permission, I'll signal General Chase." His voice echoed in Johnnie's helmet: he was using an open frequency that everyone on the bridge could overhear, rather than the command channel.

Because he was Commander Daniel Cooke, that wasn't an accident or oversight. He wanted the statement public, because he knew that every one of the pumped-up officers who heard it would regard arguments against General Chase as cowardice rather than caution.

The screens along the bulkheads, taking the place of the now-shuttered viewslits, showed a dozen pyres on the sea. The Warcock light forces were making desperate attempts to slow the hostile battleline, but the Blackhorse screen and the dreadnoughts' massed secondaries immolated the attackers as victims.

The Blackhorse battleships formed an arc with the ends slightly advanced. The Warcocks were in line-ahead, roughly centered within the pursuing arc. There were between two and six railgun installations on each Blackhorse dreadnought, and every one of them could sweep the sky above all seventeen ships in the formation.

If the Blackhorse formation broke up and each dreadnought proceeded at her own best speed, the defenses became porous.

But it was the only way the Blackhorse could be certain of running down the ships at the head of the Warcock line.

"Sir, I—" Captain Haynes began. Though he spoke to

Admiral Bergstrom, he looked across the short intervening distance to his rival.

Dan grinned at him.

Haynes' face suffused with blood and rage. He closed his mouth like a door slamming.

The Admiral turned in his seat. His expression was unreadable. He looked up at the plotting display, then lowered his eyes to his executive officer.

"Yes," he said as the eighteens fired. His lips seemed to be slightly out of synch because his voice came over the radio a microsecond sooner than air would have transmitted the words. "Let's end this, shall we?"

Dan waited an instant to be sure that he, rather than Admiral Bergstrom, was to give the order. Then, with a wink to Captain Haynes, he keyed his console and said, "Blackhorse Six to El Paso element. General Chase. I say again, General Chase. Let's have 'em for breakfast, boys! Out!"

As a period to the command, the secondary magazines of a ship near the center of the Warcock line blew up. For a moment, inertia held the dreadnought on course. Her superstructure was missing and there was a scallop from the middle of her hull as though she were a minnow bitten by a piranha.

The stricken vessel slewed to the side. Her bow listed to starboard, her stern to port.

"Sir!" said a communications tech. "The Warcocks are calling for you on Frequency 7 to discuss surrender. Shall I transfer the call?"

Another heavy shell burst, close enough to be felt but still harmlessly far in the air.

"Yes, yes, of course!" Bergstrom snapped, prodding at his console with what seemed to Johnnie to be drunken precision.

"Blackhorse to all Blackhorse elements," Uncle Dan said. "Cease firing offensive—"

The booming main guns from the battleship immediately to starboard rocked the *Semiramis*.

"—weapons. They're giving up! Cease—"

Captain Haynes rose from his seat. "You have no right to give that order, Cooke!" he shouted.

"—fire, they're surrendering. Out."

The hammering snarl of the railguns was a reminder that at this range, shells would continue to fall for almost a minute—on the Blackhorse and on their opponents.

Flashes covered the stern of another Warcock dreadnought on the display. When the blasts ended, the guns of Y Turret were cocked sideways and the deck aft was a smoking shambles.

Uncle Dan stood up. He moved gracefully and at seeming leisure, like a cat awakening. "Do you have something to say to me, Captain Haynes?" he said.

The railguns cut off. Instead of silence, the bridge filled with the sound of a voice rasping from the roof speaker, "—der unconditionally to you, Admiral Bergstrom. We, I . . ."

The voice broke. Whether it was Admiral Helwig or a subordinate promoted into his place by Blackhorse shells, there was no doubt of the sincere desperation of the Warcock commander.

Johnnie understood how the man must feel. All the few survivors of the *Holy Trinity* would understand that run-through-a-hammermill feeling.

Captain Haynes swallowed. "Remember, we've still got Flotilla Blanche to deal with," he said. His tone was almost an apology.

He started to sit down.

"If you can spare us medical help—" the Warcock officer said.

"Admiral de Lessups can do basic math, Captain," Dan said harshly. "He can match twelve dreadnoughts against seventeen in his head—and he's not so stupid that he'll try the result for real."

"—we'd be very thankful."

Haynes' face worked. Johnnie could see that the stocky captain was still trying to disengage from an argument he had lost as soon as he opened his mouth. "We're low on main-gun ammu—"

"Not so low we can't hammer Flotilla Blanche to the bottom, Captain!" Dan shouted. His face was red, and his voice was full of the ragged fury Johnnie had heard him counterfeit in Senator Gordon's office. "They know that and we know that! *You* know it!"

"That won't be possible until we've dealt with Flotilla Blanche," said Bergstrom over the roof speaker. "As soon—"

"Commander," Haynes said, looking at his clenched fingers, "I think we're both overwrought. I think we—"

"You know what the real problem is?" Dan said rhetorically. His eyes swept the other personnel on the bridge. He waved his arm. "The *real* problem is that Haynes has learned about me and Beryl, and he's willing to give up a victory just so it won't be a victory I planned!"

Admiral Bergstrom turned around and snapped, "Hold it down, for God's sake!" He straightened to resume his conversation with the Warcock officer.

Several of the listening officers gasped or turned away. Johnnie would have felt shock himself if he were able to register any emotion at the moment.

Captain Haynes blinked. He was no longer angry; amazement had driven out every other reaction.

"Cooke," he said in wonderment, "were you wounded in the head? That's ridiculous."

Uncle Dan took a step forward and reached out. His

index finger pressed the touch-plate of the visicube on the plotting table. He backed away.

"You may proceed to your home port—" Admiral Bergstrom was saying.

"*Dan, darling, dearest Dan,*" squeaked the voice from the image of Beryl Haynes. "*I wish you were here with me now so that you could kiss—*"

"—leaving only enough undamaged vessels at sea to aid those—"

Haynes went red, then white. Johnnie could barely see the seated captain past his uncle's torso.

"*—my nipples, so that you could—*"

"—which are in danger of sinking," said the Admiral's voice.

Haynes lurched to his feet. His hand groped at his pistol holster.

"*—bite my nipples the way—*"

"I'm unarmed!" Dan shouted. He raised his hands from elbow level. His holster hung from the chair behind Haynes.

Captain Haynes swung up his pistol.

Johnnie's face was calm, his mind empty of everything but trained reflex. He drew and fired twice over his uncle's shoulder.

Haynes' head swelled as both bullets exploded within his brain.

"*—that's ecstasy for me . . . ,*" concluded the visicube.

Haynes' arms, flailing as he fell, brushed the image of his wife to the floor.

Johnnie's fingers began to load a fresh magazine into his pistol.

Epilogue.

When navies are forgotten
And fleets are useless things,
When the dove shall warm her bosom
Beneath the eagle's wings.

— Frederic Lawrence Knowles

TORPEDOBOAT D992'S AUXILIARY thruster was turning at idle, enough to make the water bubble beneath her stern and to take the slack out of the lines. Despite that, if any of the vessel's crew were anxious for their passenger to come aboard, they took pains to conceal the fact.

Johnnie, wearing civilian clothes, and Captain Daniel Cooke in a clean uniform with the tabs of his new rank on its collar paused beneath a tarpaulin for a moment. The sun was a white hammer in the sky, but the storm sweeping west from the Ishtar Basin would lash Blackhorse Base before the afternoon was out.

Heavy traffic sped up and down the quays, carrying materials to repair battle damage and supplies to replace the enormous quantities used up in the action of the previous night. None of the men or vehicles came near the end of Dock 7 where the D992 waited.

Dan said, "I don't want you to misunderstand, John. You can't stay with the Blackhorse, but I can get you a lieutenant's billet with any other fleet on Venus. Flotilla Blanche, for—"

"No," Johnnie said sharply.

He looked at his uncle, then focused on the lowering

western horizon. "I wanted to learn what it was like to be a mercenary," he said. "Now I know."

His lips twisted and he added to the black sky, "I thought the Senator was a coward because he left after one battle."

"I told you that wasn't so," said Uncle Dan.

Johnnie met the older man's eyes. "You told me a lot of things!" he snarled.

"Yes," Dan replied calmly. "And none of them were lies."

A railcar carrying a section of armor clanked along the lagoon front, toward the drydock where the *Hatshepsut* was refitting from her torpedo damage. The dreadnought's gunnery control board had gone down at a critical time. Before the secondary armament could be switched to another console, a pair of Warcock torpedoboats unloaded their deadly cargo.

"Not lies?" the youth said. "Maybe not—by your standards, Uncle Dan."

Then, as his eyes blurred with memories, he said, "You *used* me. From the time you talked to the Senator, you were planning—what I did!"

"For eight years," Dan said coolly, "I've been raising you to be the man I'd need at my side when there was no one else I could trust. I never forced you to do anything— but I wanted you to have the chance to be the man I needed, *if* you had the balls for it."

"Oh, I've got the balls, Uncle Dan," Johnnie retorted. "What I *don't* have is the stomach. I see why you had to get rid of Captain Haynes—he was a normal human being. But I don't—"

The youth had been speaking in a controlled if not a calm tone. Now his voice broke.

"—see why you had to pick me to murder him. Wouldn't Sergeant Britten have dropped him in the lagoon some night for you?"

Even as he spoke, Johnnie *did* understand his uncle's cold-blooded plan. If Captain Haynes simply disappeared, his chief rival would be suspected of murder even without hard evidence. The Blackhorse was unlikely to elect a murderer to replace Admiral Bergstrom when he retired—and some friend of Haynes' might very likely choose to take justice into his own hands.

But if Captain Haynes died in a personal squabble while trying to shoot an unarmed man, then that was no mark against his would-be victim. A perfect operation—if Uncle Dan could be absolutely certain that somebody killed Haynes before the captain accomplished his intent.

And who was a more trustworthy—and lethal—bodyguard than Ensign John Gordon?

"Captain Haynes killed himself," Dan said. "He'd be alive today if he'd been a man in whose hands the fate of Venus could rest safely."

"He was a decent man!"

"Venus isn't a decent planet, boyo!" the older man snapped. "It's a hellhole—and it's all Mankind has left. I'll pay whatever it costs to be sure that Venus is unified before somebody uses the atomic weapons they figure they need to win a war. Haynes was going to be in my way for as long as he lived."

Lightning backlit one, then several of the oncoming cloud masses. Their gray and silver forms looked like fresh lead castings. Thunder was a reminder of distant guns firing.

Johnnie stared toward the clouds but at the past. "I don't care if Venus is ever unified," he said flatly. "I just don't want to see more men die."

"Well, you ought to care, boy," said his uncle in a voice like a cobra's hiss, "because if we don't have unity, we won't have peace; and if we don't have peace on this planet, then there's going to be two temporary stars orbiting the sun instead of just one."

Johnnie turned to Dan and blazed, "You don't make peace by killing people, *Captain*!"

Dan nodded. "Fine, boy," he said in the same cold tone. "Then you go down to the domes and help the Senator unify the planet his way—or some way of your own. It doesn't matter how you do it. But don't forget, boy: it has to be done, whatever it takes."

Johnnie closed his eyes, then pressed his fingers over them. It didn't help him blot out the visions that haunted his mind.

He spun around, though Dan had surely seen the tears dripping from beneath the youth's hands.

"Johnnie," said his uncle in a choking voice, "I told you there were costs. I didn't lie to you!"

I thought you meant I might be killed, Johnnie's mind formed, but he couldn't force the words through his lips.

He stumbled toward the hydrofoil waiting to carry him back to Wenceslas Dome.

"Whatever it takes!" his uncle shouted.

And the thunder chuckled its way across the sky.

Afterword:
The Stuff of Myth

SOME STORIES ARE so much a part of the culture in which they were created that they must be understood in terms of that culture—or not at all. The *Iliad* is one of those stories.

The *Iliad* is in print today in a number of English translations (and goodness knows how many translations into languages other than English). Despite this evidence of the story's continuing popularity, it isn't repeatedly worked into currently popular form the way other Greek tales of like vintage have been: Jason and the Argonauts; Theseus and the Minotaur; and particularly the varied tales of Odysseus.

The *Iliad* is a great story—arguably the greatest story ever written. Despite that, it doesn't translate out of the *culture,* rather than the language, in which it was composed. The big-budget movie Hollywood made about the Trojan War focused on the Fall of Troy—which has nothing to do with the few days covered by the action of the *Iliad*.

The *Odyssey* transcends its culture. It's a good story (or a series of good stories) in general human terms. When I reread the *Odyssey* a few years ago, I mentioned to a friend that it would make a great Western.

It certainly would, but I don't write Westerns. When I gave the idea one more ratchet in my mind, I realized that the *Odyssey* could also make a heck of a science fiction novel.

So I used it as the basis of *Cross the Stars*.

Having said that the *Odyssey* transcends its culture, I must emphasize that there are many conventions and cultural aspects to the story which are very different from those of our day. For example, since Odysseus was a mature man when he left Ithaka, he would be quite old when he returned at the end of twenty years. Modern continuations of the *Odyssey* (and even some scholarly commentators) often assume that Odysseus *is* an old man—

But he's not, in the context of Homer's story. Homer was writing about a mythical world in which a husband and wife could pick up right where they'd left off twenty years before. That was a convention appropriate to Homer's culture, though not (in adult fiction) to ours.

A problem of a more direct type occurs after Odysseus and his friends have slaughtered the suitors in his hall. The servant women who have slept with the suitors are marched outside. Short nooses are put around their necks and tied to a hawser which spans the courtyard.

Then the hawser is tightened just enough to lift the women's feet off the ground. They are left to strangle, slowly and horribly.

Could you put a scene like that in a modern adventure novel? Sure; but the villain, not the hero, would have to be responsible for the act. To Homer's culture, the punishment fit the crime.

But the *Odyssey* remains a story of enormous power. If the story is transmuted into a contemporary cultural idiom (as it was, for instance, by the tenth-century Egyptian storyteller who created some of the best parts of *The Arabian Nights*), it can retain that power for a reader who knows nothing of Iron Age Greece.

The inherent power of myth led me to base *Cross the*

Stars on the *Odyssey*. That was why I've since then adapted *Dagger* from an Egyptian folktale; *The Sea Hag* from fairy stories; and *Northworld* from Norse myth.

I've done a similar thing here with *Surface Action*. In this case the mythic basis is 1940s science fiction: the stories I encountered first (in anthologies) when I started to read SF. I went into the project by asking myself the same question as when I've worked with other mythic material: how can I make the conventions of this worldview acceptable to a modern audience?

The world of the forties is not today's world, and the differences go far beyond the obvious fact that we now know Venus isn't covered by oceans. Some of the cultural aspects have to be changed; some of them simply have to be dropped, the way I dropped Odysseus' vengeance from *Cross the Stars*.

But I've tried to create a work which would have struck a forties SF reader as being a typical part of the gorgeous tapestry of Venus tales woven by Kuttner and Moore, Keith Bennett and Wilbur S. Peacock, Brackett and Bradbury—and so many more.

I hope I've done justice to this particular myth; because it is, after all, the myth that brought me into the field in which I now live and work.

—Dave Drake
Chapel Hill, N. C.